Ghost
à la
Mode

A GHOST OF GRANNY APPLES MYSTERY

Praise for Sue Ann Jaffarian's Odelia Grey Mystery Series

What reviewers are saying...

Odelia Grey is delightfully large and in charge in Jaffarian's third entertaining romp.
—*Publishers Weekly*

Odelia Grey is definitely a force to be reckoned with.
—*ReviewingTheEvidence.com*

Jaffarian plays the formula with finesse, keeping love problems firmly in the background while giving her heroine room to use her ample wit and grit.
—*Kirkus Reviews*

[Odelia Grey] is an intriguing character, a true counter against stereotype, who demonstrates that life can be good, even in a world where thin is always in.
—*Booklist*

A sharp, snappy mystery novel... This is a fast and furious read that should be fun to see as a series with Odelia as the lead character.
—*AmaZe Magazine*

An intriguing, well-plotted mystery that will entertain and inspire.
—*The Strand Magazine*

Jaffarian's writing is sharp and sassy—like her protagonist—and she knows how to keep the suspense high.
—*Mystery Scene*

What fellow authors are saying ...

More fun than a lunch pail full of plump paralegals, *The Curse of the Holy Pail* is a tale as bouncy as its bodacious protagonist.
  —*Bill Fitzhugh, author of* Highway 61 Resurfaced *and* Pest Control

[*The Curse of the Holy Pail* is] even better than her first ... a major hoot!
  —*Thomas B. Sawyer, author of* The Sixteenth Man *and former head writer/producer of* Murder, She Wrote

Sue Ann Jaffarian does a masterful job. Once you get to know Odelia Grey, you'll love her. I know I do.
  —*Naomi Hirahara, Edgar-winning author of* Snakeskin Shamisen

A plus-sized thumbs up. Jaffarian's a new sharpshooter in crime fiction.
  —*Brian M. Wiprud, author of* Stuffed *and* Pipsqueak, *winner of Lefty Award for Most Humorous Novel*

Odelia Grey is everything you want in a heroine ... smart, funny, and completely unapologetic.
  —*Tim Maleeny, award-winning author of* Stealing the Dragon

Odelia Grey is the perfect take-no-prisoners heroine for today's woman.
  —*Camryn Manheim, Emmy award-winning actress and author of* Wake Up, I'm Fat!

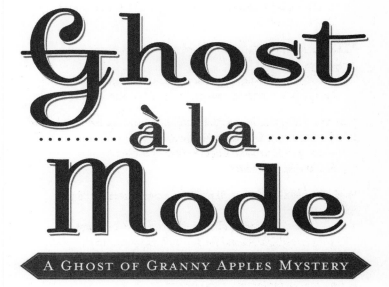

Ghost à la Mode

A Ghost of Granny Apples Mystery

Sue Ann Jaffarian

MIDNIGHT INK
WOODBURY, MINNESOTA

FIRST EDITION
First Printing, 2009

Cover design by Ellen Dahl
Cover image © 2009 Doug Thompson

Midnight Ink, an imprint of Llewellyn Publications

Library of Congress Cataloging-in-Publication Data
Jaffarian, Sue Ann, 1952-
 Ghost à la mode / Sue Ann Jaffarian.—1st ed.
  p. cm.—(A ghost of Granny Apples mystery; 1)
 ISBN 978-0-7387-1380-9
 1. Female friendship—Fiction. 2. Single mothers—Fiction.
 3. Ghosts—Fiction. I. Title.
 PS3610.A359G48 2009
 813'.6—dc22

                                                          2009011914

Midnight Ink
2143 Wooddale Drive, Dept. 978-0-7387-1380-9
Woodbury, MN 55125-2989

www.midnightinkbooks.com

Printed in the United States of America

For Barbara Moore, my former editor,
who convinced me a short story about a ghost
was worthy of a full novel and even a series.

acknowledgments

As always, a huge debt of gratitude to Whitney Lee, my agent; Diana James, my manager; and all the good folks at Llewellyn Worldwide/Midnight Ink, especially Bill Krause, Rebecca Zins, Marissa Pederson, and Ellen Dahl for their continued support, talent, and encouragement.

Thank you to the San Diego County Sheriff's Department and attorney Mark Hardiman for providing some of the police procedural and legal information.

A very special thank you goes to the warm and wonderful people of Julian, California, especially the folks at the Old Julian Drug Store, the Julian Pioneer Museum, the Julian Hotel, and the Rong Branch Restaurant and Saloon.

one
. . . .

"Mom went to a séance last night."

As soon as the words were out of Kelly's mouth, Emma White-castle wanted to kick her daughter's leg under the dining table. They were having Sunday dinner at Emma's parents' house. It was Emma's childhood home and where Emma had moved after separating from Grant Whitecastle, Kelly's father, just over a year ago. Instead of a well-landed kick, Emma scowled across the table at her daughter. Kelly was eighteen going on thirty. Graced with the long, elegant legs of a colt and the face of fairy-tale princess, she was both smart and smart-mouthed, and even though Emma would miss her daughter, she was looking forward to when Kelly would leave for Harvard in the fall. The divorce proceedings had been hard on Kelly, and Emma was hoping the move east would help her daughter start a new life without the ugliness of her parents' well-publicized relationship staring her in the face from the tabloids. Although she still would not be immune, at least in

Boston her daughter might escape the Hollywood sideshow and gossip surrounding the divorce.

"A séance?" Emma's mother, Elizabeth Miller, asked, her knife and fork frozen in midair. She stared at Emma over the top of her glasses, prim and proper, waiting for an answer.

Emma looked at each member of her family seated at the table. Besides her mother and daughter, her father, Paul Miller, a retired heart surgeon, was also waiting to see what her answer would be. She cleared her throat.

"Yes, Mother, a séance." Emma took a drink from her water glass before continuing. "Tracy asked me to go with her. It had to do with research for a class she's giving in the fall."

Tracy Bass was Emma's oldest and dearest friend. They had grown apart during the last years of Emma's marriage to Grant. Tracy had never liked Grant and had not liked the way Emma had changed under Grant's influence. And Grant, harboring a similar dislike for Tracy, had discouraged Emma from seeing her. Seeing that she lived with Grant and not Tracy, Emma had taken the easier path of acquiescing to her husband's wishes. But in the past six months, with Emma's marriage all but dead, the two women had started mending the fences of their friendship.

Tracy taught full-time at UCLA—the University of California at Los Angeles. She had begged Emma to join her the night before, saying it would be interesting. She had enticed her further with the promise of dinner beforehand at one of their favorite restaurants. Tracy had been right. It had been a very interesting evening, but outings with her flamboyant friend usually were. This one, though, had topped the list. Emma couldn't stop thinking about it. It played over and over in her head like an annoying ad jingle.

The table fell into a companionable silence as everyone resumed eating. A few minutes later, Emma asked, "Did someone from our family ever live in or around Julian, California?"

This time, Emma's mother dropped her fork with a *clunk*. All eyes turned to Elizabeth, who lowered hers as she retrieved her utensil from the middle of the plate.

"You all right, dear?" Paul asked his wife. His eyes, dark with concern, darted from his wife to his daughter and back to his wife.

"Just a little clumsy, that's all." Elizabeth put her fork back down. "I guess I'm not very hungry."

"Where's Julian?" Kelly asked.

Emma turned to her daughter. "It's a small town in the mountains east of San Diego—a historic gold rush town. I looked it up on the Internet this morning."

"A ghost town?" Kelly asked with rising interest.

"No, it's still a small but thriving community. In fact, it's known for its apples. According to the man who led the séance, we have a black sheep in our family who came from there."

"Do tell, Mom."

"Would you believe our family tree harbors a murderer?"

"No way!"

"That's what the man said. A woman who killed her husband. She was then promptly hung."

"That's pretty wild. Is this on Grandma or Grandpa's side?" Her young, eager eyes darted between her grandparents.

"I didn't do it."

In unison, Emma and her mother jerked their heads in the same direction but saw nothing. Kelly and her grandfather kept eating.

Emma turned to Elizabeth. "Did you hear that, Mother? Sounded like someone whispering. How odd."

Abruptly, Elizabeth got up from the table. "Why don't you all have dessert on the patio. It's so lovely outside."

Paul left his place at the table and went to his wife. "Are you sure you're okay, dear?"

Elizabeth patted his arm. "I'm fine, Paul, just tired from the theatre last night, that's all."

"Mother, why don't you rest? Kelly and I will clean up and get the dessert."

"Thank you, Emma. If you don't mind, I think I'll skip dessert and go upstairs and read."

Emma and Kelly were just finishing cleaning the kitchen when Nate Holden, Kelly's boyfriend, dropped by.

"We're going to a movie," Kelly announced.

"You kids want some pie before you go?" Emma cut into an apple pie and placed a slice on a dessert plate.

"No thanks, Mrs. Whitecastle. The movie starts soon."

Emma smiled. Nate Holden was a polite young man from a good family and the same age as Kelly. He was tall and slim and wore his brown hair long. They had been dating for almost two years. Emma wondered what would happen to the relationship once Kelly and Nate went their separate ways in the fall. While Kelly was heading to Harvard, Nate was off to Stanford. Seldom did high-school infatuations hold up under long-distance stress and strain. Kelly had been torn about going to Harvard because of Nate, but in the end, she knew she couldn't miss the opportunity. As much as Emma liked Nate, she had been relieved when Kelly had made her decision to go East. She didn't want her daughter to plan her life around a man as she had.

After Nate and Kelly left, Emma carried a tray holding two slices of warm apple pie with vanilla ice cream and two cups of decaf coffee out to where her father was relaxing on the patio. Emma took a seat in a chaise longue next to him. Beyond the patio, the family's black Scottish terrier, Archie, rolled around on the grass.

"Apple pie?" her father asked as he readied to take his first bite. "Where did this come from?"

"I picked it up from the bakery this morning."

Paul studied his daughter with interest. "I didn't think you liked apple pie. Thought you were a lemon meringue kind of gal like your mother."

Emma shrugged. "Generally, I am." She took a bite and chewed, savoring the homey flavor on her tongue. "It's not that I dislike apple pie, I just never think of having it. Guess it's because we never had it much while I was growing up. This, however, is quite tasty." She took a sip of coffee between bites. "Funny thing—this morning, when I was at the grocery store, I got the most intense craving for it." She laughed. "So much so, I'm surprised I didn't stop the car and dig into it on the side of the road like some junkie."

The words startled her father. He stopped eating. "This morning? You got the craving for apple pie this morning?"

"Actually, the craving started last night during that silly séance. It was quiet, just the leader speaking, and suddenly I could smell apple pie or at least cinnamon." Again she shrugged. "It was probably one of the candles they were burning. Some candles smell good enough to eat."

"Honey, how did Julian come up?"

"Julian, California?" A bit of pie escaped from her fork and landed on her blouse. Emma dabbed at it while she thought about Julian. "It was something Milo said to me."

"Milo?" Paul's graying eyebrows raised like two caterpillars snapping to attention. Milo wasn't a common name, but it was one he'd come across before.

"Yes, Milo, the leader of the séance. He said someone, a spirit, wanted very much to talk to me. Said it was important." She glanced at her father. "How silly is that? Tracy was almost green with envy since no ghosts were speaking with her. Just me and two other folks had that dubious honor." Emma's tone was filled with amusement. "Milo asked me if I had family in Julian. Said the spirit was a woman from there."

"Did he say anything more about the woman? Any details? A name?" Paul tried to hold himself back. He didn't want his daughter to sense how concerned he was, at least not yet.

"Just a woman who'd been hung for murdering her husband."

Emma looked over at her father. He was sitting on the edge of his patio chair, watching her as if she were a child ready to take a nasty spill.

"You don't believe this malarkey, do you, Dad?" When he didn't answer, she continued. "For cripes sake, you're a doctor—a scientist."

Paul took a big drink of his coffee. "As a doctor, I studied science, Emma. But during my years as a doctor, I witnessed many astonishing things. Unexplainable things. Things having to do with death and dying, and things that happen when people die. The

6

idea that spirits of the dead, or ghosts, are among us and are trying to communicate with us is a fascinating one, is it not?"

Emma gave it some thought. "Yes, it is, in theory. But I'm not so sure it's real. Last night, except for me, the other two people Milo said had ... well, visitors, is how he put it ... were desperately looking for that contact. They attended the séance hoping, even praying, that someone they loved would speak to them from the grave. It would have been easy for them to grasp at any straw."

"But what about you?"

"What about me?" Emma fidgeted in her seat. "I went to keep Tracy company. For me, it was an evening with a friend, nothing more. Maybe Milo was trying to make a believer out of me, to rope me into his scam. Considering it was fifty-five dollars a head last night, it really is quite a scam."

"Are you sure that's the only reason you went?"

Her father had a knack for digging with questions like some folks worked with shovels. Emma always thought he should have been a psychiatrist instead of a surgeon. When she looked away without responding, he continued.

"Emma, I know things have been very unsettling since you and Grant split up. Your child is about to move away from home. You don't have a career or real purpose in life, and you're floundering a bit. Maybe, in some way, you went along with Tracy to look for answers, perhaps even a focus to your life."

This time, Emma looked directly at her father. "Really, Dad, does that sound like me?"

Paul Miller shrugged with frustration. His daughter had both hardened and softened during her marriage to Grant Whitecastle. She was more cynical these days, but she also lacked the spunky backbone she'd had growing up. He missed the inner strength that used to glow from within her like a candle in a jack-o'-lantern.

"Hard to say, Emma. You used to be much more determined and focused than you are now. I know you're hurting, honey, but it's time to move on."

"You trying to get rid of me, Dad?" Her tone was joking, but in her heart Emma was a bit scared.

"No, honey, far from it. You're welcome to live with us as long as you like. You know that. We love having you here." He paused and studied his daughter before speaking again. "But I think it would be healthier for you to get on with your life. You are far too young to be holed up here with us old folks. Travel. Buy a home. Find a career. As soon as a fair settlement is reached, sign the divorce papers and get on with your life. Kick Grant Whitecastle to the curb like he deserves and be done with him."

"You sound like Tracy."

"Tracy is a smart and charming woman. I'm very glad you two are spending time together again."

Emma laughed lightly. "I'm not so sure Mother agrees with you. I think she's afraid I'll adopt Tracy's bohemian ways." It was true. Elizabeth loved Tracy Bass like a second daughter but didn't understand why Tracy preferred vintage secondhand shops to Saks.

"And I think Tracy rubbing off on you a little wouldn't hurt." He smiled at her. "And that's a doctor's opinion."

Emma and her father sat in silence, enjoying the evening. Archie brought over a tennis ball and dropped it at Paul's feet. Paul picked it up and tossed it, and the dog scampered off in the direction of the throw. Archie brought it back, and Paul threw it again.

After another throw, Paul decided it was time to tell his daughter about Ish Reynolds.

"Your ancestors did come from Julian, Emma."

"So it's true?"

He tossed the ball again for Archie. "Yes, your mother's people were originally from Kansas but settled in Julian in the mid to late 1800s."

"Is that what agitated Mother at dinner? That I found out?"

"Partly, yes."

Paul Miller sat forward in his chair and studied his daughter, locking eyes with her. When Archie came back with the ball, Dr. Miller patted the animal and gently ordered the dog to lie down. Archie obeyed.

"How much do you remember about the time following Paulie's death?"

Paulie was Paul, Jr., Emma's older brother. He had been hit and killed by a car after dashing into the street to get a wayward ball. It was a tragic accident, both for their family and for the man whose car had struck Paulie. Emma had been nine years old when it happened. Paulie was eleven.

"I remember how difficult it was on Mother—on all of us, but especially Mother." Emma swallowed. "Mother always blamed herself, didn't she?"

"Yes. That's nonsense, of course. Elizabeth was and is the best of mothers. It just happened so fast. No one could have prevented it except for Paulie. He was old enough to know not to run out into the street."

Emma watched as a gray film covered her father's face like plastic wrap. She knew her parents had never gotten over the death of their son, no matter how many years had passed.

"But what does Julian have to do with Paulie's death?"

"About six or seven months after Paulie died, your mother got it in her head to try and contact him."

"Contact him? You mean Mother went to a séance?"

Paul shifted in his chair. "Your mother went to many séances and spent a great deal of money, most of it on charlatans, trying to reach your brother. She was obsessed with it—needed to know how he was and to beg for his forgiveness—but nothing happened. Then, almost a year to the date of Paulie's death, she went to someone new: a young man recommended to her by someone she'd met at another meeting."

"Let me guess. Mother found Paulie's spirit there like a pair of sunglasses waiting to be claimed at the lost and found?" Emma snorted softly and got up to clear the dessert dishes. A slight chill wafted through the patio. She was ready to go inside and forget about spirits and séances.

Paul put a hand on his daughter's arm. "Please sit down, Emma," her father gently ordered. "This is important." Emma stopped fussing with the dishes and sat back down.

"Your mother never spoke to Paulie, but she was assured by another spirit that he was fine. It made all the difference to your mother. It brought her back to us."

"Another spirit?"

"Yes. Another spirit."

"And you believe this, Dad?" Emma stared at her father, her mouth hanging open like a marionette with cut strings.

"Like I said, there are a lot of strange things going on in the world, some we can see and explain, some we cannot. But I do know that it brought a lot of comfort to your mother and helped us get our lives back on track."

"Well, that's a good thing, no matter how it came about. And did Mother stop going to séances after that?"

"Yes, she did, but according to your mother, the spirit who helped her did not go away. She came to your mother over and over, following Elizabeth and speaking to her."

Emma's eyes grew large. "Dad, that's scary. That's psychotic."

"It certainly could be taken that way." Paul sighed, knowing the toughest part of the story was coming. "Finally, months later, I went to the man who had run the séance—a man named Milo." He emphasized the name and watched as his daughter's blue eyes widened further in disbelief. "I asked him to intercede in whatever way he could. We ended up having a private session, just he and I, during which he asked the spirit to leave your mother alone. And apparently it worked, or seemed to. Elizabeth's never had a problem since, but she's very sensitive about it, as you saw at dinner."

Emma's mind buzzed with this new information, whining and whirring until her ears hurt. Her mother had once had a spirit, or *ghost*, following her around? Her father had gone to a séance to ask the ghost to stop? Her parents were two of the most grounded and intelligent people she knew. It hardly seemed possible. And what did Milo have to do with this? There was no way he could have known who her parents were. Maybe it wasn't the same Milo, though she knew it had to be.

Emma cleared her throat and rolled her eyes, a habit of Kelly's she hated. "So who was this ghost, Dad? Did you get her business card?"

Paul let out another tired sigh. It was difficult to tell his daughter about this, but he knew she'd have to know, especially now. Whether she believed it or not would be up to her. "The spirit who helped your mother with Paulie was from Julian. An ancestor, supposedly Elizabeth's great-great-grandmother."

"Are you kidding me?"

Paul shook his head and pushed on. "Her name was Ish Reynolds. She was hung for killing her husband around the turn of the century."

Emma didn't know what to think or believe. It would take time to digest it all and come to a logical explanation. Lost in her thoughts, she ran a finger around her dessert plate. She raised the finger to her mouth and licked off the crumbs while she processed everything her father had just told her.

"One more thing, honey." Her father got up to leave. "Ish—the ghost from Julian?—her nickname was Granny Apples. She was famous for her pie." He winked at his daughter. "Guess which kind?"

two
· · · · · · ·

Emma didn't know about ghosts, but she did know she was being haunted by the leftover apple pie. It was calling to her from the refrigerator downstairs like a siren of Greek lore, enticing her with the promise of sweet, juicy fruit and comfy cinnamon.

It was after two o'clock in the morning. Her parents had long gone to bed, and Kelly had returned by eleven thirty. The house was completely silent. Emma was in bed reading, hoping it would make her sleepy. So far, it hadn't. Her mind kept drifting to the conversation she'd had with her father. She couldn't stop thinking about what he'd said about moving on with her life, and she couldn't stop thinking about her mother's attempts to contact her dead brother. And then there was that bombshell about the dead woman her father called Granny Apples.

That was it. She lightly rapped her head with her palm. That's why she wanted more pie. It was the power of suggestion from the talk they'd had. That and her growling stomach.

Restless, she padded into her private bathroom and looked at herself in the full mirror. She studied her face. In her opinion, for a forty-four-year-old woman, she wasn't bad looking, not by a long shot. She had clear blue eyes, shoulder-length honey-colored hair, a straight nose, strong chin, and perfect white teeth. Emma poked and pushed at the deepening lines around her mouth and eyes. Grant had first brought them to her attention a few years ago and had suggested she have something done to remove them.

Unbuttoning the front of her crisp white cotton nightgown, Emma took stock of the goods beneath. Although slender for her five-foot, seven-inch frame, Emma thought her figure, with its small belly pooch and soft buttocks, could do with more toning. Her breasts were average size and, like everything else, showed signs of gravitational pull.

It had been her breasts that had driven the wedge between her and Tracy—or rather Grant's obsession with her having breast surgery. It wasn't the boob job itself that Tracy had objected to but Emma's willingness to have surgery just because Grant wanted his wife to have large breasts. She had lectured Emma on the fact that it was her body, not Grant's, and if she wanted larger breasts, then great, do it. But if Grant was the only one who wanted big boobs, then let him get his own implants. Tracy's complaint had been that Emma was doing it just to please Grant. She had even gone so far as to say that Emma was addicted to pleasing Grant. In the end, Emma didn't have the breast surgery, changing her mind about it two days prior to the surgery itself. Grant had sulked for weeks. Soon after, he started having affairs with younger women with huge bosoms, affairs he didn't bother hiding. It had been humiliating.

Grant Whitecastle was Hollywood royalty. The grandson of two acting legends, the son of an award-winning producer and famous starlet, Grant himself had been a child actor from age four until he turned eleven and his changing voice and body weren't so cute any longer. He and Emma had met in college and married within a year after graduation, right after Grant went to work for his father's production company. It had been exciting to be in the swirl of show business and meet many of the celebrities and top actors at dinner parties and other social events. But Grant wasn't satisfied. He itched to be back in front of the camera, not behind the scenes.

He got a few gigs playing the odd neighbor or friend on a couple of sitcoms. That led to more work, including a small recurring role on a popular police drama. Emma had been happy for him. She knew Grant missed his time in the spotlight, and he had enough credentials and contacts to get back into acting. And he wasn't a bad actor. Not award quality, but perfect for the type of work he was getting.

Then came his big break. Four years ago, he had auditioned to be the host of a new, controversial daytime talk show, and he landed the job. In no time, he became the favorite of retirees, who remembered him as a child actor, and stay-at-home moms, who responded to his bad-boy sexiness, which the network played up and encouraged on air. Grant became the shock jock of daytime talk shows—the irreverent and rude host that brought scores of viewers to his shows like pigs to the trough of tacky and mean. It was after his first year as the host of the show that he began nagging her about tightening up her looks with surgery. And it was after she cancelled the surgery that his bad-boy persona invaded their private lives.

The straw that had broken the back of their marriage was named Carolyn Bryant, a twenty-six-year-old, red-haired bombshell with capped teeth and fake breasts. She'd come to Hollywood from Texas to be a movie star when she wasn't much more than Kelly's age. She'd been a bit player in many low-budget films, mostly slasher and teen movies where she got to show off her physical assets, but was best known for being the gal pal to some high-profile starlets with a taste for the high life. She and Grant had met at a party, and soon their photos were splashed across the sleazy rags featured at checkout counters.

Emma tolerated the affair with a stoic belief that the fling would be short-lived, as the others had been, and that Grant would dump Carolyn. She believed her husband was going through a midlife crisis fueled by both age and his rampant success, and he eventually would return to the bosom of his family. She'd been wrong. She still remembered clearly the night Grant came home, still smelling of his bimbo actress, and announced that Carolyn was pregnant and he was going to marry her. That had been eighteen months ago. For a few more months, they stayed together, battling over details, until she couldn't take it anymore and fled with Kelly to her parents' home in Pasadena. Carolyn moved in with Grant soon after Emma left and had since had a little boy, whom she named Oscar. The joke around Hollywood was that it would be the only Oscar Carolyn or Grant would ever hold.

Emma stared at her reflection in the mirror as she buttoned up her nightie. Grant deserved to be kicked to the curb, booted in the groin, and left naked in the gutter covered with fire ants. He could keep the house. She'd hated the pretentious mansion he'd insisted on buying right after his talk show became a hit. But she was hardly going to roll over when it came to the settlement. Grant had been very generous in supporting her and Kelly since she'd left, but she guessed that was more to avoid a court battle than a sense of duty on his part. Still, every time they came close to a settlement, it seemed it was Grant's lawyer, not hers, who stalled. Emma wondered if that was the game plan: a cat-and-mouse ploy to keep her off-balance until she agreed to accept less than what she was entitled to. Before she left Grant, her father had suggested that she either take or copy all pertinent financial documents in the event Grant tried to hide assets. Reluctantly, she had followed his advice, and later, when settlement talks began, was glad she did.

Emma sighed. In spite of the fact that her share of their assets would keep her comfortable for the rest of her life if she were sensible, Emma knew her father was right. She did need a focus, a career, something useful and productive to do with her life. Once Kelly was gone, she'd have even more time on her hands, and she was far too young to be retired.

Giving in to temptation, Emma slipped quietly down the back stairs and into the kitchen in search of pie. Happy to have a late-night visitor, Archie wiggled with joy as he left his bed by the laundry room to greet her. After heating up a small slice of pie in the microwave, Emma sat at the breakfast bar and savored each bite while thinking again about what her father had said about the ghost. Even though she trusted her father completely, she wasn't so sure about his take on Granny Apples. Maybe she'd make an appointment to see this Milo character one-on-one. She could question and prod him until she figured out how he knew who her parents were and what he was up to.

She was almost finished with her pie when she felt a chill. It was the wee hours of the morning, and she hadn't put on a robe before coming downstairs. She hurried to finish. As she took her last bite, Emma caught a glimpse of something out of the corner of her right eye—a shadowy movement near the door to the laundry room. Her next breath caught in her throat. Then she noticed that Archie, who was back in his bed, hadn't budged except to wag his tail. Emma shook her head in annoyance.

"Come on out, Nate," she said in a loud whisper.

It wouldn't be the first time Emma had found Nate trying to sneak out of the house in the middle of the night. The small back stairway led from the second floor to the kitchen. It was on the opposite end of the house from her parents' bedroom and next to Kelly's—perfect for late-night comings and goings. Emma was realistic enough to realize Nate and Kelly were probably sexually active but not so open-minded to allow the kids to flaunt it under her parents' roof. Even though, Emma reminded herself, Grant had done his own nocturnal traveling up and down the back steps.

When she received no response, Emma got up and went toward the laundry room. "The jig is up, Nate. You've been busted."

She snapped on the light to the laundry room. It was empty. She shook her head. She could have sworn she saw someone. Must be her tired mind playing tricks—or maybe it was Granny Apples paying her a visit. Emma tried to rub the chill out of her arms and laughed lightly.

She looked down at Archie. "You'd get the nasty old ghost for me, wouldn't you, boy?"

But even the reassuring wag of Archie's tail didn't dispel the nagging suspicion that she wasn't alone.

three
· · · · · · · · · ·

EMMA LOOKED AT THE numbers scrawled on the scrap of paper
held in her hand and compared them to the numbers displayed on
the front of the house. It was a match. The last time she'd been
here, it had been dark, and Tracy had driven. She found a parking
spot a few doors down and pulled her white Lexus sedan into it.
The house—small, white, and without pretense—belonged to
Milo Ravenscroft, the psychic who'd led the séance. It was located
in a pleasant working-class neighborhood in Los Angeles that bordered the city of Santa Monica. The streets were narrow and cluttered with parked cars and seemed a million miles away from the
manicured streets of Pasadena.

It had been a disturbing week for Emma. Ever since Sunday
night, when she'd had that talk with her father about séances and
ghosts, Emma had been sensing shadows moving near her, then
dashing away, as if playfully spying on her. And not just at home,
but almost everywhere she went. Just as disturbing was the scent
of apple pie that always seemed to linger in the air, yet no one else

could smell it. She dismissed it all as foolishness, but even so, she'd thrown the rest of the apple pie into the garbage. When she decided enough was enough, she made a private appointment with Milo Ravenscroft. She still didn't believe in the existence of the ghost of Granny Apples but was sure if she could dig deep enough into Milo's motives, perhaps she could prove him a fraud or receive some kind of explanation.

"Okay," she said to herself audibly. "Just go in there and get to the bottom of this."

Still, she sat, not making a move to turn off the engine and get out of the car. In spite of it being a warm May day, the car interior grew chilly. Emma felt goose bumps rise on her bare arms and tried to readjust the air conditioning, but it wasn't on.

"Come on now," she said to herself again. "You're just being silly."

"Yes, you are."

Emma whipped her head around to see who was speaking to her, but saw no one. "Great, first I'm talking to myself. Now I'm answering myself. Next, I'll be seeing things."

"Fraidy cat."

Unbuckling her seat belt, Emma twisted her head around to get a full view of the back seat and again saw no one. The voice she'd heard had been strong but not loud, like it was being filtered through gauze or whispered on the wind. She tried to convince herself that it was her own subconscious speaking to her and that it only seemed real. With nervous hands, she twisted the top off the water bottle she kept in the console and took a big drink. After all, what was she afraid of? Certainly not a fraud and scam artist.

She took another drink and shivered. The inside of the car was getting colder.

"I told you she wasn't right, Kitty."

At the sound of the words, Emma sprayed the water in her mouth over the dashboard and windshield of the car.

"Hush now, Granny. Our Emma's a skeptic, but she'll come around. She always was a smart, courageous girl."

Emma stared straight ahead out the car's windshield as she replaced the cap on the water bottle with shaking hands. Once more she felt the presence of a shadow but stronger this time, as if the car was stuffed with something she couldn't see but could definitely feel. Something cold and thick and smothering like dense ocean fog or a wet wool blanket.

"She don't look so good."

Like lightning, Emma flung open the car door and fled. She stood in the street a few feet away from her car and stared at it. She was still staring a few minutes later when another car came slowly down the street. Emma stepped out of the way but still didn't get near her own vehicle. The other car, an older Honda wagon occupied by a young couple with a toddler strapped into a car seat in the back, stopped and lowered the passenger-side window.

"Are you all right?" the woman asked Emma.

Emma slowly moved her eyes from her own car to them. "Yes, thank you." As she spoke, her eyes wandered back toward the Lexus.

"Are you sure?" The woman spoke slowly as her eyes noted Emma's expensive linen dress, designer shoes, and pearls snuggled at her neck and ears. To her, Emma looked like she should be heading for lunch at the Bel Air Hotel instead of standing in the middle of their neighborhood.

Emma turned and looked at the woman and saw that she was staring at her with open curiosity, then realized how crazed she must look. She forced herself to focus on the conversation, doing some quick damage control.

"I'm sorry." Emma peered inside the car at the couple and smiled. "I must look like I'm crazy, but there was a huge bee in my car, and I'm allergic."

The couple smiled back. The man leaned toward her across his wife. "We understand. My brother's like that. One little sting and he's in the ER. Want me to make sure the thing's gone?"

"Thank you very much, but I think it is. Besides, I'm visiting a friend. I'm sure he'll check it out before I leave. But I really appreciate you stopping. It was very nice of you."

They all waved goodbye, and the car continued down the street.

Once the couple was gone, Emma cautiously stepped toward her car. Part of her wanted to hop back inside and take off for home to seek medical advice, voices or no voices. The other side of her wanted more than ever to keep her appointment with Milo Ravenscroft. Either way, her purse was on the passenger's seat where she had left it, so she had to at least stick her arm back inside to retrieve it.

Looking at her watch, she saw that she still had ten minutes before her appointment. Taking a deep breath, she resettled herself behind the wheel and shut the door. The air from outside had warmed up the interior. Leaning her head against the headrest, she closed her eyes and tried to think rationally about what had just happened. Hearing voices wasn't normal for a healthy woman, she told herself. It just had to be an outcome of the stress she was under with Grant, not to mention the séance last weekend, coupled with her father's story about her mother and Paulie and that darn Granny Apples character. If she'd never see, taste, or smell another apple pie again, it'd be fine by her.

And Kitty—where'd that name come from? The voices seemed to be in conversation—conversation about her—as if they knew her. Emma only knew one Kitty, and that was her aunt Kitty, her mother's older sister, who was in a rest home in Palo Alto. Kitty had been there for the past two years following a horrendous stroke. Emma and her mother had just talked about planning a trip to visit Kitty. That must be it, she thought. Her subconscious was digging around, rooting up past conversations and piecing them together in some type of audible mirage. The theory calmed her down.

Maybe she needed a rest? Maybe all the stress of the separation and pending divorce had finally gotten to her. Kelly would be leaving soon for a long trip with her father, part of her graduation present, and her parents were shipping out on an Alaskan cruise with friends. Emma promised herself a little relaxation.

Feeling much better, Emma made her way to the front steps of Milo Ravenscroft's home and knocked. The door was opened by Milo himself. He was a small man, barely five foot five, with a slight frame and stooped shoulders. His head was bald, with a half-circle fringe of brown hair. He wore thick glasses and appeared more like an aging accountant than a clairvoyant, or what Emma thought a clairvoyant should look like. He looked at her with surprise.

"Mrs. Whitecastle," he said to her, "you could have called to cancel. You didn't need to stop by to do it." His voice was soft and comforting.

"Cancel? But why would I do that?"

"I just assumed … with the death in the family … "

Emma's eyes shot open. "Death? You must be mistaken."

Her cell phone rang. Emma pulled it out of her purse and read the display. "I'm sorry," she said in apology to Milo. "It's my father."

"That's quite all right. Please, answer it."

Emma flipped open the phone. "Hi, Dad. I'm about to go into an appointment. What's up?"

"Emma, I'm sorry," her father began in a somber voice, "but we just heard from your cousin Marlene. Aunt Kitty passed away this morning."

f our

HER COUSIN'S HOUSE IN Palo Alto was very large and beautiful, yet still maintained a homey, lived-in feel. Marlene had married an electronics executive who'd gone on to make it even bigger in the computer explosion. Her husband, Bob Singh, was the CEO of an Internet company that had managed not only to boom in the birth and growth of Silicon Valley but to survive the bloodletting of the dot-com bust that had followed.

Everyone who'd attended Kitty's funeral had gathered at Marlene's home following the graveside service. Emma, Kelly, and Emma's parents had flown up the two days before for the funeral. Elizabeth and Paul were staying over several more days, but Emma and Kelly were returning home in the morning.

Emma entered the large, sunny kitchen with an empty platter. She placed it on a counter and began replenishing it with finger sandwiches from a nearby tray.

"Let the caterer do that, Emma."

Emma turned and saw Marlene, who was busying herself filling a coffee carafe. Marlene and Emma were close in age and size, though Marlene had dark hair and eyes and olive skin, thanks to her father's Italian heritage. Emma noted the dark circles under her cousin's eyes.

"I like to keep busy at these things," Emma replied. "And I see you do, too."

Marlene Singh finished filling the carafe and passed it off to one of the catering staff. She gave Emma a sad smile. They didn't see each other often, but from childhood through college they had been close, almost like sisters.

Emma stopped filling the serving tray and wiped her hands on a nearby dish towel. "You look exhausted, Marlene. Let's go find someplace quiet, just the two of us."

She took her cousin by the arm and gently guided her out of the kitchen and toward the patio door. Upon seeing people gathered outside, she steered her down a hallway and up the front staircase, saying a quiet hello to others as they moved through the crowd of mourners.

Upstairs, they headed for the master suite. It was large and beautifully decorated with its own sitting area, complete with a small entertainment center. When Emma had first left Grant, Marlene had invited Emma to come for a visit. Bob had taken their two boys skiing for several days, so the women had the house to themselves. They had shopped, gone into San Francisco for a concert, and spent hours enjoying each other's company. For three straight nights, they'd curled up in the intimate sitting area of Marlene and Bob's bedroom, sharing a bottle of wine and talking about life.

After guiding her cousin to the loveseat, Emma retrieved a box of tissues from the bathroom and placed it within Marlene's reach. Then she sat next to her cousin and waited, giving her time, not wanting to shatter her grief with the usual words of condolence. Marlene and her family would hear plenty of that today from others. From her, she knew Marlene needed quiet time and love.

After a few minutes, Marlene blew her nose and looked up at Emma. "Silly, you know, all this blubbering. Mom wouldn't like it."

Emma nodded in agreement. Her aunt Kitty had been quite a woman, independent and full of sassy strength right up until her stroke. Emma's mother, Kitty's younger sister, was more quiet and reserved. When they were young, everyone said Emma took more after Kitty, whose real name was Katherine, while Marlene was more like Elizabeth. The family joke had been that the two girls had been switched as babies.

"Remember that summer after my brother died, I came up to spend two weeks with your family? Your mother called us Kitty's Kittens—like we were a special club, just you, me, and her."

Marlene smiled while dabbing at her tears. "That was fun."

Using her hands, Emma pretended she was straightening whiskers between her mouth and nose, first one side, then the other. Then she held up both hands like they were claws. "Meeeooooow."

Marlene laughed. Sniffling, she made the same hand gestures. "Meow."

The two grown women laughed and cried together. Marlene threw her arms around Emma's neck and gave her a squeeze. "That is exactly how Mom would want to be remembered. Thank you."

Later, after all the mourners had gone, Emma started packing her things for the flight home the next morning. She was staying downstairs in Kitty's old room. Originally maid's quarters, the Singhs had converted it into a mini suite when Kitty's health started failing and she came to live with them. Marlene, always hopeful that her mother would improve, had not changed one thing in the room since her mother's stroke. Emma's parents were staying in the guest room upstairs. Marlene's boys were bunking together so that Kelly could have one of their rooms.

Hearing a light knock at the door, Emma looked up to see Bob Singh standing at the threshold. He was of average height and built thick. Gray ran through his hair like silver threads through black silk. He had a dark, open face and gave her a warm smile. They had all gone to college together at UCLA—she and Marlene and Bob and Grant. Marlene and Bob started dating their sophomore year, while she and Grant met their junior year. The couples had been close at school and in the early years of their marriages. But Bob and Marlene were still together. Seeing their stability reminded Emma of her own failed marriage, no matter how happy she was for them.

"I have a proposal for you, Emma."

"Sorry, Bob, but I'm really not second-wife material."

After a short laugh, Bob came in and settled himself in a small rocking chair near a reading lamp.

"Kind of chilly in here, Emma. Want me to adjust the vents?"

"Thanks, but it's okay. Getting so I like it a bit cool. Maybe I'm having early hot flashes."

Bob gave her a grin. "I have a combination request and invitation for you."

"I'm all ears."

"You and Marlene have both been through a lot lately. I think it would be good for you to get away. How does a week or two sound? Just the two of you. No kids, husbands, parents, worries, or cares. Decide where, and my office will take care of everything. Shopping in Paris. Shows in London. Sunning in Tahiti. Just name it."

Emma sat on the edge of the bed and ran a hand over the lilac-print duvet. "That's quite a generous offer, Bob, but I don't know. Why don't the two of you take some time together instead?"

"We will, but I think it's important for you and Marlene to get away. With your divorce and Kitty's passing, I think you would benefit more from each other's company than anyone else's right now."

"But Kelly's graduating soon, and my parents are going away and expecting me to look after the house and Archie."

"I'm not talking immediately. More like later this summer, or maybe after school starts in the fall and the kids are off doing their own thing. Whenever it's convenient. You ladies can go somewhere and get wild and crazy. You know." Bob made a feeble attempt to do the whisker salute. "Meow."

Bob's attempt at a kitty meow came out sounding more like a Chihuahua with indigestion. Emma burst out laughing.

"I'll definitely think about it and talk it over with Marlene."

"Great." Bob got up and started for the door.

"And Bob?"

When Bob Singh turned back around, Emma groomed her whiskers and showed him her claws.

"Meow back at ya, big guy."

Following a quiet family dinner, Marlene's boys, both teenagers, had taken Kelly out to a movie. All the adults turned in early, including Emma, who retreated to her room to sit in the comfy rocking chair and read. An hour later, she wished she'd taken Bob up on his offer to adjust the air conditioning in her room. It was getting cold. She wasn't sleepy yet, so she got up to grab a sweater from her bag. When she turned back to the rocking chair, she let out a small screech, barely catching herself before it turned into a scream and woke the household.

Sitting in the rocking chair, the very chair she'd just vacated, was her aunt Kitty—or at least a misty image of Kitty.

Emma shook her head, quick and jerky like a dog shaking saliva from its jaws. She looked again at the rocking chair and once again saw a faint image of Kitty. The image was transparent and sat in the chair just as Emma had seen her aunt do so often. The figure wore a modest dark dress, the same dress Elizabeth had helped Marlene pick out for her mother to be buried in. Her hair was as Emma remembered it before Kitty had suffered her stroke, soft and white and pulled back at her nape. The only thing missing was Kitty's knitting. Kitty's hands had always been busy with one thing or another, but in the last decade her primary industry had been knitting. And Kitty had been an exquisite knitter.

Thinking it simply a mirage, a trick played on her by her mind after a day of remembering Kitty and her long life, Emma approached the chair, expecting the image of Kitty to disappear as reality took the place of fancy. Instead, the image turned its head slightly, knowingly, like a wise bird, and smiled at her. Emma jumped back, away from the chair, nearly stumbling over her suitcase in the process.

"Yes, dear girl, it's really me," the image of her aunt said, her voice sounding like the voices Emma had heard that day in the car, whispery, with no more volume than a gentle breeze, yet audible to Emma just the same.

Dashing for the bedroom door, Emma jerked it open just as she heard a second voice. It was similar in tone, yet distinct from Kitty's.

"Told you she was a fraidy cat."

Emma spun around and studied the room she was about to flee. The image of her aunt was still sitting in the rocking chair, the head turned toward her, studying her, with an encouraging smile. It was the second image, the new presence, that caused Emma to gasp.

Sitting on the bed was another filmy apparition, this one of a woman dressed in old-fashioned clothing—a simple, long-sleeved blouse and long, full skirt reminiscent of pioneer garb. Her build was small, even diminutive, but there was nothing frail about it. Her hair was pulled tight against her head with a braid circling her crown like a halo. Her face was lined and weathered. From her direction came the faint odor of apple pie. Both images were as colorless as steam, defined only by shades of gray and white.

The new apparition squinted at Emma, scowled, then addressed Kitty. "I'm not convinced, Kitty. Maybe I should wait another generation." She jerked a thumb in Emma's direction. "Doesn't this one have a girl?"

Not exactly pleased at being talked about like she wasn't there, especially by things that were not supposed to be there themselves, Emma became truly alarmed upon hearing a reference to her daughter.

"Kelly? What about Kelly?"

"Now hush, Ish. You're scaring Emma."

Ish? Emma's confused mind rooted around and didn't want to believe what was becoming obvious, if unbelievable. With wide eyes, she looked from one misty image to the other.

"You're ghosts?" Emma's voice trembled as she spoke the words.

The woman in old-time dress scoffed and addressed Kitty again. "Not very smart, is she?"

"Ish, behave yourself," admonished Kitty. "She's in shock. I'm telling you, our Emma's the one you want."

Emma pointed a manicured accusing finger at the image perched on the bed. "You're Granny Apples, aren't you? You're the one who tried to contact me at Milo's. The one who stalked my mother years ago."

"Ish didn't stalk anyone, Emma. She was looking for help."

"I helped your ma, but she didn't help me none."

"My mother had just lost a child. She was devastated." Emma turned her faced upward to address the ceiling. "I can't believe I'm speaking to something that doesn't exist."

"If Kitty and I ain't real, then why are you talking to us?"

Emma looked at Ish. Her filmy face was pinched with defiance and, Emma thought, disappointment.

Was she crazy? Was she imagining these images? Maybe she was asleep and dreaming. Her aunt Kitty was dead. She'd seen her with her own eyes in the casket the night before at the funeral home. And Ish Reynolds, Granny Apples, was dead, too—had been for a very long time. Her tired mind and exhausted body were playing tricks on her. It was that simple. Had to be that simple. Anything else was impossible, something usually reserved for Grant's low-life, trailer-trash-mentality talk show—like alien abductions and religious images found in slices of baloney.

Emma walked to the bed. Holding out a hand, she waved it through the image of Ish Reynolds. Nothing but air.

"That's not very polite," the ghost snapped. "How'd you like someone sticking their paws through you?"

Laughing, Emma yanked back the covers and dropped herself down onto the bed, falling through Ish to do so. She turned out the light and pulled the covers over herself against the cold that still filled the room.

"A good night's sleep will stop this nonsense," she announced out loud as she closed her eyes.

"You trying to convince yourself or us?" It was Ish again.

Emma opened one eye. Even with the light out, she could still make out an image. It was Kitty, now glowing slightly like phosphorous. She was still in the rocker, but Ish was gone.

"One ghost down, one to go." Emma turned over, determined to go to sleep.

Just as she was drifting off, Emma felt something soft and fluttering and as delicate as a spider web brush against her cheek. She opened her eyes and was startled to see Kitty's ghost standing over the bed. The spirit reached out a hand and stroked Emma's cheek. It felt like the lightest of feathers.

"Where's your friend?" Emma asked.

Kitty's ghost smiled down at her. "Open your heart to the unexpected, Emma. You used to be so full of adventure. So full of life."

"That was a lifetime ago." A tear rolled down Emma's cheek. "If you're real, Aunt Kitty, then please don't go. Stay here with us."

"But I must go, dear. Your uncle Tony is waiting for me. He's been waiting a long time."

Marlene's father, her uncle Tony, had died of cancer twelve years earlier. While alive, he and Kitty had been inseparable.

Kitty bent down and brushed her ghostly lips against Emma's forehead. For the briefest of moments, Emma could have sworn she felt a bit of warm breath against her skin.

"You're the one, Emma," Kitty whispered as her presence began to fade. "You're the one Ish has been waiting for. She's family, and she needs your help. You need each other."

five

"JUST TELL HER TO come back," Emma demanded.

Milo looked at Emma Whitecastle over the top rim of his wire-framed glasses. He studied her for a moment as a patient parent would study a petulant child. There was an inner strength and assurance emanating from the nerdy little man across from Emma with his dirty, crooked glasses and pill-covered blue cardigan sweater. Still, Emma had to fight the urge to reach across the table and snatch the glasses—to clean them and replace them in a straight and orderly manner.

"The other side does not take orders, Emma," Milo told her. "They come to us when they wish to come, not when we demand their presence."

"But I want to help her. Tell her that."

"Help her how?"

"I don't know exactly. She didn't stick around long enough for me to find out." She shot him a challenging look. "And besides, shouldn't you know that already? Isn't that your job, to know what these things want when they come here?"

"These 'things,' Emma," Milo cautioned her in a stern yet soft voice, "are spirits of people who have gone on before us. People who were once alive and walking this earth, just as you and I do now. Please be mindful and respectful of that."

Under his reproach, Emma squirmed in her chair like a schoolgirl and lowered her eyes. She was seated at a small wooden table in a low-lit room. Heavy drapes covered the room's two windows, shutting out the daylight. Burning candles were scattered around on various level surfaces, bathing the space in warm shadows. In the middle of the table, a large candle, white as snow and the size of a small dinner plate, flickered brightly with three lit wicks. She had returned to Milo Ravenscroft, this time with a different purpose. Initially, she had wanted to prove him a fraud. Now she wanted his help.

"I'm sorry. I didn't mean to be disrespectful." She looked up, eye to eye with him. "I just need some answers. You've met this spirit before, both with me and years ago with my mother. I must find out what she wants."

It had been a week since Kitty's funeral—an unsettling week for Emma, during which she'd been unable to eat much and had slept even less. She couldn't stop thinking about what had happened that night at the Singh's. Had she really seen two ghosts, or had she imagined it in her grief over Kitty and her curiosity about Ish Reynolds? She also couldn't stop thinking about Kitty's last words, that she and the ghost of Granny Apples needed each other. She didn't know what Kitty had meant by that, or if it was just her imagination continuing to play tricks. But Emma knew she couldn't ignore it. She had to find out what Kitty had meant and what kind of help Granny Apples was searching for. If she didn't help Granny now, would she try to contact Kelly in the future? Emma had returned to Milo Ravenscroft seeking answers.

Milo sat back in his chair. He stroked his stubbly chin with his left hand while he studied Emma once more, weighing how much to tell her, judging how much she would be open to understanding. Under his gaze, Emma again fidgeted in her chair.

"And you're absolutely sure you saw this spirit?"

"Pretty sure."

"Could you describe her?"

"You don't believe me?" Emma set her jaw. She expected disbelief from others—had she told them, which she hadn't—but not from Milo. Wasn't contacting ghosts how he made his living?

"Yes, Emma, I do believe you saw a spirit. I just want to make sure it was the same one I know as Granny Apples."

"You mean I could be stalked by others?"

"You are *not* being stalked. This entity, or spirit, obviously needs something from someone in your family. But she is definitely not a stalker. When your father came to me years ago, he wanted me to ask her to not bother your mother again. She listened and obeyed. But now that you've come into the picture, I daresay she's hopeful again."

"I never told you about my father coming here." Emma's eyebrows raised in suspicion.

Milo peered at her again over the top of his crooked glasses, but this time his mouth was set with a slight smile. "See, there are some things I do know."

"But how?"

"Granny told me."

"The ghost told you who I was?" Her mouth hung open far longer than was polite. "Today?"

Milo shook his head no and smiled. The smile was a bit too smug for Emma's taste. She was getting annoyed with whatever game he was playing.

"If not today, then when?" The hard edge of demand had entered her voice again, and this time she would not tolerate a scolding. She wanted to get to the bottom of things. She still wasn't one hundred percent sure if she believed in any of what Milo was peddling or even if what she saw that night was real. Her patience was as thin and filmy as the smoke rising from the candle.

Milo sensed her growing frustration and decided he'd played enough. He was not a fraud, but he always enjoyed tweaking the noses of those who started out believing he was and then returned for his help. Emma was not the first, and Milo knew she wouldn't be the last.

"Granny Apples told me the first night you were here—the night you came to the group séance with your friend. And she told me about Kitty's passing. That's why I knew you had a death in the family that day you came here alone." He raised his arms and pushed back the sleeves of his worn cardigan, first one, then the other. "See, nothing up my sleeves. No mirrors. No spying, wiretapping, or other sleazy intrusions."

He leaned slightly forward and locked his eyes on Emma's. "I know what I know because they tell me. I'm a medium, Emma. I speak with and see spirits. I'm clairvoyant, meaning I *see* the spirits of the dead. But I'm also clairaudient, which means I can *hear* them speak. I don't go into trances or dream it all up. I actually see them, commune with them." He laughed. "As kids might say, I hang with them."

"And what about me?" Emma sat straight up in her chair and crossed her arms across her chest. She was wearing a cotton, scooped-neck T-shirt and linen skirt and was starting to feel a chill. "Am I now clairvoyant and clairaudio—or whatever you called it?"

"Clairaudient," he corrected.

"Well, am I?"

"I daresay, Emma Whitecastle, you just might be. You see, many people want to be clairvoyant but aren't. It's not something you choose to be, just something you are." He smiled at her. "But if you do have the gift, you will have to learn to bundle up more."

"Excuse me?"

Milo Ravenscroft chuckled. "Haven't you noticed yet that every time one of them is near, it gets rather chilly?"

As soon as he said it, Emma realized that she was rubbing her arms and fighting off sprouting goose bumps with no success. The room was definitely growing colder. Now she knew why Milo was wearing a heavy sweater on such a warm day.

Rising, Milo fetched a wool shawl from a nearby chair and gently draped it across the back of Emma's shoulders. She clutched at it and drew it around her.

"The theory is that spirits gather the warmth, or energy, in the air to fuel their contact with us. It's what gives them the energy to be seen and heard. As they extract the heat, the air grows colder."

"So she's here?" Emma snuggled under the shawl. "Granny Apples is here?"

Milo nodded as he sat down.

"Then why can't I see her?"

"The spirits reveal themselves as they wish, Emma," Milo explained. "It's not a faucet you can turn on and off at will. It's their decision, not ours. Granny is here, and I can see her and hear her. Only time will tell if she'll grant you the same privilege again."

"But I want to help her. Tell her that."

"Why don't *you* tell her, Emma."

Emma swallowed hard before speaking. "Aunt Kitty told me to help you, Granny."

Not sure of exactly where the ghost of Granny Apples was situated, Emma turn her head, first in one direction, then another, as she spoke, sending her words like scatter-shot throughout the room.

"I'm not sure what she meant," she continued, "but here I am."

Not getting a response, she raised her voice. "Talk to me, Granny, tell me what you want."

"Shh, Emma," Milo chuckled. "The dead are merely dead, not hard of hearing. Just speak normally."

Emma felt a flash fire of embarrassment rise from her neck to her cheeks.

"Tell me, Granny," she repeated, trying to keep her voice steady and even, "tell me what you need. Why have you been contacting my family?"

Milo raised a single finger to halt her words. He tilted his head to one side and focused his gaze on a spot near one of the covered windows. Emma looked in that direction, too, but saw nothing.

Milo turned back to Emma. "Granny says that it's her family, too." He returned his attention to the spot by the window and was still for a moment before looking at Emma again. "And that she's not sure you *want* to help."

"I'm here, aren't I?" Emma's voice swelled with impatience.

Milo shook his head. Both Emma Whitecastle and Ish Reynolds were stubborn women. He wondered how well they would get along if they did finally team up for a common purpose. It didn't matter that one was alive and the other dead; they would butt their hard heads for sure.

"She says you might be saying you want to help only because of Kitty."

"Of course, it's because of Aunt Kitty. I don't know this Granny Apples from a hole in the ground."

Emma knew exactly when the ghost of Granny Apples left the room. The air around them returned to the warmth of before. There was an emptiness in the air, too—something Emma hadn't noticed before.

She looked over at Milo Ravenscroft. "I blew it, didn't I?"

six

· · · · · ·

"YOU LOOK GOOD, EMMA."

Emma didn't have to turn around to see who was speaking. She knew that voice, as did millions of TV viewers. She was on the patio of her parents' home, filling glasses with fresh lemonade. It was the Sunday following Kelly's high-school graduation, and Emma's parents were hosting a large party to celebrate. The Miller house and large back yard were filled with family and friends, including Grant Whitecastle, his parents, Carolyn Bryant, and baby Oscar.

"You've let your hair grow longer. I like it." He reached out and stroked her hair with a light touch, like he used to do.

She moved just out of reach of her soon-to-be ex. "Thank you, Grant."

She knew the polite thing to do would be to return the compliment, but Emma couldn't bring herself to do it. It wasn't that Grant didn't look good himself. He did. Dressed in a hip Hugo Boss shirt and perfectly faded jeans, he looked better than ever. A small bit of gray had settled in at both of his temples, only enhancing the shine of his dark, thick, wavy hair. Instead of making him look middle-aged and settled, it made him look sexier. In spite of herself, something inside Emma twitched in response. Why did gray hair make men look distinguished and women simply old? And why did their gray hair present itself in such a becoming way, as if perfectly planned by a top-notch hair stylist? If Grant were a woman, especially on TV, he would have been made to cover it up or he would have been cast off for a younger, fresher version. But then, TV or no TV, that's exactly what had happened to Emma. Grant had found himself a replacement, someone without gray hair and not averse to surgical enhancement.

Emma glanced around until her eye caught on Carolyn Bryant. A pariah amidst the family gathering, she defiantly sat off by herself in the shade of a tree with eight-month-old Oscar. Not even Grant's parents, George and Celeste, were stoically standing by her side, and they had greeted Emma and her parents with warmth and affection. While Elizabeth Miller had invited the Whitecastles, it had never occurred to her that Grant would bring Carolyn and Oscar to Kelly's party. She'd been barely able to control her anger on her daughter's behalf since they'd arrived, giving the party an underlying ill-humored hum like a disturbed hornet's nest.

Seeing how great he looked and how happy he appeared to be with Carolyn and his new child, Emma wanted to swing the glass pitcher in her hand until it connected with the side of Grant's head. Something in her gut told her that her mother would forgive the transgression of propriety. And if she did any real damage, her father could patch Grant up.

Instead, Emma tossed her chin in Carolyn's direction. "Oscar looks healthy."

"Yes, he's getting to be a big boy." Grant laughed. "I'd forgotten how much work a baby is. And how noisy."

Emma didn't share his amusement. Grant noticed and moved the conversation forward.

"Emma, we need to get our affairs in order so that the divorce can be finalized."

"I couldn't agree more, Grant."

He looked at her with frank surprise. "Really? You're ready to move forward?"

"As soon as possible." She finished with the lemonade and put down the pitcher. She looked directly into Grant's eyes, hoping hers conveyed a hardness that meant business. "But please don't read my compliance as a sign I'm rolling over on the settlement. I will take nothing less than half of our assets. Half, Grant. And that includes half of that monstrosity of a house. Plus the support for Kelly and her education."

"But Emma, you hate that house. I bought it. I should keep it."

"Then keep it, Grant," she hissed. "But I want half its value. Even in today's market, the appraisal should be pretty substantial."

"Then you can just finance Kelly and her education out of your half of the settlement." Though Grant's voice remained low, it was challenging and spiteful.

Before responding, Emma's mind calculated a fair proposal. She didn't want anything but what was fair from Grant Whitecastle. "Tell you what, Grant. We will split Kelly's education and support—fifty-fifty—providing I receive half of all our assets. You try hiding anything, and I'll go for a hell of a lot more. Play fair, and I'll be fair. And, as I recall, it was *your* attorney, not mine, who stonewalled last time. Bring him in line and give him his marching orders."

"That's telling him."

The comment startled Emma. It had not come from Grant, and the two of them were the only ones on the patio. But the minute she heard the sound, she knew what it was. It was a voice, but not a voice made of warm blood and a beating heart. She glanced around, straining to see any image or hazy form, but saw nothing.

"Be reasonable, Emma," Grant said.

She shook off what she thought she'd heard and returned her attention to him. "I *am* being reasonable, Grant. Half, or be prepared for a long siege."

Emma was surprised by her gutsiness. Not once since the divorce proceedings began had she spoken to Grant with such determination. She probably had never spoken to him like that. She could see he was surprised. She looked over at Carolyn again.

"You going to marry her?"

Grant nodded. "That's the plan. As soon as the divorce is final." He chuckled as if sharing a joke with Emma, hoping to lighten her mood. "What can I do? She's already planning the wedding."

Emma fixed him with an icy stare. "Half, Grant. Half of everything for me. And half of Kelly's support and education through graduate school. Then you can marry your bimbo. Otherwise, be prepared for a long, difficult time, both from me and from her." She jerked her head in Carolyn's direction. "I can just imagine what kind of tacky circus she's planning for a wedding."

"Kitty might be right about you after all."

Emma whipped her head around, side to side, at the sound of the words, trying in vain to catch a fleeting glimpse of Ish Reynolds. The ghost of Granny Apples had returned, and this time Emma was determined to speak with her.

Then she saw her.

Standing just off from Grant's left shoulder was a hazy transparent image with facial features and an outline, like a character in a child's coloring book waiting to be filled in. It was the same image Emma had seen that night at the Singh's. But instead of a scowl, this time Granny Apples offered Emma a smile of encouragement.

"We need to talk," she said to the apparition. The ghost nodded.

"We *are* talking, Emma," Grant said in a testy manner. "At least I was talking. You were giving commands and issuing threats."

Emma kept her eyes on Granny Apples. "I'm not talking to *you*, Grant."

Grant Whitecastle turned to look in the direction of Emma's gaze. He saw nothing.

He stepped to the side, in front of her eyes, blocking her view of the ghost. "First you say we need to talk, then you say you're not talking to me. Which is it?"

Emma returned her attention to Grant. "You, Grant, I'm through with," she announced. "You heard what I had to say. The lawyers can take it from here."

Looking around Grant, Emma no longer saw Granny Apples. She scanned the back yard until she spotted her moving through the collection of guests seated at the scattered white tables. The image, like a small column of fog, drifted here and there amongst the living. When it stopped next to Elizabeth Miller's seated form, Emma gave a slight gasp.

"You okay, Emma?" asked Grant.

"Mmm, yes, Grant." With reluctance, she tore her eyes away from the ghost. "I'm fine. I just have a lot on my mind lately with Kitty dying and Kelly graduating and getting her ready for the trip with you." She paused, then added, "Not to mention the destruction of my twenty-year marriage."

Grant let loose with a long, dramatic sigh and rolled his eyes, something that seemed to be a family trait.

Emma returned her sights to the party guests and tried to locate the ghost once again. Ish had left Elizabeth's side and had moved close to Carolyn Bryant and Oscar. She hovered there. In a moment of panic, Emma realized she didn't know much about ghosts and what they could and couldn't do. Was Granny Apples capable of harming living beings? Would she harm Carolyn, knowing that Carolyn was partly the cause of Emma's failed marriage?

Emma took two steps toward Carolyn, hoping to head off any possible problem, when she heard Grant say something. She stopped in her tracks and turned back to him.

"I'm sorry, Grant. What did you say?"

"I said, get over it, Emma. I'm never coming back."

She glanced over at Carolyn, relieved to see that Granny Apples had once again moved on. She was returning to the patio, moving like a puff of steam in Emma's direction. Trailing the ghost was Archie, ball in mouth, tail wagging. It seemed Archie was clairvoyant, too. Emma laughed.

"You think that's funny, Emma? You think I don't mean it?"

Throwing her good humor aside like an annoying cape, Emma turned on him. "I hope you *do* mean it, Grant. Otherwise, you've put me, Kelly, and both our families through a lot of pain for nothing."

Grant Whitecastle started to say something more, but Emma raised her hand, stopping him.

"Live your life, Grant, whatever way you wish to live it. All I want is what's mine. Half of our assets and half of Kelly's support and education. Nothing more, nothing less. And you'd better believe *I* mean it."

Appearing next to Grant, Granny caught Emma's eye and winked at her.

Grant stared at Emma. "What happened to you, Emma? You've become such a bitch."

"*You* happened to me, Grant."

seven
· · · · · · · · · · ·

As soon as the clump of dark blond hair fell to the bathroom tile, Emma grabbed another handful. She sawed away at it with a large pair of scissors. Soon it was on the floor with the others, creating a soft miniature haystack. She stopped cutting just long enough to grab her wine glass and take a big swig. Then it was back to work with the shears.

"Darn Grant. Darn Carolyn. Darn ghost." Putting down the scissors, she refilled her glass from a half-empty bottle resting on the bathroom vanity.

The rest of the afternoon, Emma didn't see the ghost of Granny Apples again. But she did see how young and sexy Carolyn Bryant looked in her Juicy Couture and long red hair. Even the men who were appalled by Grant's behavior couldn't keep their eyes from caressing the young home wrecker. No matter how much bravado she'd displayed to Grant, Emma felt beaten, old, and used up next to Carolyn. As soon as the last of their guests had left, Emma helped clean up, then retreated to her room with the bottle of wine.

Kelly was gone, too. She was going to spend three weeks with Grant and Carolyn, most of it in Italy at the villa of a friend of theirs—or rather, a friend of Grant's. When she and Grant officially split up, most of their show-biz friends dropped Emma like a bad review. And since most of their socializing had been centered around Hollywood, that meant she'd left the marriage with no friends except for Tracy. It had been the harsh reality of being the castoff non-show-business spouse of a powerful TV personality.

Emma was taking another drink of wine when she heard a noise no louder than the rustle of leaves coming from her bedroom. It was accompanied by a slight chill in the air.

Without leaving the bathroom, she called out, "If that's you, Granny, tell me what you want straight out or don't come back. I'm having a breakdown here. I don't have time for your nonsense."

"I can tell you what Granny wants."

Emma spun around. Standing at the door between the bedroom and bathroom was Elizabeth Miller. She was freshly showered and dressed in a nightgown and matching robe the color of ripe apricots. Her silvery hair, worn in a becoming bob, framed her lovely and comforting face. Startled at the sight of her daughter's do-it-yourself hairdo, she raised a hand to her mouth. But just as quickly, she collected herself.

"I'm sorry, dear, for the intrusion. I knocked, but I guess you didn't hear me."

Wine glass in one hand, scissors in the other, Emma stood in front of her mother as if she'd been caught raiding the cookie jar. "I was just ... um ... just ... "

"Having a breakdown?"

Instead of answering, Emma looked at her reflection in the mirror. On the left side of her head, her hair had been hacked off just below the ear. The right side was still shoulder length. Quiet tears started running down her cheeks at the carnage.

"Grant told me he liked my hair longer."

"So you thought you'd fix his wagon by cutting it off?"

When Emma shook her head, half of her hair moved. "Not really, Mother." She put down the scissors and wine glass. Grabbing a bunch of tissues from a nearby box, she wiped her face and nose. "I didn't cut it for revenge. At least I don't think so. Grant likes long hair. Look at Carolyn's hair. It's down the middle of her back."

"The tart was wearing hair extensions. I'll guarantee it."

Emma turned to give her mother a weak smile. "Maybe so, but I just didn't want to be the type of woman Grant Whitecastle likes anymore."

"Good for you."

Emma heard the words, but her mother's lips never moved. If Granny was here, she needed to get Elizabeth out of the way as fast as possible. She shifted her eyes side to side as casually as she could but saw nothing.

"Sit down, dear." Elizabeth pulled her robe tighter around her as if warding off a chill.

"But—," Emma stammered.

"Sit."

Emma sat in the small vanity chair as her mother picked up the scissors and stood behind her. They looked at their reflections in the mirror. Her mother gave her a look filled with encouragement.

"I'll just even this up for you." She started cutting the rest of Emma's hair. "Tomorrow you should go to my salon and have them style it properly."

Emma watched her mother in the mirror. She wanted to look around for Granny Apples but didn't dare.

After taking a couple of snips, Elizabeth said, "The ghost of Granny Apples was at the party today, wasn't she?"

"A ghost? Oh, Mother, don't be silly."

Elizabeth smiled at her daughter's reflection. "You never were a good liar, Emma." She made another snip at the back of Emma's head.

With a deep sigh, Emma searched her brain for something to say that would be truthful but not alarming. She need not have worried. Her mother was prepared.

"I well remember the distinct chill when Granny was near. Nothing quite like it, is there?"

Her mother didn't seem upset at all by the news that the ghost was back, so Emma came clean. "I didn't exactly invite her to the party, Mother, but I've been trying to reach her. She wants me to help her with something."

"And you should."

"That's what Kitty said." As soon as the words were out of her mouth, Emma wanted to kick herself. The wine was loosening her tongue. "I meant Milo."

Elizabeth stopped cutting. "You meant Kitty, dear, didn't you?"

Emma turned in the chair to look at her mother. Elizabeth seemed relaxed and casual about the conversation, not at all upset, as she had expected.

"Kitty came to me, too, the night we buried her."

Emma's mouth hung open, as it had many times since first learning about Granny Apples.

At her mother's urging, Emma turned back around in the chair. Elizabeth continued cutting and talking.

"Kitty told me it was time to help Granny, and that you are the one to do it."

"Aunt Kitty came to you? You saw her?"

"No, I didn't see her, but I heard her. Plain as day."

Emma saw in the mirror that her mother had tears in her eyes. Emma snatched another tissue from the box and handed it to her.

"I never saw Granny either, just heard her." She paused to dab at her eyes. "Can you see them, Emma?"

"Yes, I can. Not clearly, not like I can see you, but there is definitely a real image when I do. Almost like a hologram. And it's not all the time. Sometimes, I just hear Granny."

Behind her, Elizabeth shivered. "She's here now, isn't she? Granny, I mean."

"Yes, Mother. At least I heard her speak shortly after you came in. Should I ask her to leave?"

In the mirror, Emma watched her mother shake her head.

"No, please don't." She took another cut of Emma's hair. "I was never afraid of Granny. Your father was much more concerned about her than I was. And concerned about me."

"That's why he sent her away?"

"Yes. He thought he was protecting me."

"Did Dad ever hear or see her?"

"Not that I know of. But I think if he knows she's back, he'll become alarmed again. I really don't want that."

Elizabeth lifted her head and glanced around the bathroom. "Granny, I know you're here. I can feel you."

Emma glanced around, too, and this time saw Granny Apples. She was perched on the edge of the tub, listening.

"I'm right here, Elizabeth," the ghost said.

At the sound, Elizabeth jerked her head around, then relaxed. A small smile crossed her face.

"She's seated on the edge of the tub," Emma told her mother.

Elizabeth glanced in the direction Emma indicated, then turned back to look at Emma in the mirror. "It's quite simple, really. Granny wants someone to find out who killed her and her husband. Since we're descended from her only son, Winston Reynolds, she feels one of us should do it." She turned back toward the tub. "Is that correct, Ish?"

"Yes," the ghost replied in her whispery voice. "Someone shot my man, Jacob, and hung me. I want to know who and why."

Emma was startled. "But that was over a hundred years ago, wasn't it? How am I supposed to do that?"

"I'm sure you'll figure it out, dear," Elizabeth told her. "You were always so good at puzzles."

"But Mother…"

Elizabeth started to cut the last bit of Emma's hair. "Kelly's gone for a few weeks, and your father and I will be leaving in a couple of days. It will be a good project for you while we're gone. And it might even keep you out of mischief."

When she finished cutting, Elizabeth cupped her daughter's hair gently near her ears and examined the look in the mirror.

"You know, Emma, a really short, layered style might look darling on you. Instead of going to my stuffy old salon, why don't you make an appointment at that trendy new shop on Colorado Boulevard? I've heard good things about it. I'll bet they could give you a whole new look, if that's what you're after."

Elizabeth turned toward the tub. "What do you think, Granny?"

"Better than that ol' tart, that's for sure." Granny paused, then added, "She's no real redhead neither."

Emma and her mother snapped their heads around to stare at the tub.

Granny shrugged. "Just thought you folks should know."

eight

DRESSED IN LINEN TROUSERS, a sleeveless blouse, and a bulky sweater, Emma sat once again at the wooden table in the darkened room in Milo's house. In front of her was a large pad of lined note paper; in her hand, a pen. This time she'd come prepared.

Following her mother's advice, she'd gone to the new, hip hair salon on Colorado Boulevard and had them reshape her chopped-off hair. While she was at it, she had highlights added. The end result was a very short, stylish cut that enhanced her large blue eyes and made her look younger. It took some getting used to, but it was a stunning look and easy to care for.

Only a couple of days had passed since Emma, her mother, and Granny had had their girl's night in the bathroom, and Emma hadn't had time to focus on the task of helping Granny. But now, with her parents gone on their trip and Kelly in Europe with Grant, Emma found herself eager to delve into what had happened to Ish and Jacob Reynolds over a hundred years ago in Julian.

She'd returned to Milo for help. She felt certain that Granny would talk to her now without him, but she still was on shaky ground when it came to conversing with spirits. And Milo was eager to assist Emma. In all his years working with the dead, he'd never had a live person partner up with one for a specific purpose, and he was excited to be a part of it. He was also curious about Emma Whitecastle. It was obvious that she could both hear and see spirits, but would she also be able to discern spirits of other dead individuals beyond her own ancestors and family? And if she could, would she be open to her gift or shut it out once her mission for Granny Apples was completed?

The candles were lit, the room cold. Emma and Milo sat across the table from each other. Granny was positioned between them, her hazy image stronger than ever in anticipation of finally receiving help.

"I was in the house making pies for the church social when I heard the shots." Granny's whispery voice was steady and even. "I ran out of the house and found Jacob behind the barn. He was dead. Shot in the back."

"Did the sheriff suspect you?" asked Emma.

"No. He asked questions, that's all. There were footsteps in the dirt. Big feet in boots. And Jacob had been beaten first."

"You didn't hear anything but the shots?"

"The wind was blowing hard that day. I was in the house, busy. Winston had gone to town to meet his friend Billy."

"Do you have any idea who might have done it or why?"

"Near as I can tell, it was for the gold."

Emma and Milo looked across the table at each other but remained silent.

"A few weeks before, Jacob found gold on our property, near the stream. That's why we left Kansas, to chase gold. Jacob never found enough to get rich, but we were able to buy our homestead and settle down. It'd been nearly twenty years since he stopped panning. I thought he'd gotten over it. But I guess once you get gold fever, you have it forever. I told him not to tell anyone—that he should wait until we'd mined a fair amount before the claim jumpers and ruffians got wind of it. But Jacob didn't listen. He got drunk in town and told everyone. It'd been a fair number of years since any real gold had been found in the area, so people were excited.

"After we buried Jacob, lots of folks offered to buy the property, mostly for the gold. Winston hated farming and wanted to go somewhere to school. Always set his heart on being a lawyer. But I loved the land. Couldn't think of selling it. I figured we could find enough gold to send Winston to school, or maybe sell a couple of small claims to do it. I could always hire someone to help with the farm chores."

"So that's how Winston got up here to the Los Angeles area and started our family?"

"Not while I was alive. Never got the chance. Before we made the decision of what to do, I was killed."

Emma looked over at the ghost. Her image was pulsating between clear and fading in its visibility. "Granny, if this is too difficult, we can stop."

"I've waited over a hundred years to tell this story. By God, I'm going to tell it."

"Okay, but let us know if you want to stop."

Milo looked from the ghost to Emma, pleased with the way Emma was handling the situation. Unlike her earlier visits, she was handling this encounter with Granny well, giving the ghost the same consideration as she would a live person. It usually took newbies more time than this to get comfortable with the idea of conversing with the dead. His hopes for Emma's gift were growing.

"I was in the barn feeding the livestock. It was early in the morning, just a few weeks after we buried Jacob. I heard heavy steps. It was two men. One of them struck me to the ground."

"Did you know them?"

Granny shook her head. "They wore hoods and surprised me. When I came to, I was by the old oak with a rope around my neck. There was a third man, also hooded."

Emma shivered, but it wasn't from the cold air. "What about Winston?"

"He was out in the far field plowing, getting an early start."

The spirit's image wavered, and Milo and Emma thought they would lose her. The air got colder, and the image strengthened.

"The third man told me they didn't take to women killing their men. Said they were doing what the law wouldn't. Before I could say anything, I was gone."

During Granny's story, Emma had taken notes. She looked them over once Granny was done.

"Can Jacob tell you who shot him?" Emma asked. "I mean, haven't you seen him there—wherever you are?"

"He never saw them. He was only half conscious during the beating. Don't even remember being shot."

"Can he come here and talk to me? It might help."

"He don't want to."

Milo interrupted. "Emma, it's not like the spirits are all hanging about in some big room, waiting to be called." He glanced at Granny. "You see, we're not really sure how it works. Some believe that spirits stay on earth because they have unfinished business, like Granny. I've been working with the spirit world for decades, and even I know very little. And sometimes what I think I know is turned on its ear. But basically, I believe they come and go at random, with or without something that ties them here. Some have no desire to return to earth and commune with the living. Others are here all the time. Some have a specific purpose. Others just enjoy being around us and familiar places."

"So," Emma said, addressing him, "it's just a go-with-the-flow kind of thing."

"Pretty much, yes. Except that it does seem that they are only heard and seen when they want to be, providing the living person is able to discern them. Not everyone is, which is why people come to me. I am the bridge to those without the gift."

"Will I be able to see others, Milo? So far, I've only seen Granny and Aunt Kitty." Emma asked the questions with a slight tentativeness in her voice. It had been tough enough realizing she could see dead family members. Even though she wanted to help Granny, she wasn't eager to hobnob with the entire dead population. When Milo didn't answer right away, she asked again. "Will there be others?"

"We will have to wait and see, Emma." He paused and again looked at Granny. Her image was beginning to fade. Emma noticed it, too.

"Another thing," Milo added. "I've noticed that their physical presence doesn't last very long. That is why they come and go. You may be able to hear Granny much more than you'll be able to see her. Think of it as a flashlight with a weak battery. It can only shine for a short time before it must recharge. They can't always drain the energy from the air. Like us, they need to rest, but in a different way. Granny's done a lot of work today."

Emma turned to the ghost. "Thank you, Granny. I'll do my best." She glanced back down at her notes. "I think my first step will be to go down to Julian and look around. I want to see the town and the place where Granny died firsthand. I'm heading down there tomorrow for a few days, though I doubt I'll find any hard clues. It's been over a hundred years."

"Good idea, though," Milo agreed. "Never know what might turn up."

"Hotel Robinson," Granny added, her image becoming faint. Emma wrote *Hotel Robinson* down on her notepad just as Granny disappeared.

Emma shrugged off her sweater. The returning warmth in the room told them that Granny had not only disappeared physically, but altogether.

"That's odd," Emma said to Milo. "I was on the Internet researching places to stay and never saw a Hotel Robinson on the list. I'll check again. Maybe Google it by name this time."

"Ten." Milo announced the number in a blunt manner.

"What?" Emma had been scribbling a note about the hotel on her notepad when she heard him speak. She looked up to see Milo staring off, looking at the wall behind her.

"Ten," he repeated. "For some reason, the number ten is coming to me."

"You're a psychic, as well?"

He shook himself to bring his attention back to her. "Sometimes I have visions or see something vague that might be important. And right now I see the number ten connected with the hotel."

Emma studied him a moment. She'd come to like and trust Milo Ravenscroft. In a short time, she'd had to reconsider and believe in things she never would have several months ago, and he'd been there to help her along. She smiled at him, then wrote the number *10* on her notepad in large numbers and circled it.

"And, Emma—" He started to speak but stopped.

"You have another inkling about something?" She got ready to record it in her notes.

"It's about you, Emma."

Emma looked up at Milo, a tingle of fear tickling her heart. "What about me?"

"Changes, Emma. You're about to go through some changes."

"Considering that I'm in the midst of ending my marriage, I'd say that's pretty accurate." She gave him a small, sad smile.

"Not just your marriage, Emma. You, the person you are, is about to change."

Milo was once again looking beyond her, speaking as if transmitting a message. Goose bumps rose on Emma's arms.

Milo turned back to her and noted the concern in her eyes. "Don't fear the change, Emma." He reached over and patted her hand in comfort. "Embrace it. It will be difficult but worthwhile."

His body relaxed as if he'd just finished a strenuous chore. He leaned back in his chair and grinned at her. "Your new haircut is just the beginning."

nine

· · · · · · · ·

ACCORDING TO HER INTERNET search, the Hotel Robinson turned out to be the present-day Julian Hotel. She'd booked a room at the Orchard Hill Country Inn, the nicest place in Julian, but changed her reservation to the Julian Hotel because of Granny's comment. After boarding Archie for a few days, she'd driven nearly three hours from Pasadena to Julian, arriving at the hotel around one o'clock in the afternoon.

Once she got out of the congestion of urban freeway travel, Emma enjoyed driving the rural highways and winding country roads. Her route passed rolling meadows and rocky pastures with grazing cattle and horses. Strewn along the roadside were wild poppies and lavender. She deftly guided the Lexus through the twists and turns of the mountain roads and, for the first time in weeks, felt at peace. Thinking back, she couldn't remember ever taking a trip alone, not even for a couple of days. She'd always had her parents, Grant, or Kelly with her whenever she'd traveled. She hoped that she would enjoy Julian, and that the trip would become a needed getaway, as well as a fact-finding mission.

Granny had not made an appearance during the drive. After what Milo had explained, Emma figured she was saving her energy. Emma had gone over her notes several times the night before and wrote out a plan. She needed to find exactly where Ish and her family had lived while alive. Granny's information was sketchy at best, with possible gaps in the timeline. Milo had explained to Emma that since the spirits don't exist in accordance with time as the living know it, they often don't have a full understanding of what has occurred since their deaths. So while Granny knew that Emma and her family were descendants of her son Winston, she wasn't exactly sure when the family line moved from the country-side of Julian up to the Los Angeles area, or what happened after her death. All she wanted was to prove Granny didn't kill her husband.

With Elizabeth's help, Emma was able to trace their family lineage back several generations on her mother's side. But the trail stopped short with Winston Reynolds, Granny's son. They knew that Winston Reynolds had been a prominent attorney in the early 1900s, but the family records dead-ended there, except for references in letters that the family had originated in Kansas and settled in Julian.

As Emma entered the town of Julian, she felt like she'd stepped back in time. The town was made up of a single main street called, appropriately, Main Street, with several smaller streets shooting off to the north and south of it. There were no traffic signals, just one main intersection with a stop sign. Looking left and right, Emma noted that Main Street ran off into the country in both directions after it left town.

American flags were posted all along Main Street, and a banner announcing the upcoming Fourth of July parade was strung across the roadway. At the main intersection, there was a small grocery store, a diner/drug store, city hall, and a vacant lot. Following her directions, she turned right at the stop sign. She spotted the Julian Hotel on the next corner on the left. It looked just like the photos on the Internet. Turning left at the hotel, she pulled up next to it and parked.

Grabbing her luggage, Emma stood at the corner of B Street and Main and studied her surroundings before entering the hotel. The town itself was made up of old buildings that held a variety of businesses, such as restaurants and gift shops that catered to tourists. The buildings didn't appear to be replicas of times past but the real McCoy, lovingly maintained throughout the years, even if they didn't still house their original occupation. It was a Wednesday, so there were few visitors milling about the streets, and those that did seemed of retirement age. Take away the modern cars, Emma thought, and the place could have easily been mistaken for a back lot at one of the movie studios in Los Angeles.

The inside of the Julian Hotel gave Emma another jolt of time travel. Its lobby was meticulously decorated with antiques and period pieces, including a floral carpet and heavy drapes trimmed with fringe.

"Hello, welcome to the Julian Hotel," greeted the compact, well-groomed elderly woman behind the small lobby desk. She introduced herself as Barbara and pulled Emma's reservation to complete the check-in process.

"Since it's the middle of the week, we have several rooms available," Barbara explained. "You're welcome to go upstairs and look at them and choose which one you'd like. They are all decorated a bit differently."

Barbara wrote several numbers on a small piece of paper. "These are the rooms not yet occupied. Their doors should be open. The closed doors are rooms that already have guests."

Emma looked at the paper. Rooms 8, 9, 10, and 6 were available. Ten. She thought of Milo. He hadn't specifically said room 10. In fact, he hadn't been sure what the number ten meant, just that it was significant.

Oh, why not, Emma thought to herself. She might as well explore every possible ten that crossed her path.

She handed the paper back to Barbara. "No need. I'll take room 10." She hesitated, then added, "A friend recommended it."

"It's one of our most popular rooms," Barbara told her with a smile as she handed over the key. "Don't forget, breakfast is served in the parlor between eight and nine. Tea begins at four thirty."

When Emma first came into the hotel, she'd noticed a man sitting in the lobby reading a newspaper. He was dressed in casual attire and appeared to be in his early sixties and quite fit. Every now and then she'd glance over and catch him staring at her, appraising her over the top of his paper. She wasn't a stranger to receiving appreciative looks from men, but lately they had been few and far between. Must be the new haircut.

Barbara was giving her some last bit of information when a stocky woman with gray hair came down the stairs.

"Finally," the man in the lobby said, putting down the paper. He got out of the rocker and joined the woman at the front door. The two of them smiled at Barbara as they left.

"You have a good afternoon, Mr. and Mrs. Quinn," Barbara called to them as they left.

At the top of the stairs, the hallway branched off in two directions. She headed right. The upstairs was as nicely furnished as the downstairs. Antique mirrors and prints adorned the walls. Plants and floral arrangements were scattered about. After passing a wicker settee and a table with urns of complimentary coffee, she discovered three rooms and a small bath. Since none of the rooms down this hallway were number 10, she went back and headed down the other hallway, which took a sharp right turn. Here she found several open doors and peeked in. The rooms were very small. Each contained an antique dresser and double bed and a private bath. On the walls was vintage wallpaper. On the beds, lovely quilts. In the middle of the hallway on the right, she located room 10.

Suddenly, Emma felt a familiar chill. She glanced around, expecting to see Granny, but saw nothing.

"Granny," she whispered several times in both directions down the hallway. She dropped her bag just inside her room and strolled to the end of the hallway, where it dead-ended at an exit that led down a wooden stairway to the yard below. "Granny, you here?"

Nothing. Even if Granny was reserving her energy, she could at least say hello. Getting no response, she went back to room 10 and shut the door behind her.

Her room was similar to the others in furnishings. The bed was made of white iron, with the joints painted a dark blue that matched the heavy drapes at the single window and the swag over the headboard. The quilt on the bed had an Americana feel, with a colorful checkerboard pattern surrounded by roses. The wallpaper was yellow, with roses running in vertical stripes. To the right of the bed was a slim wooden armoire. To the left side, a single wooden chair. Across from the door was a lovely antique dresser with a mirror. The décor was fussy and busy, yet all of it worked together in a charming and beautiful manner. Tempted to forget her personal problems by escaping to another era, Emma fought the urge to climb up on the high bed and burrow herself under the quilt.

Instead, she put her bag on the bed. Toiletries in hand, she inspected the private bath. It was modern, yet still fit with the Victorian décor. It held a stall shower, toilet, and pedestal sink. She placed her makeup bag on the wooden shelf above the sink. When she turned around and faced her room, she gasped.

"I'm sorry if I scared you, Emma." Granny was perched on the edge of the tall bed, her feet swinging more than a foot off the floor.

For the first time since Emma had met the ghost, Granny's face held a smile that circled her face as her braid circled her head. In spite of her transparency, Emma noticed a twinkle in the spirit's eyes. She seemed genuinely happy.

"This place was brand-spanking new about the time I passed," she told Emma. "Of course, it didn't have these fancy privies then. Belonged to Margaret and Albert Robinson. Started out a restaurant. Margaret could cook, I'll tell ya. Put the rest of us to shame." Granny's smile widened. "Except for her apple pie. I was the best pie baker."

As Emma continued to unpack and put her things into the dresser drawers, Granny told her about the hotel, the Robinsons, and Julian. Emma tried to forget she was conversing with someone who'd been dead over a hundred years and just let herself enjoy the camaraderie. Like a thirsty sponge, her brain absorbed everything Granny told her. It was interesting and might provide some clues Granny had forgotten about her death.

A short while later, Emma found herself back on Main Street, but without her ghostly sidekick. She walked down the sidewalk, nosing about in the cute shops that sold everything from jams and baked goods to clothing, crafts, and antiques. She'd picked up a town guide along the way and studied it. It showed all the points of interest, restaurants, and shops. The hotel had recommended either the Julian Grille or Romano's Dodge House for dinner. After perusing sample menus at the hotel, she decided on the Julian Grille. It was almost three. If she had just a snack now, she could have an early dinner and turn in shortly after. The town didn't seem to have any sort of night life, and she was glad she'd brought a couple of books with her.

She stopped in at Mom's Pie House and ordered a cup of coffee with a slice of warm apple pie and vanilla ice cream. She didn't know how long she'd be in Julian but figured she'd be there long enough to sample the goods of all the pie shops. Her earlier vow of prejudice aside, she was fast becoming a fan of apple pie, and since Julian was famous for it, it seemed almost sacrilegious to order any other kind.

Needing to walk off the apple pie, Emma headed up Main Street, past the main intersection, past the Julian Pie Company, and past the Julian Grille. According to the city guide, the Pioneer

Cemetery was just up the street. Emma wondered if Granny was buried there and, if so, would she be able to find her grave. She hoped Granny would return to help her.

The Pioneer Cemetery was located at the top of a hill at the edge of the commercial part of town. Its presence was announced by a large, white wrought-iron arch over a winding, uphill path. To aid the steep climb, steps of railroad ties were embedded into the land and followed the path. Alongside the steps was a sturdy railing made of fresh lumber. At the beginning of the climb was a plaque informing visitors that until 1924, when a road access was developed, all coffins were carried up the steep hill, no matter what the season.

Looking again at the simple city map, Emma located the easier road access yet decided to make the climb. It would do her—and the pie in her stomach—good. She also wanted to take the same path Granny had taken when she'd buried Jacob shortly before her own death.

Whether they realized it or not, the inhabitants of the Pioneer Cemetery had a fabulous view of the town and surrounding hills with their lush vegetation and pine trees. Locating a bench under the leafy canopy of a large tree, Emma sat down and looked out, enjoying the countryside that was so different from Pasadena and the bustle of Los Angeles. She wished she'd brought someone with her. Julian was a romantic and peaceful place, yet she knew Grant would never have enjoyed it. Not fast enough. Not trendy enough. Not modern enough. Maybe Tracy, Emma thought. Tracy would have enjoyed this trip and this town, but Emma still hadn't told her friend about Granny Apples. Only her mother and Milo knew that Emma had embarked on a journey into the past with Ish

Reynolds. Perhaps she could bring Tracy next time. Who knew, maybe next time she'd have someone new to travel with.

Her thoughts surprised her. Not once since she'd left Grant had she thought about the possibility of someone else. Both her mother and Tracy had made some not-so-subtle hints about Emma dating again, but Emma still felt married. She *was* still married. In spite of his behavior, Emma didn't feel finding someone new was an option until it was finally over with Grant Whitecastle. Sitting on top of a hill in Julian, California, surrounded by the dead, she wondered if maybe she hadn't buried her marriage yet—if, in fact, deep down, she hoped it could be resurrected like Lazarus and given new life, even with everything that had happened between them.

After taking a deep breath of the clean mountain air, Emma put thoughts of her marriage aside. It was then she noticed the chill. Now comfortable with the feeling, Emma smiled and turned to her right, expecting to see Granny. Instead, sitting next to her on the bench was the ghost of a man.

"Oh my God!" Emma yelled as she jumped up from the bench, catching her foot on a tree root in the process. Down she went to her hands and knees. Like a crab caught on dry land, she quickly scrambled away from the bench. Once she was several feet away, she turned and sat in the dirt amongst the country graves and stared at her new companion.

"I didn't mean to give you a fright, ma'am," the spirit said to her. The image was of a young man, maybe in his early twenties, with a smooth face and dark, unruly hair. He wore work trousers with suspenders, heavy boots, and a plaid shirt.

"Who … who are you?" Emma had just gotten used to seeing Granny, and now she was seeing a new apparition. Her legs were shaking so bad, she didn't dare get back on her feet.

"Billy Winslow, ma'am."

"How come I can see you, Billy?" Emma calmed herself down enough to be able to get to her feet, but she still kept her distance.

"Not sure, ma'am. I was sitting here like I always do when you came and sat down yerself. Lots of city folks come up here, but you're the first talking to me."

Emma brushed off the seat of her trousers, knowing it would take more than her hands to get the dirt out of the good weave. She gave up on cleaning herself and studied the image. Once past her initial start, she wondered if she should ask Billy if he knew Granny or her family when he was alive. Believing she wouldn't know until she tried, she started phrasing her question when her peripheral vision caught sight of something flitting by her. She looked away from Billy Winslow and glanced around the graveyard.

"Oh … my … God!"

ten

······

"MILO, WE HAVE A problem," Emma snapped into her cell phone. "A big problem."

She was still in the Pioneer Cemetery. Across from her, the ghost of Billy Winslow kept his vigil on the bench.

"There are ghosts *everywhere*," she continued, without waiting for Milo to speak. "I feel like I'm on the Haunted Mansion ride at Disneyland. All I need is the spooky music and mouse ears."

"What do you mean by 'everywhere,' Emma? Where are you? In Julian?"

"Yes, in Julian. At the cemetery."

"And you can see them?"

"Yes! Why do you think I'm so upset? I mean, one or two, here and there, maybe I could absorb *that* idea. But this—this is like a ghost convention."

She looked out across the uneven land that comprised the graveyard. Even though it was daylight, she could make out numerous images, some more distinct than others. Some were moving, some stationary, but all were obviously spirits of the dead. Except for Billy Winslow, none had spoken to her or even looked in her direction. She started counting.

"There's about a dozen that I can make out," she said into the phone. "Various ages, both men and women." On the other end of the phone there was a long silence. "Milo, you still there?"

"This is incredible, Emma." Milo's voice was filled with excitement. "The most I've seen at any one time is three."

"What? You think this is a contest?"

Milo laughed. "No, of course not." Another pause. "Emma, is Granny there?"

"Not at this moment. At least not that I can see. Of course, she could be lost in the crowd."

"Emma, listen to me." Milo's voice was stable and comforting. "These spirits are not going to hurt you. Just go about your business. What's up with the cemetery, anyway?"

"I wanted to see if Granny and her husband were buried here. Not sure why. It was just a whim."

"Well, your whim answered our question of whether or not you'd be able to see other spirits besides Granny and your aunt. Did any of them speak to you?"

"Just one. A young man. He introduced himself and apologized for giving me a fright."

Milo laughed again. "A well-mannered ghost."

"This isn't funny, Milo. I about had a heart attack."

"Just relax, Emma. Apparently, these spirits feel very comfortable around you. They trust you."

"What about *my* comfort level?"

"You'll get used to it."

"I don't want to get used to it, Milo. I want to help Granny Apples, then be done with this."

Milo paused before speaking, taking a minute to weigh his next words. Emma again thought the call had been dropped.

"You there, Milo?"

"Emma, you may not have a choice in the matter. Now that you've opened yourself to the other side, it may be difficult to shut the door. Not impossible, but difficult."

"You mean, I'm stuck with this for the rest of my life?"

"I'm not sure. I've never met someone like you before. But for now, why don't you just go forward with your research for Granny, and ignore the others. Pretend they're not there. When you get back home, you and I can try to figure this out."

"I don't have much choice, do I?"

"Emma, these spirits allowing you to see them is a privilege and an honor. It's not a curse."

"Depends on your point of view."

After her call with Milo, Emma gave Billy Winslow a nod good-bye. He gave her a cordial wave in return.

Even though there was a narrow roadway winding through the cemetery, Emma took a deep breath and started making her way among the graves, scrub grass, and spirits lingering in the grave-yard. None of them paid attention to her. The roadway circled a knoll that contained most of the graves. On the far side of the road, facing the town, the land sloped, forming natural graded levels that contained more graves. She decided to explore the central area first.

She noted that some of the graves were arranged in obvious family plots. Others were scattered helter-skelter throughout the place. It was almost as if someone had decided to dig a grave wherever the coffin was dropped, with no eye to order and placement. The dates on the tombstones covered a wide range of years. She spotted some beginning in the mid-1800s and some that were as late as the 1930s. The tombstones marking the graves were just as diverse. Some graves were marked with solid and stately headstones, others with large chunks of weathered wood or large rocks, but most were marked with roughly hewn blocks of stone or concrete the size of a large shoebox. Names on the headstones were either primitively carved into the stone or etched on a small metal plate attached to the stone. Some of the names and dates were easily discernible, while most were difficult to read. Many featured only the name of the deceased.

At the top of the mound of graves was a redwood gazebo with a short, white picket fence surrounding the inside area. Just to the right of the gazebo, the ghost of a young pioneer woman sat under a tree and rocked a baby. As Emma approached, she noted that the woman was cradling nothing in her arms. She rocked back and forth, her empty arms comforting air.

Turning her gaze away from the rocking spirit, Emma stepped toward the gravesite. In the middle was a modern headstone with fine etching. Scattered around it were a few broken and weathered wooden crosses, some little more than dried kindling. The headstone explained that the plot was where babies were buried in the late 1870s. Emma was deeply touched. Over the years, the people of Julian had not forgotten the children of the early settlers and had erected a fitting memorial.

Emma glanced over at the rocking mother with new understanding.

"Three of my children are buried here," a familiar voice whispered from behind Emma.

Emma turned to her left, not surprised to see the ghost of Ish Reynolds. "Three?"

Granny nodded. "Two came before their time. Never had a chance to make it. Another, a girl, died of pneumonia during her first winter."

"I'm sorry, Granny."

Granny looked at the memorial. "That time, this place, was unkind to the weak."

Emma turned back toward the childless rocking mother, but the spirit had vanished.

She moved away from the children's gravesite and started again to wander among the scattered graves. Granny followed and didn't seem either bothered or excited that they were not alone. She took no particular note of any of the other spirits.

"Granny, are you and Jacob buried here?"

In response, the ghost of Granny Apples drifted through the cemetery. Emma followed, dodging scattered headstones and being careful of the uneven terrain and the spirits around her. Granny paused on the side of a small rise, several yards from the top. Emma looked down, scanning the various weather-worn headstones for a familiar name. It took her a couple of minutes before she spotted what Granny wanted to show her.

Two small hewn blocks were set side by side. Emma knelt beside them in an attempt to better read the metal nameplates. Neither displayed a date of death, only names. Close up, *Reynolds* was fairly clear on both. Touching the warm metal with her fingers, she traced out *Jacob* on the grave to the left. She did the same with the plate on the grave to the right.

She glanced up at Granny with a puzzled look. "It says *Elizabeth*."

"Elizabeth is my Christian name. When I was a girl, my younger brother had trouble saying it. It came out as Ish and stayed Ish."

"Elizabeth is my mother's name." Emma looked back down at the graves. "In looking up our family history, we found a lot of women named Elizabeth over the years." She looked back up at Granny. "Starting with Winston's daughter."

"My son did not forget me." Granny raised her head in pride.

Emma stood up. Spotting a nearby bench empty of both the living and the dead, she made her way for it and sat down. The day had been a great drain. With the long drive and now the graveyard, Emma was downright spent, both physically and emotionally. She was glad she'd made her way to Julian during the week, when visitors were scarce. She would not have liked sharing her finds at the cemetery with the usual tourists.

"Granny," she said, once she collected her thoughts, "if you never had any grandchildren while you were alive, why were you called Granny Apples?"

"It had to do with the pies," Granny explained with a slight smile. "Jacob always said I looked like an old, bent granny when I rolled out the dough. He'd tease me, calling me Granny Apples. A lot of other folks in town picked it up, especially after I won my first pie contest."

At the mention of pie, Emma realized that she was getting hungry. Looking at her watch, she saw it had been nearly two hours since she'd had the pie and coffee. She needed dinner—a good, solid dinner.

In spite of her hunger, Emma remained on the bench a little longer. Granny had disappeared and so had some of the other spirits. After reflecting on her day and what she'd learned, Emma got up from the bench and returned to Jacob and Ish's graves. Taking her cell phone out of her bag, she used the camera feature to take a couple of photographs of the graves and the surrounding area. Then she took out a small pad of paper and a pencil and made a rubbing of the nameplates. The etching on the metal plate wasn't very deep, but she was able to get a fair imprint of the names. After, she followed the paved access road down to the town and made her way to the Julian Grille, where she dined alone, without the company of ghosts.

eleven

· · · · · · · · · · · ·

"Are you sure this is where you lived?" Emma asked Granny.

Following Granny's directions, Emma had driven a couple of miles out of town. They'd left the main road and followed another paved road lined with trees before Granny pointed to a small lane branching off to the left and dipping into a shallow valley. There was a white fence around the property but no gate blocking the road.

"The trees are bigger, and we didn't have no fancy fence like this, but this is our road. I'm sure of it."

"It's probably private property, Granny. We could be trespassing."

"I've never come to it this way since I passed, but it's our property, I tell ya." Granny looked at her. "You being a fraidy cat again?"

Emma let out a big sigh. She hadn't been brought up to invade other people's property, but what harm could it do? There wasn't a gate, just fencing on either side of the road. And Granny was probably wrong. How could she be so sure after all this time? Especially since for the past hundred years, she'd been traveling by popping in and out of places and not over physical roads.

Nosing the car down the narrow road, Emma followed it through a large meadow with cattle grazing on either side. Soon the fence opened to another lane on the left. Over it was a large arch that proclaimed it to be the Bowers ranch. Down this small road, Emma could see a large house with matching barn, stables, and assorted outbuildings, all beautifully built and maintained.

"Bowers ranch. Does that name mean anything to you, Granny?"

"There was a Buck Bowers, but I don't recall him having a ranch, especially not out this way. It was just our place at the end of this road."

Emma drove a little farther until the road dead-ended at a clearing. Granny was gone when the car stopped. Emma climbed out of the car. With Granny gone, she wasn't sure what she should be looking for.

Just to the right of the road was a large clearing. A few massive, solitary trees were scattered about the area, with a large bank of trees a couple hundred yards away.

After maneuvering through a small opening in the fence, Emma made her way toward the clearing. The cattle seemed content to stay at the far end, closer to the main road.

Here and there in the grass, Emma discovered large pieces of decaying wood. She nudged some of it with her foot, only to discover it had become embedded into the ground over time. A little farther, she came upon a circular pile of carefully set stones: an old well. Someone had taken the precaution of securing a metal lid over the opening and padlocking it. Emma noted that the lid was rusty, but the lock looked fairly new. Continuing, she found odd bits of rusty metal and more chunks of wood. The wood was ragged in shape, but it was clear to see that at one time the pieces had been shaped with smooth, straight edges.

Emma continued to scrutinize the area, locating another spot of interest. This time, stones had been set into the ground in a rectangular pattern. She followed it, using her foot to trace the lines, guessing it could have been a hearth.

"Granny, you going to help me out here?" Emma called gently.

"That's where I was hung," came a voice behind her.

Startled, Emma gave a little jump. Turning around, she saw Granny staring at a large tree not far from where they stood. Emma turned her gaze upon the innocent-looking tree and studied it. It was an old oak, sturdy, with many branches that could have done the job. She shuddered.

"Was your house here?" she asked the ghost. She traced again the barely noticeable rectangle of stones in the ground.

Granny nodded. "Our cabin was there. The barn there, beyond the tree." She pointed.

Emma kicked another small pile of rocks, and a snake slithered out from under them. She gasped and jumped back.

"Not a rattler," Granny announced. "Won't hurt you."

"There are *rattlesnakes* out here?" Emma looked at Granny in horror.

"'Course there are. Lots of 'em."

Emma turned and headed for the car, slipping in her haste but regaining her balance before falling.

Granny followed. "They won't hurt you none if you leave them be."

"Rattlesnakes were not part of the bargain, Granny." In squeezing back through the fence, Emma's shirt got hung up.

"They mostly stay in the woods. Don't like people none."

Emma yanked her arm and heard a rip as she freed her shoulder. When she reached the car, Granny wedged herself between Emma and the car door.

"This ain't the city. Lots of critters out here."

It crossed Emma's mind to simply reach through Granny's hazy torso, open the car door, and hop in. But she'd done it before and knew Granny didn't like it. Snakes or not, Emma felt she should honor Granny's boundaries.

"What did you expect, Emma?" The ghost tapped her booted foot with impatience.

"I'm not sure what I expected, Granny."

Emma looked around, noticing for the first time how solitary the area was. She could see the Bowers house in the distance, but if a snake, or even something more menacing, attacked her, who'd hear? She was used to urban threats, not ones that came from nature. She wished she'd given it some thought and had come better prepared, especially in the clothing department. Her silk camp shirt was torn, and her floral capri pants looked ridiculous. She wished she'd worn her pants from last night, but they were dirty from her stumble in the graveyard. Still, better dirty than absurd. She looked down and swore softly. Open-toed, expensive canvas wedge shoes were hardly suitable for kicking around in the dirt and scrub brush, no matter how comfy and cute they were in the city. And they certainly weren't appropriate for walking in cow dung. If something did try to chase her, even an annoyed cow, she'd be dead meat.

Emma sighed deeply as she wiped the manure on her foot off on the grass. Granny was counting on her. Aunt Kitty was counting on her. Even her mother was expecting her to get to the bottom of things. She wished she had told Tracy about Granny. Tracy was a resourceful woman. She'd probably know what to do.

"Pull yourself together, Emma," she said to herself out loud. "You can do this."

"Of course you can."

Emma looked down into the weathered and expectant face of the ghost of Granny Apples—a woman who'd been wrongfully hung for the death of her husband. She'd waited over a hundred years for someone to help her.

After a moment, Emma lifted her eyes from Granny's face and scanned the area, taking in the brush, trees, nearby meadow, and last remnants of what had been a life once upon a time. It was a beautiful area. As she looked around at the peaceful countryside, Emma wondered what it would be like to wake up every morning to such natural beauty and quiet. It was probably heaven on earth.

When she turned her attention back to Granny, the ghost had disappeared. Emma opened the car door and retrieved the pad of paper from her bag. She sketched the area, noting where the house and barn had been, following the description Granny had given her earlier. Being no artist, the buildings were merely boxes. She added a few dismal stick trees, including the hanging tree and the road, for perspective. Once again, she took out her cell phone and took a couple of photos, including a couple of the Bowers ranch. Then she made a quick call to Tracy, hoping her reception would be clear.

After exchanging pleasantries, Emma cut to the reason she called. "What do you know about tracing a piece of property?"

"Not much. Why? And where are you?"

"I'm in Julian. You know where that is?"

"Julian? The apple town way the hell down by San Diego?"

"That's the place. Have you been here before?"

"Sure, years ago, on a romantic fling. The romance didn't last, but the weekend was fun." Tracy paused. "Are you buying property in Julian?"

"No, but I'm interested in the history of a piece of land here. It's a project I'm working on for a friend." Emma looked around but still didn't see Granny.

"Well, I'm not sure myself, but I have a friend from my yoga class who might know. She's a real-estate attorney, I believe. You have any information on it, like an address, lot number, owner? Anything like that?"

"Not yet, just possibly the last name of Bowers."

"Even I know that's not a lot to go on." There was a pause, during which Emma could hear Tracy giving a complicated coffee order to someone. "Sorry," she said when she came back on the line. "My turn to get the coffee for my department meeting. Why we can't just meet here, at the coffee shop, is beyond me."

"Why don't you ask your friend what's needed to search back history on property? And I mean back history, like a hundred years ago. I'll try to get more information in the meantime. I'll be—"

"Hey, wait a minute," interrupted Tracy. "Does this have anything to do with that séance we went to? That guy, Milo, didn't he say something to you about Julian?"

Emma hesitated before answering. "I don't remember."

"Bull pucky. Did you even know Julian existed a few weeks ago? I'll bet not."

With distaste, Emma looked down at the pucky still on her shoe. "I was curious, that's all. Had some time to kill while my folks and Kelly are away, so I thought I'd check it out."

"Uh-huh. And now you want to know the history of some property in Julian?"

Before Emma could answer, Tracy let out a loud gasp. "Oh my God! I remember now. That spirit at the séance was from Julian, wasn't she? You know, the one who wanted to chat you up?"

"Tracy, please, keep it down." Even though Emma was nowhere near the coffee shop, she was embarrassed to have her situation broadcast to the world.

"How long are you going to be in Julian?" Tracy's words came in a rush. "If I leave right after my one o'clock meeting, I can be down there in time for cocktails and dinner. Where are you staying?"

"I don't need you to come down here, Tracy. I'm simply looking into some interesting facts. Seems our family did come from Julian after all."

"Uh-huh. So why do I have goose bumps right now?"

"The air conditioning's set too high in Starbucks?"

"Oh, please tell me, Emma. Did the ghost follow you home like a lost puppy or something?"

"Tracy, I just need to know how to trace some property that might have belonged to my family a very long time ago. That's all."

"Then why don't I believe you?"

"Because you're cynical and have trust issues."

Tracy laughed. "Okay, I'll call this woman and see what she can tell me. You still going to be there later today?"

"Looks that way. It's nice down here. Sweet and peaceful. Might stay a couple of days to think things through about Grant and me."

"I saw at Kelly's party that the two of you were getting into it. Everything okay?"

"Yes. Great, in fact. We're moving ahead to finalize the divorce."

"Emma, don't take this the wrong way, but I'm both sad and happy for you."

"You and everyone else I know, including me."

"It'll be fine. You'll be fine. You'll see."

"Thanks, Tracy." For a brief moment, Emma almost asked Tracy to hop in her car and join her in Julian. It'd be nice to have some live company.

twelve
· · · · · · · · · · ·

"I'D LIKE THE VEGGIE burger," Emma said to the pretty Latina waitress at the Rong Branch Restaurant. "And what do you have in the way of cold beer?" After spending the entire morning traipsing around the Julian countryside in the June sun, she was both famished and dry.

"We don't serve alcohol," the waitress announced.

Emma looked down at the menu, which clearly stated the place had a full bar. In fact, the establishment's name was the Rong Branch Restaurant *and Saloon*.

"But it says here—," Emma began, pointing a finger at the full bar announcement.

The waitress shook her head and cut her off mid-sentence. "We lost our liquor license last month. It was in the paper."

Emma knitted her brows. "I must have missed it."

Her subtle sarcasm lost on the waitress, Emma ordered an iced tea to go with her burger. While she waited, she reviewed the photos on her phone and starting sending them, one by one, to her e-mail at home for safekeeping. The waitress brought her tea. When she set it down on the table, Emma glanced up and smiled. The smile quickly turned to wariness.

Standing a few feet behind the waitress was a man, and he was staring at Emma. When the waitress moved away, the man approached her table.

"A fancy lady like yourself must be the owner of that Lexus parked out front." The man's voice was neither harsh nor friendly, just matter-of-fact words spoken in a medium tone.

Emma frowned. "Do I know you?"

The man in front of her was tall and solid. He wore a trimmed moustache, and his face was lined. Emma guessed him to be in his early fifties. He was dressed in faded jeans and a white knit polo-style shirt with dirt smudges. Before he answered, he took off his cowboy hat to reveal a bald pate. Positioned between his head and moustache were a slightly crooked nose and serious gray eyes. He reminded her of the actor Gerald McRaney, whom she'd met once at a party with his wife, Delta Burke.

"Name's Bowers. Phillip Bowers."

Bowers, Emma thought, like the name on the ranch next to Granny's homestead. She continued to look at Phillip Bowers, saying nothing, waiting for him to make the next move. He, in turn, seemed to be waiting for her to recognize the name and say something.

Without giving him her name, Emma asked, "What can I do for you, Mr. Bowers?"

A tight smile edged his lips. "I'd like to know what your business was on our land."

Emma continued to look at him without saying a word. She was weighing what and how much to tell him. Meanwhile, the stranger stared back. Their little standoff was interrupted by the waitress delivering her burger and fries.

"Can I get you anything, Phil?" the waitress asked him.

He tossed the waitress a smile, then returned to studying Emma. His smile vanished.

"A cup of coffee would be nice, Anna," he told the waitress without taking his no-nonsense gray eyes away from Emma's face.

A bit rattled by the commanding presence of Phillip Bowers, Emma busied herself with adding the lettuce and tomato to her veggie burger. By the time she'd poured a small lake of ketchup next to her fries, Anna had brought Bowers his coffee and he'd plunked himself down at the table across from her. She felt her face flush with uneasiness.

After cutting her burger into two halves, she looked up at her uninvited guest. "I don't recall inviting you to join me, Mr. Bowers."

"And I don't recall inviting you onto our property." He paused to take a drink of coffee, quite comfortable with his style of intimidation. "But since we're going to have a chat, why don't you call me Phil."

It was an obvious opening for Emma to tell him her name, but she didn't. Instead, she picked up a half of her sandwich and bit into it. It was delicious, even if the company wasn't. As she chewed, she studied Phil Bowers. If he could play tough, so could she. She was, after all, the soon-to-be ex-wife of Grant Whitecastle, the reigning TV king of rude and tacky. And she hadn't done anything to hurt the Bowers property.

Phil Bowers took another long slurp from his coffee mug before speaking. "Okay, Fancy Pants, if you won't tell me your name, then why don't you tell me why a gal from Los Angeles is trespassing on private property out in the middle of nowhere."

Emma stopped chewing and swallowed. "How do you know I'm from Los Angeles?"

He chuckled. "I could say it's obvious from your expensive duds, but the truth is your car's license plate frame says *Lexus of Beverly Hills.*"

"I never said I drove a Lexus."

He put down his coffee cup and glanced around the restaurant. "Look around, Fancy Pants. There are only a few folks in here right now. I know most of them, and not one of them drives a luxury car. That leaves you, through the process of elimination."

Emma flushed again, this time with embarrassment. The man had a point.

While she quickly thought through her dilemma, she picked up a fry, dragged it through the ketchup, and polished it off in two determined bites. Should she ask this annoying man about his property, or should she keep her mouth shut? She weighed the possibilities.

Bowers leaned back and leisurely sipped his coffee. The waitress swung by with the coffeepot and refreshed his mug. Something told Emma he was going to take all the time necessary to get to the bottom of her trespassing. She thought about getting up, paying her tab, and leaving, but she was hungry and the food was good. More importantly, she realized she was enjoying the little banter. At first blush, Phillip Bowers, albeit rather brusque, was intelligent and witty and not too hard on the eyes in a rough and tumble, middle-aged way. He had no proof it was her. And if he did, what harm had she done? Why would this man care that she'd hopped a fence and wandered through a meadow mined with cow patties? Maybe, she thought, she should just 'fess up and say it wouldn't happen again. And maybe, just maybe, he could tell her something about the property. After all, it wasn't like he'd murdered Granny himself.

As if able to read her mind, Granny materialized next to their table.

"Ask him how he came to own our land," Granny demanded of Emma.

Emma glanced at her and frowned. When she did, Phil Bowers looked over in the same direction but saw nothing.

"Go ahead, ask him. What are you waiting for?"

Emma started to reply to Granny but caught herself in the nick of time. It wouldn't do to have Phil Bowers, or anyone for that matter, see her gabbing away at nothing.

Ignoring both of her companions, Emma took another few bites of her burger and ate a couple more fries before she finally pushed her plate away. While she ate, Phil Bowers drank his coffee, never taking his eyes off of her. After a long drink of her iced tea, Emma dabbed at the corners of her mouth with her napkin and leaned back against the leather booth.

"Okay, you got me," she began. "That was me out by your ranch." She leaned slightly forward. "But if you saw me, why didn't you approach me then? Why wait until now and interrupt my lunch? After all, I might have driven off and not come back into town."

"True, you might have." He nodded his head. "But I wasn't the one who saw you. I took my chances that you were heading back here. Not a lot of places for a car like yours to hide in this town." Phil reached forward, grabbed a fry from her abandoned plate, and stuffed it into his mouth. "They make a good burger and fries here, don't they? They go great with beer."

"They lost their liquor license. It was in the paper." Emma said the words with a straight face.

Phil took another fry, never taking his eyes off her while he ate it. "You read the local newspaper, do you?"

"Every chance I get."

He chuckled. "Yeah, I bet you do. Probably have it delivered to your home right along with *Vanity Fair*."

"Are you always this charming to tourists, or is it just me?"

"Depends. Are you a tourist? Or a trespasser?"

Phil Bowers studied the attractive woman across from him. She seemed to be thinking hard about her response. He waved at the waitress and she immediately scooted over to refresh his coffee and Emma's iced tea.

"Most tourists don't find their way onto our property unless they take a wrong turn. And then they don't get out, jump a fence, and wander about talking to themselves and taking photos."

Emma's eyes widened. Someone had been watching her, and closely. But from where? The Bowers house was quite a distance from Granny's homestead.

"I wasn't talking to myself."

"No? Then you must have a mouse in your pocket."

"Whoever was watching me was mistaken. I made some phone calls, that's all." Fighting to seem nonchalant, Emma drank some tea.

"According to my aunt Susan, at one point you even appeared to be arguing with someone—someone who wasn't there. And, believe me, my aunt is quite accurate with her binoculars. And she gets nervous when crazy people come onto the ranch."

Binoculars, Emma realized, that's how she was spied on with such detail. This woman must have heard her car on the road and investigated. She probably saw everything—the slip in the dung, her attempt to leave, facing off with Granny—everything. She could hardly tell the imposing man in front of her that she wasn't alone, she was with a ghost. He was barely tolerant now. Something like that would really tip him over the edge. She had to think fast.

"I have one of those Bluetooth gizmos," she explained. "And I can get quite animated on the phone sometimes."

Granny had moved closer to Phil Bowers and was trying to get Emma's attention. It was all Emma could do to keep from yelling at her to stop and go away.

"You're not wearing the earpiece now," Phil said.

"Huh?"

"The Bluetooth. You're not wearing it now, yet I get the feeling you're talking with someone besides me. Your eyes keeping darting, and your facial expressions are changing constantly."

"Um, I'm thinking. I'm an animated thinker as well as an animated talker."

Phil Bowers studied her some more while Emma worked hard at ignoring Granny. The ghost was waving her hands, trying to get Emma's attention, talking constantly and insisting that Emma ask about the property. It was as annoying as an angry bee and just as distracting.

"Uh-huh. Still doesn't explain what you were doing there, Fancy Pants."

"Will you please stop calling me that? My name is Emma—Emma Whitecastle." She braced herself for the usual comments. Most folks, upon hearing the name Whitecastle, either made a joke about the hamburger chain or asked if she was related to Grant Whitecastle. She preferred to be associated with the tiny burgers. Phil Bowers made neither comment.

"Okay, Emma Whitecastle, now that *that* formality's out of the way, why don't you tell me what you were doing on the ranch."

Deciding to lay her cards on the table and hopefully get some help researching the history of the property, Emma gave him the truth. "It's simple, really. I just found out that my family used to live here in Julian over a century ago, so I wanted to check it out." When Phil said nothing, she continued. "It seems their homestead was, or might have been, located on that patch of land I visited this morning."

Phillip Bowers' body language changed. Although it was slight, Emma noticed it right away. His gray eyes clouded over like two storm clouds heavy with electricity. His shoulders straightened. His jaw tightened. He leaned forward, going partway through Granny.

"Don't tell me," he said, his voice laced with angry sarcasm. "You're a descendant of that Reynolds woman, too. Granny Apples, isn't it?"

"Too?" Emma's interest perked up. "You mean you're related to Jacob and Ish Reynolds, as well?"

"Noooooo, not me. No murderers hanging from our family tree."

"I didn't kill anyone!" Granny insisted, looking straight at him, but only Emma heard her.

Phillip Bowers got up from the table, going through the indignant Granny to do so. He dug into his pocket and produced a couple of dollar bills, which he tossed onto the table. Before stalking away, he leaned down toward Emma, his face naked with anger. She pulled back.

"The next time you see Ian Reynolds, Fancy Pants, you tell him sending you to do his dirty work is a new low, even for him. The property's not for sale. Not now. Not ever." He paused and studied her at close range. Emma could smell the coffee on his breath. "And if I ever see you anywhere near the ranch again, I'll have you arrested."

He turned on his booted heel and made for the front door of the Rong Branch.

"Wait," Emma called out.

She jumped up from her booth and started after him, then realized she hadn't paid for her meal. Like a dog digging for a bone, she rooted around in her bag for her wallet, keeping her eye half on Bowers' retreating back.

"Wait," she called again. "Who's Ian Reynolds?"

thirteen
· · · · · · · · · · · · · · · ·

THREE HOURS LATER, EMMA was back in her room at the Julian
Hotel armed with a small assortment of jeans and casual shirts, as
well as a pair of sneakers and a few pairs of socks, all purchased from
the Kmart in Ramona, located about fifteen miles from Julian.

By the time Emma had paid her lunch tab and dashed from the
Rong Branch Restaurant into the street, there had been no sign of
Phil Bowers.

When she asked Granny about Ian Reynolds, all the ghost
could tell her was that he, like Emma, was a descendant of her son
Winston. But beyond that, she didn't know much about him. She'd
tried to contact him once, but he couldn't see or hear spirits so
Granny had found no use for him in her quest to find out about
her murder.

Emma was tired and dirty after running around the Julian
countryside all day. In a few hours, she'd have to think about dinner, and if she wanted to eat, she would have to shower and dress

and leave her room. As charming as the Julian hotel was, she would have killed for room service and cable TV.

She removed the tags from her new clothes and put her dirty ones in one of the Kmart bags. She wasn't quite sure what to do with her shoes. The fabric was stained from the cow manure and looked and smelled disgusting. Tucking them inside the box her new sneakers came in, she made the decision to take them home and see if a shoe repair shop could salvage them. Considering the ruined shoes and torn blouse, the trip to Julian had been costly in the wardrobe department.

The shower stall was the size of an upright coffin, but the water was hot and the water pressure good. While shampooing, Emma thought about Phil Bowers. He'd been tolerable while he grilled her, but as soon as she'd mentioned that her ancestors used to live on that land, he'd gotten as riled up as a disturbed bull. When he said the name Ian Reynolds, he'd been bordering on rage. If Phillip Bowers had been a cartoon character, steam would have shot out of his ears. Emma laughed at the thought of the image.

And he knew about Granny and the fact that she'd been hung for murder. The hanging may have happened a century ago, but it was still remembered, at least by Phil Bowers.

As she toweled off, Emma felt a chill come into the bathroom from the bedroom. Granny must be back. She wanted to ask Granny again about Ian Reynolds, hoping that maybe she'd remember more if she thought about it again. Emma stumbled out of the bathroom, her head down, towel-drying her hair. When she removed the towel and looked up, she let out a small, short shriek and dashed back into the bathroom, slamming the door behind her.

Several seconds later, there was a knock at her room door. "Ms. Whitecastle, are you all right?"

Emma slipped into her short summer robe. She needed to let the person outside her door know she was fine, but at the same time she wasn't sure she wanted to leave the bathroom.

There was another knock. "Ms. Whitecastle? Emma? It's Barbara, the manager."

Emma steeled her shoulders and opened the bathroom door. Milo had said that ghosts wouldn't hurt her, but he'd said nothing about scaring her to death. Collecting herself, she opened the room door.

"Are you all right?" the hotel manager asked. "I was down the hall and thought I heard a scream."

"I'm so sorry, Barbara, but I'm fine. Just thought I saw something, but it was nothing. Just my imagination."

Barbara gave her a sly smile. "Perhaps you saw our ghost."

"Your ghost?" As she said the words, Emma turned her body slightly and looked at the far corner of the room. It was still there. *He* was still there. "This hotel is haunted?"

"Oh, dear. I thought you knew the legend. Especially since you asked for room 10."

"Room 10? This particular room is haunted?"

"Well, the entire hotel supposedly, but especially this room. People come from all over to stay in room 10." She paused, then added with a wink, "But don't worry. I've been here over twenty years and have never seen him yet. Guests have claimed they have, but I think it's more wishful thinking on their part."

Emma shot a quick glance at the image in the corner. Her wishful thinking was that he'd disappear. But no matter how hard she tried, he remained, sitting calmly in the straight-backed wooden chair next to the bed.

"I didn't see a ghost, I can assure you," she said to Barbara with a nervous laugh. "I thought I saw a huge spider, but it was nothing. I feel so foolish."

"Nonsense," Barbara told Emma with a gracious smile. "It happens, especially in new surroundings." She started down the hallway to the staircase, then turned back around. "Don't forget, we'll be serving tea shortly."

"Oh, by the way, Barbara?"

"Yes?"

"Who is the ghost who supposedly haunts the Julian Hotel?"

Barbara gave her a bright smile. "Albert Robinson, the original owner. We have many photographs of both him and his wife, Margaret, downstairs in the parlor, where you had breakfast this morning."

Emma glanced again at the spirit in the corner. "A very distinguished-looking black man, right?"

"Yes, that's correct. A freed slave who came here after the Civil War. He became one of our most prominent citizens."

"Yes, I remember seeing the photos at breakfast." It was a lie. Emma hadn't taken notice of any of the photos in the parlor.

After shutting the room door, Emma waited a few heartbeats to make sure Barbara was out of earshot before taking action.

"Granny, where in the world are you?" she said to the room in general in an urgent whisper. "We have company."

Emma eyed the ghost of Albert Robinson while she waited and hoped for Granny to appear, or to at least say something. He sat in the chair erect and alert like a proper gentleman, dressed in a dark suit with a high starched collar. His hair was thick, his face dark and lined and punctuated with a thick moustache. As she studied him warily, he studied her with curiosity.

Emma called for Granny again. When she received no response, she approached the visiting ghost, careful not to get too close, just in case Milo was wrong.

"What are you doing here, Mr. Robinson?"

"This is my hotel. I like to make sure my guests are comfortable."

"I see." What Emma didn't see was Granny—the one ghost she wanted to appear.

Emma pulled her robe tighter around her body. The room was as chilly as a deep freeze, and while Albert Robinson may have been a ghost, he was the ghost of a man and in her room while she was half naked, although he didn't seem to be taking any notice of that particular point. Maybe it didn't register with him. Maybe spirits didn't care about such things. She made a mental note to ask Milo about that the next time she met with him. If she was going to keep company with ghosts, she wanted to make sure none of them were lecherous for the fun of it.

"Mr. Robinson."

"Call me Albert, please."

"Okay, Albert. I'm Emma." She smiled at the ghost. The gesture was more to put herself at ease than for him. After all, this was his hotel, and he appeared quite at home.

He tilted his head in polite acknowledgment.

"I'm related to Granny Apples—I mean, Ish Reynolds. Do you remember her from when you were alive?"

"That I do." He smiled. "She and my wife always had a friendly competition over pie baking." He gave Emma a conspiratorial wink. "Don't tell Margaret, but I always preferred Granny's pies over hers. Margaret's were a little heavy on the cinnamon for my taste."

She gave a little laugh. "You're secret's safe with me."

In spite of her initial discomfort, Emma was enjoying chatting with Albert Robinson. He appeared to be intelligent and charming. She sat on the edge of the iron bed and faced him, thinking that Phillip Bowers could take etiquette lessons from this ghost.

"Albert, were you still alive when Ish Reynolds died?"

"You mean when she was hung?" His words were as blunt as the final yank of a rope.

"Yes, I mean when she was hung. It was for killing her husband, wasn't it?"

As easily as a flicked light switch, the ghost's demeanor changed to troubled. "That happened a long time ago, but I remember it well." He paused to think. "Ish Reynolds was never convicted of killing Jacob. She never received a trial. She wasn't even arrested."

"Then why was she hung?"

"She wasn't hung properly. It was done by vigilantes—by men who thought she should die for something she might have done but probably did not do." He looked out the nearby window into the tree tops. "Shook up the whole community. Brought a lot of bad memories back to some of us folks."

A respectful silence fell between them. Emma was sure Albert was thinking back to when he was a slave and the things he'd seen and experienced. She waited a moment before speaking again.

"Albert, do you think Ish killed Jacob?"

He turned back to face her. "I certainly do not. No one did. Ish could be a difficult woman. She was independent and feisty, even bossy." His face grew stern with conviction. "But she was an honest woman and fiercely loyal to her family and friends. If a neighbor took sick, she was the first there with soup and help. Jacob was a good man, but he was not as smart as his wife. She was the backbone of that family."

"Who do you think killed Jacob? And Ish?"

"Not rightly sure. No one was ever caught. There were rumors, but that's all."

"How did Buck Bowers and his kin get our land?"

The voice came from behind Emma. She turned to see Granny standing near the door. It was then Emma noticed that it had gotten a lot colder in the room. She was still wearing only her thin robe. She pulled up an edge of the quilt on the bed and wrapped it around her.

If Albert Robinson was surprised to see Ish Reynolds, he didn't show it.

"Buck never owned your property," Albert told her. "Buck Bowers was just a mine worker. Spent all his pay in saloons on whiskey, women, and gambling. Never had no money for nothing, let alone land."

"His people own it now."

Albert Robinson stared once again out the window. He seemed to be thinking, digging into his memory with an imaginary shovel. Soon, he turned back around.

"As I recall, Ish, your boy sold the place to Big John Winslow." As if to underline his words, the spirit of Albert Robinson nodded his head up and down as he spoke. "Yes, I believe that's right. John Winslow bought it."

"Winslow." Emma said the name more to herself than to the ghosts. She looked from Albert to Granny. "Last night at the cemetery, I met the spirit of a young man who called himself Billy Winslow."

"That would be Big John's boy," Granny said. "He and my Winston were good friends."

"Granny, did you notice Billy last night?"

Granny shook her head.

The ghost of Billy Winslow had been young, only in his early twenties, if that. It suddenly occurred to Emma that perhaps the ghosts appeared as they had when they died, as if frozen in time. She studied Granny's image as if seeing it for the first time. She got off the bed and moved closer, right up to her, like a poor-sighted woman trying to read a pill bottle. She reached out to touch Granny's neck area, but her hand only went through the hazy apparition.

"What's ailing you?" Granny asked Emma, but she didn't move away. She looked over at Albert. "Sometimes, she acts a bit tetched in the head, but she's harmless."

"Turn your head for me, Granny, like this." Emma demonstrated. Granny seemed annoyed with the request, but she complied. Emma noted that there was no sign of her neck being broken or even of a rope mark.

Emma added another mental note to her list of things to ask Milo.

"There's no evidence of how you died, Granny."

"You don't believe I was hung?" From her voice, Granny was getting her back up. Emma hoped she wouldn't disappear.

"Granny was hung, Emma," Albert added. "There's no doubt about that." He sounded peeved at her, as well.

"That's not what I meant." Emma paced at the foot of the bed as she sorted through her thoughts. "Listen, guys, I'm just learning about ghosts and spirits—kind of like on-the-job training. Please give me a break."

She looked from Albert to Granny and added Billy's image to the mix. "It's just that Billy Winslow's ghost was very young. But his ghost, your ghosts, don't seem to show the method of your deaths. I'm just curious, that's all."

Granny looked at Albert. "Tetched, see?"

Emma looked at Albert. "Do you remember how Billy Winslow died?"

"Aye, I do." Albert Robinson's face drooped in sadness, and the image slowly started to fade. "Young man like that, tragedy shook the whole town." He looked back out the window, lost in the remembrance of grief. "Billy was a good boy, both he and Winston. But shortly after Winston left town, he took a shotgun into his daddy's barn and blew his head off."

Emma shuddered. Granny turned away.

"Broke Big John's heart," Albert continued. "He was never the same. Took to drinking after his wife and daughter left. Got worse after Billy died."

"Did Billy leave a note? Any reason for what he did?"

The ghost of Albert Robinson shook its head. It continued to stare out the window as its image shimmered like dust in the sunlight.

fourteen

AFTER ALBERT AND GRANNY left her room, Emma got dressed in her new clothing and wandered out of the hotel. She'd made a list of things to do. She wanted to visit the Pioneer Museum. Barbara had told her that it contained a lot of artifacts and memorabilia about the town, and that the people who ran it were very knowledgeable about local history. It was too late for the museum today. It would already be closed, as were most of the shops in town. She also wanted to talk to Phil Bowers again. She wanted to know what Ian Reynolds wanted that made Phil so angry. Being June, it would be several hours before it got dark. She was pretty sure she could find her way out to the Bowers place without Granny as long as it was daylight.

And then there was Billy Winslow. She didn't know if he could help her with the murders, but after hearing how he died, she felt a strong maternal urge to see him again, if only to sit by his side on the bench and gaze at the town.

Before she left town, Emma stopped by the small grocery store and picked up a good bottle of wine. Then she made her way to the Bowers place.

As she got out of the car, Emma heard dogs. From the angry barks, it sounded like several. She glanced around, ready to jump back into the car to save her skin, but no dogs materialized. As she made her way to the front door, the cacophony of canines continued. It was no surprise that the door to the large home was opened even before she rang the bell.

"Well, what do you want?" the woman at the door asked.

She was short and plump, with cropped silver hair, dressed in jeans and a short-sleeved knit top. Emma thought her to be about her mother's age. She had a full face with a rosy complexion—a face that would have been considered open and friendly had it been fixed with a smile instead of a scowl. She had a growling German shepherd by the collar. Looking at the strong jaws and sharp teeth, Emma prayed the woman's grip was tight. She could hear other dogs barking from somewhere in the house behind the woman.

"I...um...," Emma stammered.

"You're the same woman who was out here this morning snooping around." The woman tossed her chin. "I recognize the car."

"Uh...."

"Spit it out, girl, I haven't got all day."

"Is Phillip Bowers here?" She felt like a child asking if little Phil could come out to play.

Emma steeled her shoulders with faux confidence but couldn't help glancing every now and then at the growling dog just a few feet away. Where was Granny? Archie liked the ghost. Maybe spirits were good with animals. Maybe Granny could calm the savage beast licking his chops over her leg bone. And maybe she was on her own.

"He's not here right now."

"Are you his aunt Susan?"

"That I am."

Emma held out the bottle of wine. "I brought this to say I'm sorry. For my intrusion this morning."

"And what about your intrusion now?"

It was clear to Emma that charm and good manners did not run in the Bowers family. She fought the urge to roll her eyes. Instead, with nothing to lose, she cut to the real purpose for her visit to the Bowers ranch.

"Who is Ian Reynolds?" Her eyes met the woman's.

The woman narrowed her blue eyes and studied Emma for what seemed like a month of dental work. The dog continued to growl.

"Down, Baby," the woman commanded. The dog ceased growling, plopped its butt down on the floor, and looked up with adoration at its master, the intruder forgotten.

"You really don't know who Reynolds is, do you?"

Emma shook her head. "Not a clue. I tried to tell Phil that, but he stormed off before I had the chance."

For the first time, the woman smiled. "Sounds like Phil. He was pretty mad after he saw you."

The two women and the dog continued to stand at the front door. Finally, the woman seemed to make up her mind about Emma.

"Come on in. I just made some iced coffee. Decaf. Would you like a glass?"

Emma nodded but eyed the dog.

"Don't worry about Baby. He's harmless once he knows you're okay."

Emma followed Susan through the front foyer back to the kitchen. The Bowers home was spacious, with a modern, open floor plan. Toward the back of the house, it opened into a huge space with kitchen, informal dining area, and family room flowing easily from one into the other. The place was comfortably decorated with country-style furnishings, pine wood, and oversized sofas and chairs. A brick fireplace took up one wall of the family area.

Baby laid down by sliding doors that led out to a large deck. The unseen dogs continued to bark and growl.

"Quiet," Susan yelled. The barking ceased.

She walked toward a closed door. As soon as she opened it, two more dogs spilled into the room. They beelined straight for Emma. One was a German shepherd almost identical to Baby. The other, a bichon frisé, was pure white with button eyes and looked more like a child's stuffed animal than a living dog. The shepherd gave her a few short sniffs, then joined Baby by the door. The little dog sniffed her with an intensity that bordered on obsession.

"Stop that, Killer," Susan said to the little dog. "Don't pay him no mind," she said to Emma. "He thinks he's a tough guy. The other dog, the other shepherd, is Sweetie Pie."

Emma glanced over at the two big security dogs, then down at Killer, who continued to sniff and give off little growls. At least the Bowers family had a sense of humor where their animals were concerned.

Susan held up a pitcher of iced coffee and asked, "Or would you prefer iced tea? We have both."

"Iced coffee would be wonderful, Mrs. Bowers."

"It's not Bowers, it's Steveson."

"Iced coffee then, Mrs. Stevenson."

"Just Steveson, without the *n*. But call me Susan. My maiden name was Bowers."

Susan Steveson busied herself pouring iced coffee into tall glasses. "And what is your name? I'm afraid my nephew never told me before he took off." She glanced up at Emma. "He did say you were pretty though. And he's right."

Feeling a blush forming, Emma put the wine down on the counter and looked out the sliding doors. Beyond the deck was a gorgeous view of a rolling meadow, and beyond that, a wooded area.

She looked back at Susan. "My name's Emma. Emma White-castle."

Susan set a full glass and long spoon in front of Emma, then pushed a sugar bowl and creamer toward her. "You'll have to sweeten it yourself. I also have artificial sweetener, if you'd like."

Emma took a small sip. The coffee had a faint taste of vanilla. It didn't need sugar. She poured in a little milk and stirred. "It's delicious."

"Whitecastle." Susan rolled the name around on her tongue like a gumdrop while she stirred sugar into her own coffee. "Unusual name. You related to that fool on TV?"

"That fool is my husband."

"Sorry. Guess I shouldn't have called him a fool."

"It's okay. He's actually a soon-to-be ex-husband." She paused to take a sip of coffee. "And he is a fool."

Susan eyed Emma over her glass. "Something tells me he's a bigger fool to let you go."

Emma blushed again. "I don't think Phil would agree with you. He's sure I'm in cahoots with this Ian Reynolds person."

"My nephew has his own problems. He's in the middle of a divorce himself. Married over twenty-five years, then one day his wife runs off with someone else. Fortunately, his kids were already grown and out of the house."

"I'm sorry to hear that. About his divorce, I mean. I have one daughter, Kelly. She leaves for college in the fall."

In spite of the rocky start, Emma liked Susan Steveson. She might be able to get more information out of her about Ian Reynolds than her rude and cranky nephew.

They adjourned to a table on the deck. The three dogs followed them outside. The afternoon sun was half hidden by the trees, leaving it warm but not too hot.

"I was surprised by how hot it is here," Emma remarked. "Being in the mountains, I thought it would be cooler."

Susan shook her head. "We get the full four seasons up here. Summers can be scorching, and winters bring snow." She turned to look at Emma. "But we like it. Glen and I moved away shortly after we were married but came back here to live when Phil's parents died. He was a young teenager, a bit older than our kids. We raised him along with our own son and daughter. They've both married and moved away, but they loved growing up here."

"No wonder Phil is so protective of the land. It's his heritage."

"That it is. He's actually a lawyer. Has his own practice down in San Diego. Goes back and forth a lot. But I think as soon as his house sells and the divorce is final, he'll move here full-time and commute to his office. Or maybe he'll work from here."

"There must be a lot of work to running a ranch."

"The Bowers ranch isn't a working ranch anymore. Most of our land is leased to other ranchers for grazing. We keep a couple of horses for our own riding, but it's been years since we ran it as a real ranch."

Susan got up, emptied two big bowls of water that were sitting on the deck, and refilled them with fresh water from a nearby spigot. The two big dogs lapped with gusto while the little dog jostled for position for his own drink. Baby stepped aside for him.

Susan laughed and pointed at the little dog. "Despite his size, Killer rules the roost around here, believe me."

The two women settled into companionable silence for a while, enjoying the peace and watching the three dogs play. Emma thought about Archie. Although he was boarded at a doggie 5-star hotel, she really needed to get home and release him. Also, she had only booked her room at the Julian Hotel through tonight. Barbara had told her when she made her reservation that the hotel was booked solid for the entire weekend. So unless she made other lodging arrangements, Emma would have to go home tomorrow. But there was still more she wanted to know.

"What can you tell me about Ian Reynolds, Susan?"

"Hmm, not much, I'm afraid. He's mostly dealt with Phil, and the dealings have not been pleasant. I do know that he claims to be a descendant of that Granny Apples woman, just like you." She looked at Emma, her blue eyes measuring and weighing. "Are you really? You know, related to that murderer?"

"I am not a murderer!"

Without notice, Granny had appeared next to the table. Outside, with a slight breeze in the air, Emma hadn't noticed the usual accompanying chill. The spirit stood with her hands on her bony hips and glared at Susan Steveson.

Emma ignored her, or tried to. She and Susan were getting along so well, she didn't want to take the chance of spoiling it by looking like a nut job.

"Yes. I'm related on my mother's side. I just found out about Ish Reynolds and Julian and the story of her hanging. It's a fascinating story, so I decided to look into it."

"Tell her, Emma," Granny insisted. "Tell her I didn't kill nobody."

"However," Emma continued, trying not to look at Granny. "We have reason to believe that Ish Reynolds didn't kill her husband—that they were both murdered."

Susan Steveson's eyebrows raised in curiosity. "Really? And how did you come to that conclusion?"

Spinning the wheels in her head as fast as possible, Emma searched for a plausible lie—something other than *her ghost told me.* The irony wasn't lost on Emma that the truth was stranger than the fiction.

"I was going through some old letters and documents." Emma prayed Susan wouldn't see through the fabrication. "There were references to the hanging and the property." Keep it simple, she told herself. It's easier to lie if you keep it simple.

"I understand that Ish and Jacob's son, Winston, sold the property after his parents died to a John Winslow, but there was no mention of how it got into the Bowers family."

Emma was so glad that the ghost of Albert Robinson had paid her a visit. The information she was able to regurgitate to Susan Steveson made her sound credible and not crazy, as long as she didn't have to reveal her source.

While Susan considered what Emma had just told her, Granny started pacing. Emma noticed that the two big dogs, who were sprawled on the deck, watched her movements but overall seemed uninterested. Killer, on the other hand, started pacing with the ghost, keeping at her heels as if she were his trainer and he the best-behaved dog at puppy school.

Susan pointed at Killer and laughed. "Look at that fool pacing back and forth. It's as if he is keeping time to a silent marching band."

Emma laughed along with her. Catching Granny's eye, she tried to get her to stop walking back and forth. The ghost looked down, noticing the dog.

"Darn animal," Granny said, finally coming to a stop. The dog halted with her and looked up, its tail wagging. "Doesn't it have anything better to do?"

Susan laughed again. "Even for Killer, that's pretty strange behavior."

Emma wanted to go back to the hotel and crawl under the quilt and stay there until it was time to go home. Keeping company with ghosts was stressful, and Granny wasn't helping any.

"Well, Emma, I can tell you how the Bowers family got that particular piece of property." Susan turned from Killer's peculiar behavior and looked at her. "If family legends are to be believed, we didn't come by it honestly, I can tell you that."

fifteen

SUSAN STEVESON WAS ABOUT to tell Emma how the Bowers family got their hands on Ish and Jacob's land when the three dogs started barking and leapt to their feet. They charged off the deck and disappeared around the side of the house toward the garage. Killer, having abandoned Granny, brought up the rear, his short little legs pumping like pistons in the wake of Baby and Sweetie Pie. Emma, on the edge of her seat waiting for Susan's explanation, hung her head in frustration.

Susan didn't make a move to control the animals, and Emma noted the barking, though loud, was different than the angry protests upon her arrival. Through the barking, the sound of tires on the driveway reached their ears.

Susan glanced at her watch. "I'll bet that's Phil. Still early for Glen. He's off playing golf with his cronies. Goes to the coast, makes a full day of it."

"Maybe I should go," Emma suggested.

"Go?" Granny stared at Emma, her hazy face scrunched in disbelief. "Just when we're about to find out about my land?"

"I'm not sure Phil will be happy to see me here." Emma glanced at Granny, then at Susan, confused herself about which woman she was addressing.

"Nonsense," Susan said, patting Emma's arm. "Stay where you are. We can clear the air between you two."

"She's right," Granny said.

Emma wasn't so sure.

She heard a door in the house open, and the three dogs came charging back out onto the deck. Right behind them was Phillip Bowers. He filled the door from the family room to the deck, glowering at her.

"What in the hell are you doing here, Fancy Pants? I thought I told you to stay away or I'd have you arrested!"

"Now, Phil," Susan started, trying to calm him.

Ignoring his aunt, he continued addressing Emma. "You think I'm kidding?"

"Phillip." Susan put a little edge into her voice. "Emma came here to apologize for her intrusion. We've been having a nice chat."

He looked at his aunt like she had three heads, then back at Emma. "Out of here. Now," he ordered.

Emma looked at Granny. The ghost had her arms crossed in front of her and was tapping her foot in annoyance. She looked at Phil, who was just as angry but for a different reason. She needed to decide on the spot what to do: stand her ground or flee.

"Phil," Emma began, then stopped to clear her throat. "I have no idea who Ian Reynolds is. But you didn't give me a chance to tell you."

"I don't believe you."

"I believe her, Phil," Susan chimed in.

"Damn it, Aunt Susan. You'd invite the Manson family in for coffee and scones."

Emma stood up and bristled. "Your aunt's been very gracious to me, and she's been kind enough to listen—something *you* failed to do."

"That's the way." Granny started hopping around like a diminutive prize fighter. "Don't let him boss you around." Killer circled the ghost, hopping up and down in an erratic pattern. The other two dogs sat alert, their attention divided between the live people and the dead.

Phil started to snap at Emma, but Killer's antics kept grabbing his attention. "What in the hell is wrong with that animal?"

"He's been acting a bit strange all afternoon," said Susan, glad the dog had diverted her nephew's attention, at least for a bit. "Stranger than usual."

Phil Bowers turned back to Emma. "No doubt your visit has something to do with this."

"Me?" Emma clapped a hand over her heart in protest. "That dog has hardly paid me any mind since I arrived." She wasn't about to add that it was her unseen companion that the dog was in such a dither over.

Susan got up and moved between Phil and Emma. "Tell you what, kids. Why don't you both sit down and talk rationally. I'll just whip us up some steaks for dinner."

"She's a vegetarian," Phil said to his aunt.

"How do you know that?" Emma was surprised, and the surprise raised her hackles. She didn't like the way this man made assumptions, but what got her goat was that his assumptions were almost always correct. "Was that tidbit of information on my car's bumper, too?"

"No self-respecting meat eater goes into the Rong Branch and orders a veggie burger."

"No problem," chimed in Susan with a forced smile. "Do you eat fish, Emma? Or are you a strict vegetarian?"

"I eat fish."

"Good. I have some fresh salmon, too. You two can just go to your own corners and chow down on your individual preferences." She patted her nephew on his shoulder. "Maybe with a full belly, you'll be ready to be civil."

Emma took her narrowed eyes off of Phil and looked at Susan. "I don't want to be any trouble, Susan."

"Nonsense, no trouble at all."

"You've been trouble ever since you set foot on the property, Fancy Pants."

Susan was halfway through the door to the house when she spun on her heels and returned to stand in front of Phil. He towered over her. "Okay, enough!" she snapped, looking up at him. "Emma is curious about her family's history. That's what she told me, and I believe her. Now sit down and behave yourself. I'll get you a beer. Maybe that will take the edge off your ugly mood."

She turned to Emma. "Would you like a cold beer, Emma?"

"Yes, that would be great, Susan. Thank you."

"A beer sure sounds good to me." Emma turned quickly at the sound of the whispery voice. For a moment, she'd totally forgotten about Granny. The ghost had stopped hopping about and was sitting on a bench at the side of the deck. All three dogs lay at her feet. Emma scowled at the ghost, ordering her without words to behave.

When Emma turned back around, Phillip Bowers was staring at her, deep furrows carved into his forehead like fields waiting to be planted.

"Hearing things, Fancy Pants?"

"What?"

"The way your head turned and your ears pricked reminded me of the dogs when they pick up a sound from the woods. You did the same thing in the Rong Branch."

She rolled her eyes at him. "Stop calling me Fancy Pants."

He filled his lungs and expanded his chest like a cocky rooster, then he looked her up and down. "Well, at least you're dressed sensibly now. And you don't stink of manure."

Emma started to say something, but Susan Steveson interrupted her snippy retort by returning to the deck with two cold beers. She handed a bottle to each of them.

"Now, you two just relax and behave yourselves. We're going to sort this all out. You'll see." She went back into the house.

After sitting down, Phil took a long swig from his beer and leaned back in his chair. He stared out at the woods bordering the property. He may have quieted down, but his body language announced that his surly demeanor was not going away any time soon.

Emma sat back down at the table and took her own drink of beer. It was cold and refreshing. She'd wanted a beer ever since lunch. "At least the Bowers ranch didn't lose its liquor license."

Phil Bowers took another long drink from his bottle. Then slowly, almost without notice, one corner of his mouth curled upwards under his moustache. It was a smile. A small smile, but it was a start.

Susan returned to the deck with a bowl of pretzels and two more beers nestled in a small bucket of ice. The bucket was silver, with star cutouts along the rim. "Good. Nice to see you kids at least trying to get along." She placed the bucket and bowl on the table along with a few napkins.

Phil downed the rest of his beer and reached for one of the bottles in the bucket. With a quick twist, he removed the cap, his body language a little less hostile with each slurp of suds.

"You know, Phil, you two have a lot in common." Susan started back into the house, still talking. "Emma here is going through a divorce, too. She's divorcing Grant Whitecastle—you know, that idiot talk-show host on TV."

sixteen

· · · · · · · · · · · ·

PHIL BOWERS DIDN'T EXACTLY send Emma sprawling into the side of her car, but Emma felt that the only thing that stopped him was that she was a woman, or maybe it was the presence of his aunt. She was sure, given his druthers, he'd have splattered her over the hood of the Lexus like bird droppings.

As soon as the churlish Bowers heard that she was connected to Grant Whitecastle, he'd slammed his beer down on the table. Foam erupted from the bottle like lava from a volcano. Grabbing her purse and then her arm, he yanked Emma up and started marching her roughly down the steps of the deck and around the house to her car, half dragging her across the scrub grass like a sack of grain. He never uttered a word the whole time.

Trotting behind them was Susan, yelling at Phil to let Emma go. Granny was beating on Phil Bowers with her fists, but each blow went through his body like a knife through water. The dogs circled them all in a barking frenzy.

"Get your hands off me!" Emma yanked her arm away. Even free, she could still feel where his fingers had dug into her skin. "What in the world is wrong with you?"

Phil Bowers stared at her without saying a word, barely keeping a lid on his rage. The scent of his anger bubbled and stank like week-old garbage.

"Phil," Susan demanded, "what is this about?"

"She's a plant, Aunt Susan." He spoke without taking his burning eyes from Emma's face. "Reynolds said he was going to the media if we didn't give in. Said the history of the land would make good TV."

Susan Steveson turned eyes wide with disbelief on Emma. "Is this true, Emma? Were you playing me like some country rube?"

"No, Susan, it's not true." Emma's eyes darted from Susan to Phil. "It's true, I'm the estranged wife of Grant Whitecastle, but I have nothing to do with his show. In fact, except for our daughter, I have nothing to do with him anymore." She paused, sifting through her brain for something that might convince them, but all she came up with was garbled mush. Still, she forged on, hoping something would come out that would convince them she was on the level. "And it's true that I'm a descendant of Ish and Jacob Reynolds."

"So, after all this time, you chose *now* to investigate your roots?" Phil's voice was shrouded in sarcasm. "Now, right on the heels of Reynolds' threats and claims? How convenient."

"I have no idea who Ian Reynolds is, I swear."

"Tell them about me, Emma," said Granny, dancing about with nervous energy.

Emma glanced at the ghost but said nothing.

"So just how did you find out about the old Reynolds property?" Phil emphasized his question by tossing Emma's bag on the hood of her car and crossing his thick arms across his chest. "Seems odd that you knew exactly where it was located."

"Tell them about me," insisted Granny. "That'll convince 'em."

"I can't," Emma hissed at the ghost without thinking.

"You can't tell us how you found out?" Susan's face clouded with suspicion.

Emma turned away from Granny so as not to be distracted. "It's a bit complicated."

"Lies usually are." Bowers uncrossed his arms. Picking Emma's bag up from the hood of the car, he tossed it to her. She caught it and clutched it to her chest like a life vest.

"Now get the hell out of here," he ordered. "Before you find yourself in real trouble."

"But I'm telling you the truth." She looked at Susan, her eyes pleading for understanding. "Look, I don't know what this Ian Reynolds wants, but I don't want anything but information about something that happened over a hundred years ago. My interest is purely academic."

Susan's stance and face softened a bit. "But why now, Emma? Why now, right on the heels of Reynolds' threats?"

"I don't believe in coincidences," added Phil, still looking at her with contempt.

"I don't know why." Emma's voice got higher in frustration. She was on the verge of tears. "As I told you, I just found out about Granny Apples and the hanging a few weeks ago. I got curious and looked into it. From what I've learned, both Ish and her husband were murdered—that Jacob Reynolds wasn't killed by his wife." She paused and took a deep, exhausted breath.

"Finally," said Granny with satisfaction.

Emma gave Phil a challenging look. "I guess as a spoiled, almost-divorcée without a job, I have too much time on my hands. So I came up here to learn more about Julian and my family."

Susan approached Emma. "You told me you found some old documents—that the information was in them. Can you produce those?"

"I don't have them with me." Emma felt panic rise in her throat like bile. The few old family documents her mother had come up with had mentioned nothing about the Julian property or the hanging.

Bowers scoffed in disgust. "Another convenience."

Emma glanced from Phil to Susan. "I know this looks fishy, but I honestly just want to know what happened to Jacob and Ish Reynolds."

Bushed from trying to plead her innocence, Emma steeled herself for one last pitch before they ran her off with a shotgun. Even though there were still a couple hours of summer daylight left, the sun was making its descent, leaving long shadows across the small valley. Once again, she felt the pull of the comfortable bed back at her hotel.

"I know that their only surviving child, Winston Reynolds, sold the property to John Winslow right before he left town. He eventually became a very well-known attorney in Los Angeles. I'm descended from him." Emma's voice, chocked with emotion and exhaustion, sounded like it had been dragged over a dirt road.

"I also know that shortly after Jacob was killed, three hooded men came to the Reynolds farm and strung Ish up for murdering her husband. They hung her from that big old oak, right over there." Emma pointed in the direction of Ish's farm, across the road in the distance. Tears tracked down her cheeks. "She was never charged with her husband's death, she was killed by men with their own agenda. Probably to get their hands on the property." Emma was babbling, unable to stop herself. "Jacob found gold on the land shortly before he was shot in the back behind his own barn. After he died, people tried to buy the land, but Ish wouldn't sell."

"That's an astounding story, Emma," said Susan.

"Sounds more like the movie of the week to me," scoffed Phil Bowers, but Emma noticed that his body language had relaxed a bit. "And you got all this from a few old documents?"

Emma didn't say yes or no. She just stood there, wiping her tears away with the back of her hand.

Susan, Emma's one hope for an ally, shifted her head from side to side slowly. "I've lived here all my life, Emma, and I've never heard that story. And this town thrives on colorful history like that. If it were true, don't you think it would be common knowledge amongst the old families who still live here?"

"Not if it was a cover-up." Emma didn't know if there was a cover-up or not, but it was the closest straw to grab.

"A cover-up?" Phil let loose with a deep, short laugh. "You've been watching too many cop shows, Fancy Pants. A turn-of-the-century cover-up, that's rich."

"Why not? You think cover-ups were invented just last week?"

When Phil didn't answer, Emma turned to Susan Steveson. "You said yourself that your family didn't come by this property honestly." She swallowed, her throat dry and strained. "What did you mean by that?"

"Well, nothing to do with murder, I can assure you." Susan looked at her nephew a moment, then turned her attention back to Emma. "Our own black sheep of the family was Buck Bowers."

"He was a mine worker," Emma added. "Given to drink and gambling. Correct?"

Phil started to say something, but Susan gestured for him to remain still.

"Yes, that's true. He was also a cheat and a thief. Buck Bowers won the Reynolds property from John Winslow in a poker game, and he most likely cheated to do it. Several years later, he was shot and killed during a game after he was caught red-handed."

"John Winslow was probably a broken-down drunk by the time he lost the property," Emma declared.

"What do you mean by that?" Susan leaned forward with interest. "John Winslow was a pillar of the community. One of the founding fathers. He wasn't a drunk."

Emma caught herself. She'd let too much slip. Obviously, the town history didn't include the tale of Winslow's breakdown after his wife left and his son died.

"I meant, he must have been drunk to have lost the property like that."

"No, you called him a *broken-down drunk*." Phil Bowers was staring at her. "Sure you're not making this up to pump up viewer interest?"

"You still don't believe that this is not about Grant Whitecastle, do you?"

"Not for a minute. I think Ian Reynolds contacted you or that slimy husband of yours, and you smelled a sensational story—a bit of colorful history to tweak the old folks." He stepped closer.

Emma stepped back a bit, then stopped, determined to hold her ground even if she did it half crying. There was less than a foot between them.

"I'm not making this up," she insisted, going eyeball to eyeball with Bowers. She could feel tears of frustration, big as bowling balls, ready to roll again.

"But how could you know all this otherwise?" asked Susan.

Granny stood to the left side of Susan Steveson. "Tell them, Emma," she pleaded. "If you don't, they'll think you're a scalawag."

At wits' end, Emma swung her attention to Granny. "And if I tell them, Granny, they'll think I'm nuts."

The silence that followed was thick and fluffy, like cotton batting, shutting out everything but the three of them and Emma's last words. Everyone stopped. Time hung like a tethered helium-filled balloon.

"Emma, dear," Susan said in a soft voice, "who are you speaking to?"

Phil started to steer his aunt away from Emma. "Aunt Susan, go into the house. I'll take care of this."

Emma continued to look at Granny, too embarrassed and afraid to look at Susan and Phil—especially Phil.

The ghost gave Emma a weak grin. "At least the cat's out of the bag."

If Ish Reynolds wasn't already dead, Emma might have killed her on the spot.

seventeen

. . . .

"ARE YOU HAPPY NOW?" Emma tossed the question into the emptiness of her car. From the warmth inside the vehicle, she didn't think Granny was with her as she drove back to town, but she didn't care. She was going to rant at her anyway.

Granny had disappeared as soon as the spook hit the fan, so to speak.

Despite her nephew's efforts to protect her, Susan Steveson remained rooted to the ground in front of Emma, looking like she'd been goosed from behind. Unable to get Susan to go into the house, Phil Bowers stepped forward, trying to put his aunt behind him.

"I'm counting to ten," he said to Emma in a slow, moderated voice. "Get in your car and leave. If I ever see you around here again, I'll shoot first and ask questions later."

Emma started to open her bag to dig out her keys. Bowers stopped her by snatching away her purse.

"If you don't mind, *I'll* do that." He opened her bag and dug through it—every inch of it—like he was on a tiny scavenger hunt.

"I don't have a weapon, if that's what you're looking for."

He tossed the keys to her. Emma, still in shock from her confession, let them drop to the ground. When she stooped to pick them up, Phil Bowers dropped her designer bag at her feet. It landed with a dull thud in the dirt. She collected both the keys and the bag and started to climb into her car. Halfway in, she stopped and turned to face Susan and Phil. She had nothing to lose, might as well go out spilling the whole pot of beans, whether they believed her or not. And why should they believe her? She didn't believe it herself half the time.

"I really have no idea who Ian Reynolds is or what he wants."

Phil Bowers shifted on his feet, unsure of whether to stop her and shove her into her car or let her continue. Susan stared at Emma, her face an uncommon blend of anger and compassion.

Phil shook his head in disgust and took a menacing step toward her. "Don't tell me, some spirit from god knows where told you about the Reynolds property. Right? You seeing things that aren't there, Fancy Pants? Is that your gimmick?"

She held up her hand, palm out, to stop his advance. "It's no gimmick, but yes, the ghost of Ish Reynolds, Granny Apples, told me about the property—and about the hanging."

"Oh, Emma," began Susan, shaking her head, her eyes filling with tears of concern. "Why are you doing this?"

"Can't you see you're upsetting my aunt?" Phil's voice was deep and angry, a canyon of rocky cliffs and treacherous trails.

"I'm sorry, Susan, but it's the truth. Strange as it might seem." Emma took a breath. "When Granny first came to me, I didn't believe it either."

Bowers tried once again to maneuver his aunt away from the scene. "And," he said, "I suppose your murderous ancestor also told you the tall tale about John Winslow being a drunk?"

Emma stuck out her chin. "No, she didn't. The ghost of Albert Robinson told me that."

With both Phil Bowers and Susan Steveson staring at her, their open mouths resembling side-by-side caves, Emma got into her car and headed down the long drive.

After pulling up next to the Julian Hotel, Emma sat in her car for a long time. Her mind and body felt drained and tinny like an empty soda can. She wanted to go home. She wanted to leave these people behind. She certainly never wanted to see anyone from the Bowers family again.

She looked at her watch. It was nearly seven o'clock. If she packed her bag and left now, she estimated she could be home by ten thirty. Emma saw no good reason to stay one more night after the day she'd had. After all, what would it matter if she proved Ish innocent? It wouldn't change the ownership of the land, and it certainly wouldn't change the fact that Ish was dead. Even if she hadn't been murdered, she'd still be dead now, if only from natural causes. Home beckoned her like a beacon of hope, offering comfort and sanity. It called to her with the promise of familiar surroundings and the lure of sleeping late in the morning. Three and a half hours on the highway and Julian would be just an embarrassing memory.

She leaned forward, resting her forehead on the steering wheel, and closed her eyes. In spite of the call of homey comfort, the idea of driving for three hours seemed as difficult a task as crossing the desert in August barefoot and without water. She should just go upstairs to her room and go to bed. Just crawl under the covers and sleep until it was time to check out in the morning and head home. If Albert and Granny showed up, she'd tell them to get lost. She was out of the ghost business.

Lifting up her head, she rolled it around in a circle, then from side to side, listening to the pops and cracks of stress. Emma promised herself a full body massage when she got home. After her bones protested, her stomach took its turn. She needed to get some dinner but didn't want to sit in a restaurant. She got out of the car, locked it, and headed down the street toward the market on the corner of Main and Washington. She would pick up a sandwich or anything that could hold her until morning and breakfast.

The market was about to close, but Emma managed to grab a couple cartons of yogurt, a plastic spoon, a bottle of water, and a small box of crackers. Just outside the entrance to the market was a bench. The day was cooling off, promising a comfortable evening. Small clusters of lavender and poppies like brooches of purple and orange gems dotted the vacant lot across from the market. Beyond the lot was the Rong Branch Restaurant. A few cars were parked in front of it. It seemed like several days, rather than just hours, since her lunch at the Rong Branch and her initial meeting with Phillip Bowers.

Emma sat down, opened a yogurt, and dug in. She took a spoonful, leaned back, and closed her eyes, letting the banana-strawberry cream slide down her throat in cool satisfaction. After a moment, she opened her eyes and took another spoonful. Then another. She was hungrier than she thought. She opened the box of crackers, gobbled up a couple, and washed them down with a swig from the water bottle. She was feeling better.

She looked around, studying the quiet town. Few cars were on the road, and fewer people were on the streets. The little town was shutting down for the night. In spite of her run-ins with Phil Bowers, Emma liked it here. She wasn't sure why, but she did. The slower pace was refreshing, giving a person time to think. Even hopping with weekend tourists, Emma was sure it would still be a sleepy little place that time had almost, but not quite, forgotten. That must be why the tourists liked it. It gave them a chance to unplug from the grind of their daily lives, shop for trinkets, eat pie, and relax.

While eating her second yogurt, Emma dug her cell phone out of her bag. She'd shut it off during her visit with Susan. After turning it on, she saw that she had received one text message and three calls. The text message was from Kelly, telling her she was having a great time and that she had spotted Leonardo DiCaprio that morning. The first call was from Milo, checking up on her. She called him back but only reached voice mail. The second call was from her divorce attorney, giving her the good news that it looked like Grant and his attorney were ready to come to a reasonable settlement.

The last message was from Tracy, saying that her friend confirmed that more information would be needed to track the history of a property, especially one that old. As soon as Emma had more information, Tracy told her in the message, the woman would be happy to help trace the property. Tracy also asked again if she should join Emma in Julian.

Now that she knew for certain who owned the old Reynolds property and the path it took to get there, Emma didn't feel she needed to know more about it. She really just wanted to find out who killed Jacob and Ish. Once she did that, Ish would be considered innocent and would be satisfied.

Mid-thought, Emma sat up straight on the bench and ran a hand through her short hair. Twenty minutes ago, she'd told herself she was off the case. No more ghosts. No more snooping around. She was only staying in Julian to get a good night's sleep before hitting the road in the morning. Yet here she was, still trying to fit the puzzle pieces together. She let out a deep sigh. There was no denying that no matter how much she tried to push it out of her mind, the story intrigued her.

Finished with her yogurt, Emma sat back and munched a few more crackers. A couple of cars went by. Two people left the Rong Branch, climbed into a pickup truck, and headed out of town on highway 78. There was a nice breeze, but not a cold one, letting Emma know she was ghost-free, at least for now. Relaxing, she reflected on what she'd learned so far, reviewing the information in her head like notes before an exam.

Big John Winslow had bought the land from Winston, Granny's son, when he left town. John Winslow was the father of Billy Winslow, a close friend of Winston's. For whatever reason, Billy's mother left her husband and Billy killed himself. John Winslow drowned his misery in drink and lost the Reynolds' land to Buck Bowers, a known card cheat. She wondered if John Winslow was a big drinker before his personal tragedy or if it was something that came about only after Billy's death.

Emma's eyes traveled up Main Street toward the cemetery. It stood high on the hill, the dead keeping watch over the living. At least Billy Winslow kept watch. Emma's mind traveled back to her meeting with the ghost of Billy Winslow and to what Albert Robinson's spirit had told her. The cemetery closed at dusk. It was getting close to that time, but thanks to it being summer, there was still a bit of daylight ahead. Before she left town, she wanted to talk to Billy again.

Her dinner complete, Emma tossed her trash into a nearby bin and stuck the half-empty water bottle into her bag. She needed a bathroom. There were public toilets nearby, but her hotel was just a block away. At the Julian Hotel, she decided to travel light and left her bag behind. She tucked her hotel keys and cell phone into the pockets of her jeans. After a slight hesitation, she added a few dollars in case she decided the yogurt wouldn't be enough until morning. Before leaving her room, she called out for Granny several times, but she never materialized. Neither did the ghost of Albert Robinson.

Moving at a steady, slow jog, Emma quickly covered the distance between the hotel and the cemetery. It felt good to run. Emma couldn't remember the last time she'd run anywhere except on a treadmill at the gym. She sucked in the fresh air and tossed a smile at the moon. Passing the drug store and the market, she crossed Main Street at an angle in front of the Julian Pie Company. Except for the Rong Branch and the Julian Grille, everything at this end of town was closed for the night. Soon she was climbing the railroad tie steps up to the Pioneer Cemetery.

At the top, Emma paused to get her breath and look around. Although it wasn't quite dark, the large trees dotting the burial ground like sentries cloaked the graveyard in a fringe of foreboding darkness. Emma kept a small emergency flashlight in her car and now wished she'd thought to bring it.

The ghosts won't hurt you. She kept replaying Milo's words over and over in her head like a mantra as she picked her way forward.

At first glance, she didn't see any ghosts. Then, as she slowed her mind down and let her eyes adjust, Emma began to see a few shimmering images. To someone else, they might have appeared as light patches of fog, but Emma knew better. Before her watchful eyes, the small puffs of mist took shape, and soon several were clearly defined. They moved about slowly, these men and women from the other side of life. As the numbers increased, so did the chill in the air. Still dressed in one of her new tee shirts and without a jacket, Emma hugged herself against the increasing cold.

Without full light, Emma moved carefully from the small paved road toward the bench where she'd last seen Billy Winslow. Tree roots like the tentacles of a giant sea creature lay in wait to grab her feet. The larger tombstones were easy to maneuver, but the small, blocky ones stuck up from the ground like uneven teeth. Making her way over the bumpy ground, she finally reached the bench and plopped herself down, facing the town. From her viewpoint, and with night creeping in, the town below looked like a toy village. Were it snowing, it would look like the quaint inside of a snow globe.

Billy was nowhere to be seen, but other spirits were active and plentiful. Turning away from the town, Emma sat on the bench and watched, her arms still wrapped around herself for warmth. She looked for Billy in the crowd of ghostly men and women dressed in old-fashioned garb. She even looked for Granny and Albert Robinson, but she didn't see them. As the town below tucked in for the night, the town of the dead was wakening.

"I'm here, Miss Emma."

eighteen

. . . .

THE FRIGHT NEARLY GAVE Emma an out-of-body experience. She placed her right hand over her heart as if saying the Pledge of Allegiance and felt it pounding like a tom-tom calling tribes to war. Collecting herself, she turned toward the polite, whispery voice so close to her ear.

Without so much as a *boo*, Billy Winslow had appeared on the bench beside her. His face was blank, as unreadable as an empty slate.

"You know my name?"

"Mr. Robinson told me."

"Do you know why I'm here? Who I am?"

The hazy image nodded. "He said I should talk to you if you returned. Said you're kin to Winston."

"Yes, I am. You and Winston were good friends. Isn't that right, Billy?"

"Yes, ma'am. He was my best friend. Played together since we was babies." The ghost looked toward the quiet town. "Then he went away."

Granny had told Emma and Milo that it did not surprise her that Winston left Julian after their deaths. With them gone, there was nothing to hold him there.

"Your mother left, too, didn't she?"

"Yes, ma'am, and took my little sister."

"Why didn't you go with her?"

"She wanted me to, but someone had to help Pa with the farm. I was grown. I had to stay and help him."

"Billy, do you remember why your mother left? It was before you … you died, wasn't it?"

Another nod. "She left because of Pa. Something he did."

"Do you know what that was?"

"Yes, ma'am."

He didn't look at her, and he offered no further information. Emma studied him. He couldn't have been much older than Kelly when he died. She tried to place a comforting hand on his young shoulder, but it slid through the air instead of resting on solid flesh.

Treading lightly so as not to frighten off the reluctant spirit, Emma prodded him again. "Billy, did you kill yourself because your mother and Winston left?"

For the first time since the questioning began, Billy Winslow turned and looked Emma fully in her face. He had been a good-looking boy with broad, friendly features.

"I didn't kill myself, Miss Emma." He spoke the words without expression, with the same flatness as if telling her he'd locked the door and put out the cat.

"Albert Robinson told me you did. Said the whole town was upset about it."

Billy looked back toward the town. "That might be what folks thought."

"So you didn't go into the barn and shoot yourself?"

The young spirit shook his head. "No, ma'am." He turned toward her again. "I was kilt in the barn, but not by my own hand."

Smelling important information, Emma leaned forward, almost coming nose to nose with the ghost. "You're sure?"

He didn't pull away. "I think I'd know if I was kilt or not."

Billy had a good point. If anyone should know if he took his own life, it would be him. Emma glanced around, looking for Granny, wanting her to hear this. But while the graveyard was a regular ghostly cotillion, there was no sign of Ish Reynolds. She never seemed to be around when Emma needed her, only when she could be a pain in the neck, like at the Bowers ranch.

Emma was struck by another thought. Didn't the ghosts talk amongst themselves? Albert Robinson only knew what the town assumed. Why hadn't he asked Billy about it once they met up in ghost land or wherever it was they all congregated? He had taken the time to communicate to Billy that he should talk to her, but hadn't, in all these years of death, asked about Billy's suicide?

Emma ran her hand through her hair. It was becoming a habit. By her side, Billy Winslow waited patiently.

The ghosts didn't seem to be interested in anything beyond themselves. She looked around. Although there were many ghosts milling about the graveyard, it wasn't like they were gossiping in clusters over backyard fences. While there were various pairings, most kept to themselves and had their own reasons for walking the earth. Albert wanted to keep watch over his hotel. The young mother wanted to rock her dead baby. Billy kept vigil over the only home he'd ever known. Their personal histories ended when their deaths occurred, and they'd seemed neither nosey or dishonest in their interactions with her. What you saw was what you got. Albert simply told Billy her name and suggested he talk to her if he saw her again. Billy didn't seek Emma out. He'd waited until she came to him without even knowing if she would.

Then there was Ish Reynolds. The ghost of Granny Apples seemed to be the most animated of the bunch. She got excited and chatty from time to time, though it only seemed to be with Emma, and that night in the bathroom with her mother. Maybe it had something to do with them being her descendants—kin, as Billy put it. But there were times when even Granny Apples seemed devoid of emotion and flat in her responses.

It was clear to Emma that she and Milo were going to have to compare notes when she got home.

"Billy," she said, returning her attention to him. "Do you know who shot you?"

"No, ma'am. They had hoods on."

Hoods, just like with Granny. "There were three of them?"

He shook his head. "Two."

Emma looked back over the now-dark cemetery. The ghostly figures shimmered like her aunt Kitty had the night she'd visited

Emma, giving off faint pools of iridescence. Watching them, she wondered what had happened to the third assailant. Granny specifically said three men in hoods had attacked her.

"Two—and my pa."

Emma whipped her head around to face Billy. "Your father was there? He saw you get shot? Didn't he do anything to stop it?"

"One of the men had a gun on him. Told him it was too late."

Too late. Emma wondered what the assailants had meant by that.

"But why you, Billy?"

He shrugged his young shoulders in their leather suspenders.

Emma rephrased the question. "Why do you think you were shot?"

"Most likely 'cause I knew what Pa had done."

"Did your father do something to these hooded men?"

"No, ma'am. He did it with them."

Emma was getting frustrated waiting for Billy to say what it was he knew about his father, but obviously it was going to have to be pulled it out of him like an impacted wisdom tooth. It finally dawned on her that Billy wasn't embellishing his answers with comment but simply giving direct answers to her direct questions. She would have to come right out and ask him what she wanted to know.

"Billy, what did your father do that you found out about?"

Before he could answer, Billy disappeared.

It was then Emma noticed that it wasn't just Billy. As the air went from cold to merely cool, Emma cast her eyes around the graveyard. All the ghosts were gone, vanished to wherever they go, leaving behind an empty darkness that made her sad on top of surprised.

Emma stayed on the bench, listening to the sounds of the night, her ears keen, her eyes adjusting to the darkness illuminated only by slivers of moonlight penetrating the canopy of trees. She went on alert; all her senses were primed and ready, seeking out what had made the spirits disappear as quickly as a switch being thrown. There had been no warning, no indication from Billy that he had to leave. No slow fading from him or the others as she'd seen from Granny when her physical presence was weakening. One minute they were here, the next—*poof*—gone, like the puffs of mist they resembled.

When she saw nothing to have caused the mass bolting of ghosts, Emma concluded maybe it was just another one of the quirky things about them that she needed to learn.

After another moment of reflection, Emma decided it was time to leave. She needed to think about what she'd learned tonight. Billy had told her that he was murdered right in front of his father, and probably because of something his father had done. Emma wondered if Big John Winslow had something to do with Jacob and Ish's deaths too. Maybe that's what Billy discovered. And maybe that's why Mrs. Winslow took off. It's too bad Billy left just as he was about to tell her what it was. Emma would just have to seek him out again.

Deciding it was too dangerous to take the long, steep stairway in the dark, Emma started to make her way across the uneven ground to the narrow, paved road that ran through the cemetery. From the guidebook, she remembered that it would lead her to the town below.

She was almost to the road when she heard something. It sounded to her like the snapping of a branch. She froze. The hairs on the back of her neck stood up like a mini blond forest. *Remember, Emma,* she reminded herself silently, *the ghosts won't hurt you.*

Then she remembered that the ghosts didn't make noise, except when she heard them speak. She remained still as a statue, too frightened to turn around, too frightened to move. Something scampered across her path and she gave a slight, short shriek. Then something else ran by. It was small and close to the ground. When it crossed the road where the moonlight wasn't blocked by the trees, Emma saw that it was only a couple of squirrels. *Critters.* She could hear Granny's words as she gave a sigh of relief.

A few more steps and Emma reached the road. To her right was the uneven and steep staircase, a shorter but more uncertain path in the dark. To her left, the road continued, circling the graveyard until it wound its way out of the cemetery and down the hill. In front of her was a several-foot drop to a lower level of graves—the most dangerous path of all.

She was about to turn left and take the safer, more even road when a chill ran through her. It wasn't the same chill she experienced when she had ghostly company. This was an icy, foreboding chill that started within her and traveled outward. It was the chill of danger.

Very slowly, Emma started to turn, trying to seem as natural as possible. All her senses stood at attention, ready to see, hear, feel, or even smell something that didn't belong. But it was her sixth sense, the one that knew things beyond sight, touch, taste, smell, and hearing, that told her someone was out there. Another living being was in the cemetery and was watching her.

Emma started backing up toward the stairway. Whatever—whoever—was out there was on the other side. The road side. Her eyes struggled to see a form, an outline, anything, giving her the location of her watcher. In the dark, her ears fought for the tiniest sound.

"Who's there?" she called out.

No answer except the slight snap of a twig.

She thought about pulling the cell phone out of her pocket but realized by the time she did, the person could make a move on her, using any small amount of her divided attention as a window of opportunity to attack, if attack was what they had in mind. She wasn't going to stick around to find out.

Still making her way slowly backwards, Emma held out a hand until she felt the unfinished wood of the stairway railing. She grasped it. Feeling with first one foot, then the other, she descended the first step. Still moving backwards, she covered the broad step, and her foot found the next drop. Her eyes scanned the graveyard as she made her way painstakingly down each deep, wide step. She was halfway down when she spotted him. Just a glimpse, but it was enough to know he was moving with stealth, taking advantage of the dark and the old, thick trees. He was moving toward Emma.

Fight or flight. The words crossed Emma's mind as quickly as the ghosts had disappeared. She chose flight.

Turning, she scampered down the steep funereal steps as fast as her new Kmart sneakers could carry her. Halfway down, she stumbled. She tried to regain her balance by grabbing onto the railing. A sharp pain shot through her right palm as her hand slipped on the raw wood. Totally off kilter, Emma pitched forward, landing roughly on the step below her. She cried out as she landed.

"Miss Whitecastle!" came a voice from above her.

Slightly dazed, Emma heard someone running down the steps. She tried to get up and scramble away, but strong hands grabbed her from behind. She fought like a wildcat, pounding her assailant with her fists. Finally, she connected with the side of his head.

"Ow!" He ducked his head to avoid another blow but continued to hold tight to her. "Miss Whitecastle—Emma—please, I'm trying to help you."

Emma stopped fighting and tried to shake off her confusion. The hands repositioned her from a very unladylike sprawl into a sitting position with her back against the step above. The hands then traveled up and down her left leg, checking it for breaks. They did the same with the right leg.

"I know you can move your arms."

Emma demonstrated by lifting both arms and wiggling both wrists. Her right palm hurt like hell. She was banged up, but nothing was broken.

In the dark, Emma couldn't see the man's face. She only noted that he was slim and smelled of expensive soap.

"Can you get up?" His voice was even and crisp, almost perfect in its diction and clarity, like a trained speaker.

Without answering, she got one leg under her and hoisted herself upright. He helped by steadying her with an arm tight around her waist and the other holding one of her elbows. She stood still for a moment, testing her ankles and getting her bearings. Then she remembered. This man had been lurking in the graveyard.

He'd been following her. He may be helping her now, but if not for him, she wouldn't have fallen in the first place.

She shook off his hands and grabbed the wooden railing for support. Taking in his size and fitness, she realized there was no way she could outrun him, fall or no fall.

It was time for the fight portion of the program.

"Who are you?"

In the patchy darkness, the man studied her a second in silence. Emma stared back at him, her strong chin firmly turned up in a challenging posture. Crossed by narrow shadows, his face looked like a photograph pieced together after tangling with a paper shredder.

He gave her a sliced smile and stuck out a hand. "Ian Reynolds. At your service."

nineteen
· · · · · · · · · · · · · · · · · ·

"At my service? You nearly got me killed."

"I'm sorry. I assure you, I meant no harm."

"Then why didn't you answer me when I called out?"

In the semi-darkness, Emma thought she caught a grin.

"Forgive me, but it's a bit embarrassing to be caught lurking in the shadows like some peeping Tom."

He took a step toward Emma, but she backed away, going down to the next step. Supposedly long-lost kin or not, he was a stranger, and they were alone—in a dark cemetery. It wasn't like the ghosts could come to her rescue.

"Lurking *and* spying," Emma added, continuing to slowly ease herself down the remaining steps without taking her eyes off of Ian Reynolds. "Why are you here?"

This time, Emma did catch a glimpse of a broad smile.

"I could ask you the same thing. But truthfully, I came here to see you."

She made it down the last few steps. Ian was moving with her, keeping pace with her bit-by-bit progress yet keeping his distance so as not to scare her off. Back on the flat surface of the street, Emma felt safer. The Julian Grille was still open and not too far away should she need help. But she was still shaken from her fall and not ready to make a run for it, even for that short a distance.

"To see me?" She started back toward the midst of town, walking with the upper half of her body turned in order to keep an eye on Ian. If Ian Reynolds wanted to talk to her, he was going to have to follow her. She wasn't hanging around the graveyard anymore tonight.

"Yes." Ian walked next to her with a few feet between them. "I had just parked by the hotel when I saw you running. I followed you on foot but took the back way up. There's an access road up to the cemetery, you know."

"I know." Her words were sharp, her voice tight, letting him know she wasn't warming to him. "I was about to take it back when you spooked me."

"Speaking of spooks, Emma, who were you talking to up there?"

The directness of his question jarred her. They were almost at the intersection of Main and Washington. Emma stopped dead in her tracks by the vacant lot. The Rong Branch was to her right on the other side of the lot. She could see a truck and a car parked in front. She felt safer but still as uneasy as Archie on his way to the vet.

"Okay, what's this all about?" She put a low growl into her voice and placed both hands on her hips, ignoring the pain in her right hand. She didn't think she'd look tough worried about a few scrapes and splinters. "How did you know I was in Julian? And how did you know where I was staying? More importantly, how do you even know who I am?"

Ian Reynolds took in the determined set of her strong jaw and the growing fire in her eyes. He gave her a relaxed, almost sexy smile and reached forward, toward her head. She recoiled.

"You have twigs in your hair."

"Never mind the twigs. Answer my questions."

He took her by the elbow and started guiding her toward the Rong Branch.

"A little bird told me they saw you with Bowers earlier today and overheard part of your conversation. The same little bird knew I was interested in anything having to do with the old Reynolds property."

Emma pulled away. Ian stopped and looked at her with self-satisfaction.

"The same little bird told me your name and where you were staying. Apparently, we're long-lost relatives."

"Industrious little bird. Should be working for the FBI instead hanging out in Julian."

Reynolds offered up a smarmy grin. "I see them too, Emma."

"See who?" She felt her heart stop.

"You know what I'm talking about—the ghosts. I see them too."

Emma took a half step back.

"Must be a family trait," he added. "And I know all about Granny Apples and Jacob—even Billy Winslow. You were talking to Billy tonight, weren't you?"

Something wasn't right. Emma could feel it in her gut but couldn't quite grasp what it was. Like a bowl on a top kitchen shelf, it was just beyond her tired mind's reach.

"So, cousin, how about a cup of coffee and a little chat? I think you'll be interested in what I have to say."

Emma felt as pulled as saltwater taffy. It wasn't even nine o'clock, yet she wanted to go back to the Julian Hotel, take a hot shower, and crawl into bed. The single day had turned into several days' worth of activities crammed into one short time slot. Her brain was muddled and saturated, her body tired and bruised. Yet, at the same time, she wanted to go with Ian and hear him out. She wanted to know why Ian had gone out of his way to track her down, but the biggest draw was the unknown—the bit of unremembered information that was nagging at her about his self-professed talent.

He tried to take her arm again, but she yanked it back. In return, he sent her another oily smile. It curved his lips at one corner, giving his face a disturbing quality. He started walking. She followed next to him, careful not to make physical contact. Before entering the restaurant, she ran her hands through her hair, finger-combing out debris. She doubted it helped much.

The Rong Branch was mostly empty. The waitress, who was not the same one from lunchtime, seated them at a booth. Emma slid into the bench seat facing the door. Ian tried to slide in next to her, but she silently blocked him. Amused, he took the seat across from her.

"We close in just over twenty minutes, folks," the waitress told them. She was in her mid-fifties, with long, gray hair pulled back and fastened at her neck with a large clip, a handsome woman with a friendly face and plump figure.

Emma declined the offered menu. "Do you have soup?"

"Today we have beef with barley and vegetable."

"A bowl of vegetable, please."

"What about pie?" asked Ian.

"Best apple pie in town," the waitress boasted. "We also have cherry and lemon meringue today. We had chocolate cream, but that sold out."

"I'll take a piece of warm apple pie and a cup of coffee."

"Want ice cream with the pie?"

"Just the pie, please."

"Could you add a cup of decaf to my order?" added Emma. She picked up a napkin and dabbed at her injured hand.

The woman squinted through her wire-framed glasses, taking in the injury along with Emma's dirty clothing and disheveled appearance. "You okay?"

Emma looked at Ian, then at the woman. She wasn't about to tell this woman she fell while being chased through the graveyard by the same man now having coffee with her. Ian busied himself looking around the restaurant, but Emma knew he was listening.

"I'm fine, just clumsy." Emma laughed lightly. "I tripped and fell." Emma turned her hand over and displayed the abrasions on her palm where her hand had dragged over the unfinished banister.

"That's a nasty scrape. Why don't you go wash that up while I get your order? The ladies' room is right down that hallway."

"Good idea. Thank you."

Her hand still hurt when Emma returned to her table, but at least it was clean. There were several wooden slivers embedded in her palm. As soon as she returned to her hotel room, she'd take care of those with the tweezers from her cosmetic kit. She'd also shaken out her hair and washed the dirt from her face.

Her soup and coffee were waiting for her, but so was a big surprise. Standing next to her table in a heated discussion with Ian Reynolds was Phillip Bowers. He was in a clean shirt and jeans, with his back to Emma. She suddenly wished she could disappear into thin air as easily as Granny and Billy Winslow.

Standing awkwardly a few feet behind Bowers, she checked out the other people in the place. Only two other tables contained customers. One held the Quinns, the older couple she'd seen in the lobby of the Julian Hotel when she'd checked in. At the other table, two men were finishing up their dinner. They looked like locals, a fact confirmed when the waitress wandered over to clear their plates.

"Not the same around here with the saloon closed, hey Beverly?" one of them said to the waitress.

"Sure isn't," she replied. "Tips aren't the same either." All three of them laughed.

One of the men, a clean-shaven redhead, said, "I hear everyone's heading to the casino at Santa Ysabel to do their drinking."

As the waitress left their table, she spied Emma, who was now casing the place for a back door.

"Everything okay, honey?"

Seven sets of eyes stared at her. So much for trying to make an unobserved getaway.

"Fine," she squeaked out. She headed to her table and slid into her seat, not looking at Bowers. A piece of apple pie and coffee had been set in front of Ian.

"Well now, isn't this cozy?" Phil Bowers hovered over her in a menacing stance.

Emma glanced up at him, giving him a dose of the family eye rolling. Then she picked up her spoon and started eating. His eyes pierced her as she worked on her soup. Ian watched her also. She seemed to be the dinner show.

She was waiting for Phil to accuse her of lying about knowing Ian Reynolds and about the two of them being in cahoots. But at that moment, she didn't care what he thought. Nor did she care what Ian thought. She'd placed them in the same category as Grant Whitecastle—men determined to have their own way, regardless of her feelings. Right now, men in general were on her crap list.

"Soup, pie, and coffee are always cozy," she said after swallowing. "Comfort foods like chocolate chip cookies and milk, don't you think?"

Phil Bowers leaned closer. "You're a little old to be acting coy, don't *you* think? Not to mention looking a little ragged around the edges. You get your fancy ass dragged behind a truck today?"

"It's not polite to reference a lady's age," chimed in Ian.

Emma stared at Ian Reynolds, letting him know she didn't find his comment cute or helpful. She needed to find out more about him, but now Bowers was spoiling it all. Or was he? She looked from one man to the other and decided that Phil Bowers' presence might help. It could be that his badgering personality might prod Ian into saying something useful.

She looked at Phil. "Why don't you pull up a chair and join us?"

He cocked an eyebrow at her.

"Or you could always squeeze in next to Ian."

The two men eyed each other. Emma noticed that besides the mutual distrust and dislike, their eyes silently asked each other what was going on. Bowers grabbed a chair from another table and set it, seat facing out, at the end of their booth. Then he straddled it in a macho move that almost made Emma groan.

She waved at Beverly, who had just finished cashing out the two men. "Would you please bring Mr. Bowers a cup of coffee?" When the waitress hesitated, Emma added. "I promise we'll be out of here so you can lock up on time."

"Make it decaf, Bev," Bowers called to the waitress.

Emma finished her soup while waiting for Phil's coffee to arrive. Ian sipped his coffee but hadn't touched his pie. Once Phil had his coffee in hand, Emma dabbed at her mouth with a paper napkin.

"Okay, gentlemen, enough is enough." She took a sip of coffee. "I have no idea what's going on here, but I want to know, and I want to know now."

Neither man made a move.

"First, you." She looked pointedly at Bowers. "Until a few minutes ago, I hadn't met Mr. Reynolds here. I hadn't even heard his name until you mentioned it today." When Bowers started to growl something, she held up her hand. "It's the truth, whether you want to believe it or not, and frankly, I'm sick and tired of trying to convince you of it."

Ian Reynolds started to laugh. He picked up his coffee mug and pretended to drink to hide his pleasure at Bowers being dressed down.

Emma turned to him. "Not so fast. At least Phil here had the decency to approach me openly. He didn't track me down through informants, then stalk me through a dark cemetery until I was so frightened I fled, falling down those steep stairs."

Upon hearing her words, Phil Bowers stared at Reynolds with open disgust. Ian started to say something, but Bowers had already turned his attention back to Emma. "What in the hell were you doing up in that graveyard after dark? It's dangerous."

"Is that a caution about my safety or a warning of a more menacing nature?"

"Just saying it's not smart to be up there after dark, Fancy Pants. We're not Los Angeles, but crimes do happen here."

Ian settled comfortably back into the corner of his seat. He draped one arm across the back of the booth and held his mug in the other hand. In the light of the Rong Branch, Emma was able to check him out better. She placed him in his late thirties or very early forties; average height and slim. His hair was light brown with highlights, cut short and spiked with gel in planned chaos. His face was fashionably stubbled and populated by dark brown eyes, a long, thin nose, and thin lips that framed slightly crowded teeth. He had the sort of looks that some women might find handsome; others, not so much. For Emma, the jury was still out. Dressed in designer casual wear, he wore it with the same air of self-satisfied elegance as Grant did. He was slick like Grant, too, Emma noted. Slick and calculating, and very show-bizzy. *That* was it, Emma thought, studying him. Ian Reynolds reminded her of the dozens of metrosexuals—straight men with the same fashion phobias and obsessions normally attributed to gay men—she'd met over the years as she accompanied Grant to one Hollywood event after another.

Emma was about to say something to Ian when Bowers put his mug down on the table with a solid thud. Coffee sloshed. He seemed to have a problem setting beverages down without making a mess.

"Oh my God!" Phil said, his sarcasm bright enough to illuminate the room. He stared at Emma. "Please tell me you weren't up at that cemetery communing with the dead."

"That she was." From behind his coffee mug, Ian smiled like the Cheshire Cat. "I saw her."

twenty

· · · · · · · · · · · ·

WHILE PHIL LOOKED AT the two of them in disbelief, Emma shot Ian a look of indignation sharp enough to poke out an eye. She'd noticed he didn't say anything about his own alleged talents. Ian Reynolds took it all in stride.

"Would you forget about ghosts," Emma snapped at Phil. "You, too," she said to Ian. "You saw *nothing*."

It was then that Emma remembered they were not alone. The older couple was staring at her. So was the waitress. She didn't have to look in a mirror to know that her face resembled a wildfire. She could feel the heat traveling up her neck to her hairline.

She gave the couple a sweet-as-pie smile. They continued to stare.

"Great. The whole world's going to think I'm a crackpot."

Ian gave her his signature smug smile. "No, just this hick town."

Both Emma and Phil scowled at him.

"Okay," Emma began again, "let's get down to business. What's going on with the Reynolds property?"

"It's simple," Ian explained. "I want it, and he won't sell it."

Phil Bowers smacked his hand on the table. "It's not for sale. And even if it were, I wouldn't sell it to *you*."

Ian's eyes challenged his opponent. "Maybe we should let the law decide that."

"I am a lawyer, damn it. You have no legal right to that property."

"Hold on a minute." Emma stretched her hands across the table to keep them apart. The two men measured each other like boxers in a ring. "Now, I'm not a lawyer, and I don't know squat about real estate, but it seems to me, Ian, if the Bowers family doesn't want to sell that property, you can't make them."

Ian looked at her with surprise. "One would think, cousin, that you'd be more on board with recovering that property. After all, if Ish Reynolds hadn't been murdered, it might still be in the family."

"And if she hadn't been murdered, Winston might not have left Julian, and you and I might never have existed."

Phil chuckled. "Touché."

It was then that Emma looked up toward the door and saw Granny Apples. Her image was hovering by the cash register, near the area where the Rong Branch displayed local gift items for sale, such as jams and candies. But the ghost didn't come near and remained silent. Emma squinted, trying to see if Granny was attempting to give her a signal, but she couldn't make out anything. The two men noticed Emma's concentration, and both turned in the direction of the door. Granny disappeared.

It was then Emma remembered that Granny didn't have any problem showing up when Phil Bowers was around. She had even tried to defend Emma when Bowers dragged her to the car earlier. Phil couldn't see or hear the ghost, so Granny didn't mind being visible and talking to Emma around him. Ian, on the other hand, told her he could see them. So why had Granny disappeared just now? Could it be she didn't want to be seen by Ian?

She leaned against the back of the booth and tried to pry open that portion of her brain that might reveal what she was forgetting. Phil was sitting still. He was studying her, full-blown skepticism tattooed across his sturdy face. Ian also studied her, but his look was one of observance gift-wrapped in a smirk.

Then she remembered.

A chill shot through her body like an icy stream. She wanted to run, to get away from Ian, but there was still much to find out. More than ever, she needed to know who he was and what he wanted—and what his connections were to the spirit world. She cleared her throat and got down to work.

"Why do you want that property, Ian? You don't look like you're from around here any more than I do."

"He's from Los Angeles, Fancy Pants, just like you. A real-estate developer. You're both a couple of damn carpetbaggers. How do I know the two of you are even related to the Reynolds clan?"

"You're going to build on that land?" Emma's question was accusatory.

"Condos. Low-level ones, of course, that blend into the natural environment."

"Over my dead body," added Phil. He stood up from the table.

Ian took a sip of coffee and gave Phil a bored look, as if he were dealing with an annoying child. "Cut the drama, Bowers."

The words played like gasoline on Phil's already angry flames. "Even if you manage to cheat your way into that property, I'll make sure you never get a building permit. People here are fussy about new construction."

Ian chuckled. "Trust me, the permit will be no problem." He shook his head. "You may have a law degree, Bowers, but you're still a hayseed."

Phil Bowers flung the chair out of his way and started for Ian in the booth. Ian threw his coffee at Phil's face, but Phil turned just in time for the warm brown liquid to strike his right shoulder.

Emma shot out of the booth. "Stop it! Both of you!"

As Phil grabbed Ian by his shirt front and pulled him from the booth, Emma got an idea. Using the fight as cover, she pulled her cell phone from her pocket and snapped off a few quick photos of the fight.

Beverly rushed over, furious. "Okay, folks, closing time. Phil, I'm surprised at you."

The elderly couple quickly got up and headed for the register. The man tossed the bill and money on the counter. "Keep the change," he called as they scooted out the door.

After the brief but explosive fight, Beverly ejected them all with a few well-chosen curse words. Outside the restaurant, the only vehicle in the parking area was Phil Bowers' truck. Emma started to cross Washington at an angle, heading for the city hall on the corner. Beyond it, just a block down Main Street, was her hotel. She was anxious to reach it for many reasons.

"Wait, Emma, I'll go with you."

She stopped and turned to see Ian walking toward her. Phil leaned against the tailgate of his truck, watching them both.

She stopped halfway across the empty street and pointed a finger at Ian. "Oh, no, you don't. You stay away from me."

"I have a room at the hotel. We can walk together. We still need to talk."

"No, thanks. I'd feel safer walking alone."

"The lady doesn't want you near her, Reynolds." Phil Bowers left his truck and covered the few step to Ian, his fists poised to take a swing. He looked at Emma. "I can walk you back. I came by to take Bev home tonight, but she still has a few things to do."

Emma considered his invitation. She wasn't a big fan of Phil Bowers, but at least she trusted him more than Ian Reynolds. He was gruff and had a bad temper, but she was pretty sure he was exactly who he said he was.

"Do me a different favor, Phil. Stand here and make sure this creep doesn't follow me for at least five minutes. I'll be inside my room by then."

"I don't like the idea of this joker being at the same hotel."

Emma stared at Ian Reynolds. He stared back, his dark eyes fixed on her face, all trace of earlier pleasantries gone.

"I'll be fine, Phil. It's a small hotel. If he tries anything, everyone will hear."

Phil Bowers stepped between Emma and Ian. He turned to face Ian and crossed his powerful arms across his chest.

"There's no need for this, Emma," Ian called to her.

"You heard the lady, Reynolds." Bowers stepped closer to him. "And just to be sure, we're giving her a ten-minute head start."

In spite of her bruised legs, Emma started for the Julian Hotel in a dead run.

The hotel was locked up for the night, and the lobby was empty as she made her way up the narrow wooden staircase to the second floor. As soon as she got into her room, Emma locked the door and barricaded it with the straight-backed chair. She didn't know which room Ian Reynolds was staying in tonight, but she wasn't taking any chances.

Yanking her cell phone out of her jeans pocket, she tried to call Milo again, but it went straight into voice mail. She left him a message saying it was urgent. Noting her battery was low, she dug out her charger from her luggage and plugged it in, thankful she'd remembered to bring it. Then she called Tracy.

"Are you busy tomorrow?" she asked as soon as her friend answered.

"No," Tracy said eagerly. "Want me to come to Julian?"

"Trust me, I'd love to see you, but I'm coming home tomorrow."

"Then let's have dinner, and you can fill me in on all the juicy ghost stuff."

"Dinner sounds good, but first would you go by the pet hotel and get Archie, just in case I'm not home before they close? You still have the key to the house, don't you?" When Emma's aunt Kitty had died, Tracy was given a key to the Miller house to keep an eye on Archie the few days they were gone.

"Yep. Still have it."

"Good. I'll call the pet place and let them know you'll be picking him up."

"You okay, pal? You sound funny."

"I'm fine. Just exhausted. Took a nasty spill down some stairs."
Emma laughed lightly so as not to concern her friend. "I'm okay,
but I'm sure I'll be stiff tomorrow."

"A few cosmopolitans tomorrow night will fix that."

After the call, Emma took a hot shower, put on her nightgown,
and crawled into the comfy bed she'd dreamed about off and on all
day. She wished Milo would call. She didn't know his e-mail address
or she would have sent him the photos. She lay in the dark, the
phone clutched in her hand, as her mind raced over the events and
information of the day like a race car over a fast oval track. Every
noise put her on alert for Ian Reynolds. She heard people chatting
in low voices as they made their way down the hall to their room.
From the room next door came the sound of the shower. Outside,
beyond the curtained windows, a soft breeze rustled the trees. Every
sound was amplified and grated on her nerves.

In spite of feeling the familiar chill, she was even startled when
Albert Robinson walked through the closed door. The ghost of the
hotel's founder sat down in the chair that was tipped against the
door and made himself comfortable.

Emma sighed in relief, happier to see a spirit than a live person
at that moment. "Good to see you, Albert." The ghost gave her a
courtly nod.

"Where's Granny?" asked Emma.

"Don't rightly know."

"Thank you for telling Billy Winslow to speak with me."

The ghost nodded, maintaining his proper and distinguished
posture.

"Do you know who Ian Reynolds is?"

"I'm afraid I don't."

After a long pause, Emma said in a small voice, "I'm scared, Albert."

"No need, Emma. I'm here now. You get some sleep."

. . . .

MILO CALLED EARLY THE next morning while Emma was putting her bags in the trunk of her car. She told him about Ian Reynolds and what he'd said about being able to see spirits.

"Maybe it runs in the family," Milo offered as a way of explanation. "Can't your mother at least hear them?"

"But I don't think this guy is really Ian Reynolds. Granny told me that she had tried to contact Ian Reynolds once, but he couldn't hear or see spirits. This guy claims he can, and from what I've witnessed, he's telling the truth, at least about that. And the strange thing is when he's around, the spirits disappear."

"That is odd. It usually means they don't trust or like the person."

"Give me your e-mail address. I have some photos of him on my phone. They're not the best, but maybe this guy is someone you've seen as a client or something."

"Okay, but it may take awhile. I don't have the fastest system, and I'm not that computer savvy, especially with stuff like this."

After sending the photos to Milo, Emma headed into her last breakfast at the Julian Hotel. She'd almost skipped it, not wanting to bump into Ian, but so far she'd seen no sign of him.

The hotel had been almost completely booked the night before, and the small, square tables in the dining room were nearly full. In the corner nearest the kitchen was a table set for four with only two people seated at it. Emma's heart sank when she recognized the older couple from the Rong Branch the night before. They spied Emma about the same time. The man frowned. The woman looked embarrassed. Emma chose a small table near the opposite door occupied by two older women—one large and round, the other thin and angled. Both had short gray hair.

"May I sit here?" she asked.

"Of course, dear," said the plump woman.

Someone came in from the kitchen and set a bowl of homemade granola in front of Emma. It was the same cereal they'd served her yesterday. It was delicious. She'd even bought a bag to take home to her mother. She began to pour milk over it when she noticed that the two women, who'd been chatting with great animation prior to her arrival, were silent.

"Please," said Emma, "just pretend I'm not here."

The two women exchanged glances. Finally, the smaller one spoke. "We didn't want to upset your breakfast."

The other woman added, "We mean, in case you hadn't heard the news yet."

"News?" Emma stuck her spoon into her cereal. "What news?"

A few people, including the older couple, finished and filed out of the dining room. It was then that Emma noticed the low, urgent hum of conversation among most of the diners. Even the servers seemed high strung. Emma looked at her dining companions for an explanation.

"What news?" she asked again.

Emma stuck some cereal into her mouth and began crunching down on it. She was only half listening, mentally making a list of her plans for the morning. Among them were a trip to the drug store for some ointment for her palm and a visit to the Pioneer

Museum to see if they knew anything about the Winslow family, especially Billy's death and the transfer of the property. Ian or no Ian, she intended to finish her mission. By early afternoon, she planned to be on the road back to Pasadena.

Again the women at her table exchanged glances. "Might as well tell her," said the large one. "She'll hear soon enough."

Her friend looked around, including over her shoulder, before leaning toward Emma with wide eyes magnified even more by her thick glasses. "Someone was found *dead* last night. Right here in Julian."

"Murdered," the other said, dragging out the word dramatically. "Just like in one of those Agatha Christie novels."

twenty-one

AN ELECTRICAL CHARGE TRAVELED throughout Emma's body at the word *murder*. She ordered herself to calm down. Probably a domestic quarrel gone bad. Phil Bowers had warned her that crimes did happen in Julian. But Emma was sure murder wasn't a common occurrence like it was in other parts of California. Then she began to worry that the two men had gone back to fighting after she'd left.

Her two breakfast companions were all a-twitter about it. She turned her attention back to them, hoping to learn more before she jumped to any conclusions about Phil and Ian.

"We've been coming here every year for over ten years," the plump one said. "We teach school in Riverside, and every year as soon as school's out we leave our husbands and get away to Julian for a long weekend."

"Something like this has never happened before, has it, Hilary?" commented the slender one.

"Absolutely not," replied Hilary. She leaned toward Emma again. "The manager at the hotel told us specifically *not* to visit the Pioneer Cemetery today." She looked around as if the FBI had the placed bugged. "Apparently, that's where *it* happened."

Emma dropped her spoon with a loud *clunk*. Quickly, she picked it up again and smiled in apology at the remaining guests who'd turned her way.

"The cemetery? You mean the historical one up on the hill?" She gave a sigh of relief. If Phil and Ian had tried to kill each other, they wouldn't have taken the time to go all the way to the cemetery.

The women stopped talking as a server approached with a plate of fruit and homemade bread for Emma. Along with it was served a baked egg dish nestled in a ramekin.

"That's the one," Hilary whispered, once they were alone again. "Alice and I just love going up there and poking around." She turned to her companion. "Don't we, Alice?"

Now it was Alice's turn to lean toward Emma. "I heard Barbara, the hotel manager, say that the victim wasn't a local." She paused to look at Hilary. "You know, Hil, I'll bet it was drug related, being so close to Mexico and all."

"Julian's also a big stopover for lots of rough bikers," added Hilary. "Could have been one of them."

Emma could see this was exciting news to the two Miss Marple wannabes, but it rattled her like marbles in a jar. Drug related or not, she'd been in that same cemetery last night just as it had gotten dark. Bumping into Ian had been scary enough. She shivered at the thought that they might have ended up in the middle of a drug deal gone bad.

After breakfast, Emma checked out of the hotel and walked down to the Old Julian Drug Store. Most of the shops were just opening up for the day. After picking out some antibiotic cream and a package of large bandages for her hand, she wandered the small drug and sundry store, looking at the various souvenirs and products. They had a nice assortment of books on the history of the area, and Emma bought a couple. At the cash register, she asked about the murder.

"I heard this morning that there was a murder at the old cemetery last night. Any idea who it was?"

The man running the register took her money and put her purchases in a bag. "No word on his name, but I did hear he wasn't from around here. Most of us are thinking it was drug related. Can't imagine what else it could be."

Drugs again. Well, she thought, drugs had nothing to do with her. Outside on a bench, Emma doctored her hand before heading to the Pioneer Museum.

The museum was housed in a building a few blocks down Washington, just beyond the Rong Branch on the opposite side of the street. Next to it was a small park with mature trees and picnic benches. As she entered the museum, she was warmly greeted by a small woman sitting at a desk. She appeared to be in her sixties and wore her gray hair pulled up on her head. Her figure was trim and dressed in jeans and a Western shirt. After collecting a small entry fee, she told Emma if she had any questions, to just ask.

The museum consisted of several rooms crammed with artifacts and photos from the pioneer and gold rush days of Julian. Emma wound her way through the various displays of mining equipment, clothing, and household goods, reading the descriptions and bits of history along the way. She studied the photographs. There was a photo of Albert Robinson and several other folks in front of the Hotel Robinson back when it first opened. Albert looked much the same as he had last night in her room, just younger.

A chill wafted through the cramped space. Emma looked around, relaxing her eyes and mind in order to better see images that weren't quite there except to those who knew what they were looking for. A few seconds later, she spotted the hazy image of a ghost sitting on one of the upholstered display chairs. The ornate velvet chair was set off to the side. Across its seat was a velvet rope to ward off tired live bones. Tacked to the back of the chair was a printed note asking visitors to please not sit on the furniture.

The ghost appeared to be an elderly woman with thick gray hair swept back into a bun. Her dress was long and dark with a tight bodice. A cameo fastened a high collar close to her neck. Across her shoulders was a lace shawl. She sat erect, as if receiving callers on a Sunday afternoon. Looking at Emma, the ghost gave her a small, warm smile. Emma smiled back and realized that the ghost and the curator looked very much alike. She wondered if the woman at the door realized she had company.

Emma continued through the displays until her eye caught a photograph that made her breath catch. It was of a man and woman in the stiff formal pose so common in photographs of the time. They were dressed in their country best. The man, thin and rangy with a full beard, was seated. Behind him stood a diminutive pretty woman with a hand on his shoulder. Even though she was younger, Emma recognized Ish Reynolds immediately. The note below the photo confirmed it. It also noted that Ish was hung for killing her husband.

"I was quite a looker, wasn't I?"

Emma jumped. She'd been so engrossed in the photo, she hadn't noticed or felt Granny's presence. Granny stood beside her, looking at the picture.

"Yes, Granny, you were."

Granny Apples pointed to the caption. "I didn't kill my man, Emma. I didn't."

"I believe you."

Emma looked around. They were in a separate room, away from the main door. Still, Emma wanted to make sure the curator wasn't near before speaking again. "But that was a long time ago, Granny. Why is it so important now? Even Albert said he didn't believe you did it. Probably others didn't, too. So why not just let it be?"

Before Granny could say anything, Emma had a new thought, one associated with Ian Reynolds. "You're not thinking that by proving your innocence, the family will get the land back, are you?"

Granny started to move away. Emma followed.

"Granny," she hissed. "That land was sold fair and square to the Winslows, even if you and Jacob were murdered. Winston sold it."

Granny's image stopped by other photos. She pointed to one of a family. The caption said it was John Winslow, his wife Helen, and their children. Emma looked closely at it. The boy in the picture was only about ten or twelve, but Emma saw a resemblance between him and the ghost in the graveyard.

"No, Emma, I don't want the land back. Wouldn't do me no good now, would it? I just don't want folks thinking I'm a killer. Not now. Not ever."

"May I help you?"

Emma jumped. It was the curator, peeping around the corner at her.

"Sorry to have startled you, but I thought I heard you say something."

Emma slapped a sheepish grin on her face. "Sorry, but I was reading the captions aloud to myself. Bad habit."

As the woman started back to her desk, Emma stopped her.

"Excuse me, but I do have a few questions."

She turned and walked over to Emma. "Of course, that's why I'm here. Name's Maude."

"Emma Whitecastle." Emma held out her hand, and the two women shook politely.

"Maude, I'm a descendant of Elizabeth and Jacob Reynolds—the couple in that photograph." She pointed to the picture of Ish and Jacob.

"Really?" Maude looked surprised. "I was going to ask if you were related to that fool on TV."

"Actually, I am, but only by marriage." She walked over to the photograph. "I'm related by blood to the Reynolds, on my mother's side. We've traced our line back to Winston Reynolds and to Julian."

"Funny, someone else was asking about the Reynolds family recently. About two or three months ago."

"A tall man, nice looking but flashy, from Los Angeles?"

Maude scrunched up her face in thought. "Can't say. The inquiry came by telephone, but I do recall the number being from Los Angeles, and the gentleman said his name was Reynolds. I might still have the number somewhere." She started back to her desk. Emma and Granny followed.

After scrounging through her cluttered desk, Maude produced a scrap of paper with a Los Angeles phone number and the name *Ian Reynolds* printed neatly under it. "He gave me his number in case I remembered anything more to tell him."

"And did you? Remember anything more, I mean."

"Why, yes, as a matter of fact, I did." Maude sat down at her desk. "I wasn't sure it would help, but then I remembered that the records show the Reynolds property was sold to John Winslow, one of the town's prominent citizens. The Winslow family history is very tragic. John's wife, Helen, left Julian and took their daughter with her. Soon after his mother left, young Billy Winslow committed suicide. Story is, John's heart broke so bad he took to drinking, and he gambled away everything he had. One night he was so drunk, he wandered into the woods during a snow storm and died of exposure."

The story made Emma remember what Granny had said about the early days being unkind to the weak.

"What did that have to do with the Reynolds family?"

"Maybe nothing, but then a librarian called me and told me that they had come into possession of some letters written between John and Helen Winslow after she left Julian. Apparently, a patron left the library a lot of books when she died, and the letters were stashed inside some of them. They were probably handed down through the daughter's line."

Maude excavated another piece of paper from the depths of her desk. "Here it is. Her name's Jill Patterson. She's with the La Habra Library. Said she knew about our museum and wanted to know if we'd like copies of the letters since they contained history about the town and its people. Of course, I said yes. Then I called Mr. Reynolds and told him about the letters, to see if he might be interested since they involved the family that bought the property. I offered to send him copies as soon as I received them, but he said he'd get them directly from the library since it would be faster. I gave him Ms. Patterson's number."

Emma's brain absorbed the information like a cracker dipped in milk. It could be nothing. But then again, the letters between Helen and Big John Winslow, written after Mrs. Winslow left Julian, might contain clues as to why she left and to what happened over a hundred years ago when Julian wasn't a sleepy, sweet tourist attraction but a rough-and-tumble town emerging from the heat of a gold rush.

Letters from the grave.

It had already occurred to Emma that John Winslow might have been one of the three men who attacked Ish Reynolds and strung her up from the old oak tree on her homestead. Billy might have found out and was killed for it. Or his father might have had remorse, and Billy was killed to shut him up. Both were plausible, but based on what little information she'd gleaned from Billy's stiff responses, Emma's money was on the former—that Billy somehow found out and paid the price for his knowledge. And that his father had been unable to stop it, causing him to sink into the depths of a bottle.

"Do you have the letters?" she asked Maude.

"Yes, I do. They came in several weeks ago." Again she rummaged around her desk, coming up this time with a large manila envelope. "I'm afraid we haven't had time to review them yet." She handed the envelope to Emma.

The envelope had been opened, but it didn't look like the contents had been disturbed. Inside were copies of several letters written in a tight hand. Emma examined them, noting that the originals must have been written on small sheets of paper, as the words were edged on the copy paper with a slightly ragged frame. She noted, too, the dates—definitely after Granny was hung. The letters were addressed in two variations: *Dear wife* or *My dear Helen*. All were signed: *Your devoted husband, John.*

As she scanned the correspondence, Emma became excited. Though stiff and formal, the letters begged for forgiveness and contained professions of love and confessions of dark deeds. She looked around for Granny and found her hovering nearby, next to a display case.

Granny came to Emma. "Those there letters, they're important?"

After noting that Maude was busying herself at her desk, Emma gave Granny a smile and a nod. Granny wrung her hands and closed her eyes in hope.

Emma approached the curator's desk. "Maude, is it possible to get copies of these letters?"

"Yes, but I'll have to charge you for the copies."

"No problem. While you're at it, can you make me two copies of each?"

While Maude disappeared into a small room just behind her desk, Emma thought about Ian Reynolds. The land properly belonged to the Bowers family, but she wondered if he was intending to strong-arm them with this historical information into selling it to him. And now she could see why Phil Bowers had reacted so strongly to her being Grant Whitecastle's wife. This *was* a good story; it was a historical murder-mystery come to life—the type of story that would capture the imaginations of viewers and put public sentiment on Reynolds' side, possibly pushing the Bowers family into making a guilt sale.

But something was amiss. She still didn't think the Ian she'd met last night was the real Ian Reynolds. So why would an imposter be interested in this land? Was it really about building condos? She doubted it. Condominiums could be built anywhere, especially somewhere amenable to new construction and not so far out, off the beaten path. Was there really an Ian Reynolds somewhere?

Emma cocked her head toward the back room. Maude was still making the copies. Casting her eyes about the messy desk, she spotted the note with Ian Reynolds' telephone number and quickly jotted it down on a scrap of paper. She'd just replaced the original note when Maude returned with the copies.

"By the way," Emma said to the curator as she paid her for the copies, "Ish Reynolds did not murder her husband, as that tag under the photograph says in the other room."

"All the historical accounts say that she did and was even hung for it." Maude looked at her with curiosity. "Do you have proof of it being otherwise?"

"If I did, would you change that photo caption?"

Maude thought a minute before speaking. "Yes, I believe we would. After all, we'd want it to be accurate."

She pointed to the papers clutched in Maude's hand. "Read those letters. That's the proof."

Emma grinned. Not at Maude, but at the ghost of Granny Apples. As if on springs, the spirit hopped up and down in joy before disappearing.

Happy to have fulfilled her promise to Granny, her aunt Kitty, and her mother, Emma was now ready to go home. But first she was going to drive out to the Bowers ranch and leave a copy of John Winslow's letters with them. She didn't care what transpired over the property, but she wanted them to know she'd been right about Granny. Her family tree was murder-free, at least that she knew. She also wanted Susan and Phillip to have the same information Ian Reynolds had and know what he was planning to use in his bid to grab the property.

She had taken a few steps away from the museum, toward the park, her head down as she concentrated on tucking the letters into her bag, when she heard a whispery voice.

"Emma."

Snapping her head up, she saw nothing.

"Emma," came the slightly shrouded male voice again. This time from behind her.

Snatching off her sunglasses, she pivoted 180 degrees, coming face to face with a ghost. Emma staggered, grasping the trunk of a nearby tree to steady herself. She felt the blood drain from her face like water from a bath.

"Emma," the ghost said again.

Emma stared at the spirit, recognizing it on the spot.

It was the ghost of Ian Reynolds.

twenty-two

. . . .

THE GHOST SAID NOTHING further, just spoke her name a couple more times before disappearing. Emma stumbled to the nearest picnic table and dropped on a bench, her teeth chattering like castanets.

With great care, her mind computed what she had just seen. She was sure it was Ian Reynolds. The ghost looked exactly as she had seen him last night. The same clothing. The same hairstyle. The same voice. Everything the same as when she'd last seen him standing in front of the Rong Branch with Phillip Bowers. But if the ghost was truly Ian's spirit, that meant—she put the brakes on her thoughts, not wanting to enter the dark cave of probability.

Emma looked up into the trees that shaded the table. Heard the birds chattering like old friends. Felt the heavy heat of the June sun and smelled the clean, fresh mountain air. Cars and trucks went by. So did a small covey of motorcycles. The streets were starting to feel the pitter-patter of vehicles belonging to early weekend travelers. People who hadn't heard yet that a murder had taken place in the quiet little town.

Shaking herself, Emma willed her brain to complete her earlier thought. If the ghost that had just visited her was indeed Ian Reynolds' spirit, that meant Ian was dead.

"Ian's dead," she said to herself out loud in a barely audible tone. From her bag, her cell phone rang. In her shock, Emma didn't hear it. It rang again.

"Dead." She repeated the word, drawing it out into two syllables, forcing her reluctant memory to make note of it, to understand and hold on to what it meant. If Ian was dead, did that mean Phil Bowers was a killer? Or had Ian returned to the cemetery and stumbled upon something unsavory?

She looked in the direction of the Pioneer Cemetery but couldn't see it from where she sat. Yet she knew it was there and that a body had been found. Was Ian's body the one in the graveyard, or was that someone else, and Ian's body was still to be discovered?

The third ring penetrated Emma's dazed thoughts. She pulled her phone out of her bag and looked at the display, taking a moment to let the name register. It was Milo Ravenscroft. On the fourth ring, she answered.

"Emma, thank God I reached you." He sounded anxious. "Are you still in Julian?"

She looked around the park, still thinking about Ian Reynolds, looking to see if his ghost was present. She saw nothing, not even Granny.

"Yes, but I'm leaving soon." She shook herself, demanding that her mind and body concentrate on Milo's call. Milo was the one person who might be able to answer her questions.

"Soon is not soon enough. Get in your car and leave now. Right this minute."

"Why?" The urgency in his voice put her on alert. "What's the matter? Did you look at the photos I sent you?"

"Yes, but forget that for now. Right before I called you I had a vision. I think there's going to be a murder in Julian."

"There already has been, Milo." She said the words slowly and with care, like eggs being carried over rocky terrain. "I heard about it this morning." She swallowed hard before speaking. "And I think his ghost just visited me."

"His ghost?"

Still shocked and confused, Emma nodded up and down before realizing Milo couldn't see her. "Yes, at least I think so. Unless there are two bodies."

"I saw a body, Emma, in a graveyard—an old graveyard. But I couldn't see his face." Emma heard him take a deep breath before continuing. "And I saw you."

A vibration ran up and down her spine like strings on a stroked cello. She put her sunglasses back on, as if they could hide her from harm like an invisibility shield.

"You were running in the graveyard, frightened and hurt."

"That's a pretty accurate description of last night. I was in the graveyard and frightened, and I stumbled and hurt myself. Not badly, just scrapes and bruises. But there was no body. At least no fresh ones."

She thought about Ian, both alive and dead, and how quickly he'd gone from one state of being into the other.

"Last night I was frightened by a man who was following me. But today, just before you called, a ghost came to me that looked like him."

There was a long silence on Milo's end. Emma stayed quiet, knowing he was thinking it over.

"And you're sure it was the same man?"

"Pretty sure."

"And last night you're sure he was alive when he chased you? That it wasn't his ghost trying to scare you?"

"Considering he and I had coffee together soon after, I'm pretty sure he was alive in the cemetery last night. And he wasn't exactly chasing me. He was following me, watching me."

While she talked, she watched the traffic on the road several yards away. People were coming and going in a normal manner while she sat in the park talking about murder and ghosts.

"What's more, he heard me talking to the ghosts in the graveyard last night, and he wasn't at all surprised by it."

When Milo didn't respond, she added, "As I told you last night, the ghosts scattered as soon as they sensed his presence. Granny, too. She wouldn't let him see her."

Again Milo didn't answer. His silence was making her more nervous. She plowed on, clarifying. "The ghost who just visited me and the man who chased me last night are one and the same. It's the man in the photos I sent you. The young one, not the bald one."

She hoped at some point he'd stop her and offer words of advice and comfort. He did not.

"Do you know who the man in the photos is, Milo?"

"Yes, I do. And you're right, Emma. His name isn't Ian Reynolds. It's Garrett Bell."

"You know him?"

"Yes, I do. Professionally, at least."

"He was a client?"

"No, Emma, he wasn't. He's a professional clairvoyant, like me. Or at least he was."

In the warmth of day, Emma started shivering again. Taking off her sunglasses, she made sure there were no spirits around before attributing her bone-numbing chill to fear. She was alone.

"I'm puzzled, Milo. If Ian, or this Garrett person, could see ghosts, why did they flee from him? Is it because they didn't like him or trust him, as you said last night?"

"I'm not entirely sure why, but probably a bit of both, especially the trust part. Garrett...," Milo started to say, but his words were broken up by static. Then the call was dropped.

Emma immediately dialed him again but got a busy tone. Frustrated, she put the phone down on the table and waited for Milo to call her back. She resumed watching the street. A sheriff's vehicle went by. So did another small group of bikers. It seemed like forever before Milo rang through again, although it was less than a minute.

Without saying hello, Emma said, "I lost you just as you started to tell me about Garrett Bell."

"Garret Bell was a clairvoyant who used his gifts unethically for his own benefit and to benefit others with dishonest motives. He wasn't interested in helping people or in comforting them over lost loved ones."

"You mean he used the spirits for financial gain?"

"Yes. He'd help people locate spirits who could help them find out things that could be used for other purposes. People would come to him with information about old bank heists or stolen gems, missing artwork, stuff like that, and he'd contact spirits to help locate them. If the items were recovered, he received a large fee."

"That doesn't sound illegal."

"Most of the stolen items were never returned to their proper owners. That is illegal. His services were used mostly by fortune hunters. And though he'd been charged with illegal activity on several occasions, he'd managed to slip out of it. He'd even been suspected of using spirits to convince elderly folks to change their wills in favor of other family members, who then paid Garrett a hefty fee when they collected. Usually, collection was sooner rather than later."

Emma shivered again. "That's despicable."

"Yes, it is. And the worse part is, often the spirits don't even realize they're being used in such a manner. But like us, they can often sense when someone isn't right. That could be why they fled when Garrett was around."

"You mean buzz about Garrett Bell's activities has made it to the Ghost Gazette?"

"Go ahead and laugh. But while I doubt the spirits have broadcast his shenanigans, I'm sure most of them have picked up the negative vibrations, or aura, that has built up around him over the years."

Emma was on the brink of making a nervous crack about a disturbance in the Force, but she decided to keep the joke to herself.

"Emma, are you in a visible, public place?"

"Yes, I'm in a park. Lots of people driving by. Some even walking by."

"Good. Stay public as much as possible. Don't go anywhere where you can be trapped alone. And above all, stay out of that cemetery."

"Do you think Ian's ghost—I mean Garrett's ghost—will hurt me?"

Just as Emma asked the question, the sheriff's SUV drove by again, this time moving slowly. Emma watched it. The people inside watched her.

"No, I don't think his ghost will hurt you. I'm more worried about the person who killed him. That's the real danger. That person is alive and at large."

Emma thought again about Phillip Bowers. He was with Ian/Garrett the last time she saw him. And Phil had quite a temper. But try as she might, she couldn't see Phil Bowers going up to the cemetery to have it out with Ian. Besides, he had said he was going to take the waitress home. Then she remembered that Ian was supposed to stay at the Julian Hotel last night. Emma wondered if he'd ever checked in.

"Why did Ian's—Garrett's—ghost come to me?"

"Hard to say. He knew you could see him. Could be he wanted to tell you something, perhaps warn you or let you know about his death. But more likely, Garrett's spirit probably hasn't adjusted yet to being dead."

"Uh-huh." Emma watched the sheriff's SUV drive by again, then do a U-turn and head back in her direction.

"Sometimes spirits are in shock for a while," Milo continued explaining, not picking up on Emma's hesitation. "Some eventually pass over and never return to earth. You might never see it again."

"I see," she murmured, watching the SUV park in front of her. A woman in plain clothes got out of the passenger's side. A uniformed officer climbed out of the driver's side. They were looking right at her.

"The other man in the photo—he might have been one of the last people to see Garrett Bell alive. Quick, Milo, any vibes on him?"

"Interesting character, that one. His bark's worse than his bite. I don't think he did the deed, but I've been wrong before."

The officers started walking her way.

"Milo, gotta run. I'm about to be visited by the authorities."

"Be careful what you say to them, Emma. Police aren't always the most open-minded beings. But," he cautioned before ending the call, "don't try to lie to them. They can smell a lie. It's what they do. Tell them the truth, but be smart about it."

"Are you Emma Whitecastle?" the woman asked.

Emma nodded as she closed her phone.

"I'm Detective Jani Hallam of the San Diego County Sheriff's Department. This is Deputy Jorgenson." The woman turned toward the officer. "Let them know we've located her."

twenty-three

. . . .

"How did you know who I was?"

"Mr. Bowers described you. We went to your hotel, but you'd checked out. The woman at the hotel said your car was still parked there, so we knew you couldn't have gone too far."

The detective moved closer to Emma and took a small pad and pencil from the jacket of her pantsuit. She was compact and fit, with dark hair that curled slightly below her ears. "We'd like to ask you a few questions, Ms. Whitecastle."

"May I ask what this is about?"

"We'd like to ask you about Ian Reynolds. We understand you were with him last night at the Rong Branch Restaurant."

"Yes, I was. In fact, so was Phillip Bowers."

"Yes, we know that."

Emma was about to say more when she caught sight of an image slightly to her left. It shimmered in the shadows of a nearby tree before becoming more pronounced. Taking off her sunglasses, she turned her head slightly, just enough to get a better view and hopefully not enough to catch the attention of the officers. But she couldn't hide her surprise. The ghost of Garrett Bell was back. As soon as she saw him, he started moving toward her.

"Is something the matter, Ms. Whitecastle?"

"Huh?" She turned her attention back to Detective Hallam. "Uh, no. I thought I saw something, but it was just a reflection on my glasses. Sorry." Emma straightened her shoulders. "You were asking me about Ian Reynolds?"

"When was the last time you saw Mr. Reynolds?"

Now there was a trick question. Alive, she saw him last night. Literally, she was seeing him this very moment. Sensing that the detective meant alive, and realizing that Detective Hallam hadn't mentioned yet the fact that Ian was dead, she assumed the former.

"Last night. The three of us were the last customers to leave the restaurant. Ian and Phil were standing in front of it when I went back to my hotel."

"And you never saw him again?"

Emma's mind did some quick gymnastics. Technically, that was the last time she'd seen Ian Reynolds. The entity she was seeing now was really Garrett Bell. She knew she was splitting hairs, but it wasn't really lying to say she'd never seen him again, was it? Milo had warned her to be truthful but careful.

"No, I didn't. He said something about staying at my hotel, but I never saw him again last night or this morning at breakfast."

"May I sit down, Ms. Whitecastle?"

"Of course. And please, call me Emma." She gave the detective a small smile, noting at the same time that the deputy remained standing.

"Is there a problem, Detective? I mean, why all the questions about Ian? We just met for the first time yesterday."

"You'd never met him before? Ever? Never talked to him on the phone? Or through correspondence or e-mails?"

"Never."

"Mr. Bowers seems to think he was a relative of yours."

Emma shrugged. "That's what he claimed." She peered at Detective Hallam, then shifted her gaze to the young, scrawny deputy standing just behind her, shifting from foot to foot. "You said *was* a relative, Detective. Past tense."

"Ian Reynolds was murdered last night. Up in the old cemetery."

Even though Emma already knew, hearing the official pronouncement shocked her all over again. "I heard about a murder at breakfast this morning, but I had no idea who it was."

"Phil Bowers says you and Mr. Reynolds were up in the cemetery together yesterday."

"Not together, no. I went up there and he followed. It was near dark, and he scared the tar out of me. I tried to run away and fell down those steep steps. You know, the wooden ones that go up the hill." Emma held her palm out and stripped off the bandage, showing the officers the still raw and ugly scrape from the night before. "I did this on the railing. My legs are bruised also."

"Why were you trying to get away from him?"

"He was a stranger, Detective, and it was almost dark. He didn't announce himself, even when I called out to whoever was there. Instead, he crept behind trees, getting closer to me. Wouldn't you try to get away, too?"

"I see your point. Was this before or after you were at the Rong Branch with him?"

"Before. Like I told you, after the Rong Branch, I went to my hotel. I was very tired and went straight to bed."

"I'm confused, Emma. If Mr. Reynolds frightened you, why did you go with him to the Rong Branch?"

Emma told the detective about coming to Julian to learn more about her family and stumbling into the fight between Bowers and Reynolds over the old homestead property. She continued to answer questions about the property and its history, and why she was in the graveyard—conveniently leaving out communing with the ghosts. She explained to the detective that she was doing last-minute research on old family graves before going home the next day. She even dug in her bag and produced the rubbing. She answered all questions, keeping anything about spirits and ghosts out of it. Partway through the interrogation, the ghost of Garrett Bell disappeared. Emma gave a sigh of relief. Then the detective tossed her a hardball.

"Emma, did anyone at the hotel see you come in last night?"

Emma knew what that meant. The detective wanted to know if she had an alibi for the time Ian was murdered. Emma thought through the night before. The hotel had been quiet when she got there, and she hadn't seen anyone on the way to her room. She'd heard folks come in later, but they hadn't seen her. Only one person knew she'd been in bed all night and never left: Albert Robinson. But somehow she doubted they'd look him up for verification.

"No, no one. It was very quiet when I returned. I showered, made a couple of calls on my cell to friends, then went to bed. I heard people out in the hall a bit later, but I don't know who they were, and they never saw me."

Detective Hallam smiled. "Not uncommon for that hotel. My husband and I have stayed there many times."

The detective closed her notepad and got up from the table. "I think that's all for now, Emma. Are you going home today? Back to Pasadena?"

"Yes, I am. Shortly." She'd never told them where she lived. The detective noticed her surprise.

"We got your contact information from the hotel," she explained. She rattled off a phone number. It was the number to Emma's parents' home. "Is this the best number to reach you?"

Emma gave Detective Hallam her cell phone number, and the detective jotted it down, saying, "If there is anything else you'd like to tell us or add, just call us or stop by the station." She handed Emma her card. "We may be contacting you if we have further questions."

As the officers were about to leave, Emma was being nagged by a last thought. The police probably didn't know Ian wasn't Ian. But then again, how would she explain how she knew? Quickly she reasoned that they would check his fingerprints and know soon enough. She didn't need to get involved any more than she was already.

As she watched the sheriff's vehicle pull away, Granny popped up, her image quickly taking shape right in front of Emma. The ghost did not look happy.

"You can't go home yet, Emma."

"Oh, yes, I can." Emma got up and stretched. She'd been sitting on the bench a long time. "I cleared your name. Isn't that what you wanted?" She put her sunglasses back on and started walking up Washington toward Main Street, pulling out her phone along the way. She dialed Milo, but it went into voice mail. She tucked her phone into a side pocket of her bag so she could hear it better if he called back.

"But Emma, it's important. Our land is still in danger."

Emma turned and faced the ghost. "Right now, Ish, all I want is to pee and get something to drink, in that order. Then I'm getting into my car and heading home. Besides, it's not your land any-more—hasn't been for a long, long time. And the man who was trying to get his hands on it is dead."

There were public restrooms just behind city hall. Emma made a beeline for them, then prayed she had a quarter when she noticed they were pay toilets. Granny continued hounding her while she dug out her wallet. Not finding any quarters, she started digging through the bottom of her large leather bag until she produced a stray coin. She quickly entered and shut the door on Granny.

"Now you listen to me, Emma Whitecastle. I'm still your elder." Granny had come through the bathroom door and was shaking a finger in Emma's face.

"A dead elder," Emma reminded the spirit. She was sitting on the toilet, praying that Garrett Bell didn't come in and join them. She finished, pulled up her jeans, and started washing her hands. "Just how old were you anyway, Ish? You know, when you died."

Granny crossed her arms in front of her and frowned, letting Emma know that no woman likes to be asked her age, not even a dead one. "I had just passed my forty-first year."

"Aha!" Emma dried her hands. "I'm forty-four. That makes me the elder here. And I'm taking my elder butt home, where there are no murders or murderers, past or present."

Before leaving the bathroom, Emma put on some lipstick and ran her hands through her short blond hair, trying to bring some order to it. She might be older than Granny, but she wasn't going to go through the rest of the day looking it.

She glanced at Granny Apples. The ghost was standing in a corner of the small bathroom wearing a thunderous scowl. Emma hung her head and gripped the side of the sink.

"Ish, be happy. You've been exonerated. You won't be considered a murderer any longer. Those letters even said who killed you."

"They did?" The ghost's face lightened a bit.

"Yes. John Winslow confessed in the letters. He confessed in the hope of gaining his wife's forgiveness for that and for the death of their son Billy. I'll bet the letters were written shortly before he died. And I'll bet his wife knew about his part in it. That's why she left him."

"Big John Winslow," Granny repeated, shaking her head.

"Yes, he and two other men, a guy named Parker and someone he called Bobcat, did it."

"Bobcat Billings," the ghost added. "He was a good-for-nothing drifter. Tom Parker owned property on the other side of the stream from us. Mean as a snake."

"It was over the gold, Ish, just like you thought. They did it knowing Winston would probably sell and leave town."

"Winston would never have sold the land to Parker or Bobcat."

"But he trusted John Winslow, didn't he? He was his best friend's father."

Granny nodded, her face down, her eyes locked on the cement floor of the public toilet.

"Billy was probably killed by Parker and Bobcat because his father was about to go to the authorities and confess. They did it to keep him quiet, making it look like a suicide. According to Winslow's letters, they also threatened to find Winslow's wife and daughter."

Her head still down, Granny said, "Senseless killings, all over some fool gold."

Emma leaned over and kissed Granny's cheek. Her lips fell through the air, but she knew Granny would appreciate the gesture.

twenty-four

"WHO YOU TALKING TO in there, Fancy Pants?"

Startled, Emma spun around. She'd just walked out of the public toilet when she heard Phil Bowers' voice. He was standing next to the door to the bathroom, leaning against the building, one foot up behind him flat against the wall. He was dressed in jeans and a light blue polo shirt and wore his cowboy hat pushed slightly back. He was relaxed and confident, a man sure of his place in the world. In spite of herself, Emma thought he looked finger-licking good.

"Are *you* following me now?"

"Just wanted to talk to you. I was walking back from the sheriff's office when I spotted you up ahead and saw you duck in here."

"Nothing to talk about, Phil. Now leave me alone. I'm leaving for home as soon as I get to my car."

She put on her sunglasses. Looking for the quickest way out of the city hall parking lot, she saw it was the way she'd come in, past him. She started walking that way. Phil left his post and fell in step next to her. Before they reached the street, he took her gently by the arm, stopping her.

"First, tell me who you were talking to in there."

Emma yanked her arm away. "It's none of your business, but since you insist on making it so, I was on the phone."

"Difficult to talk on the phone without one, isn't it?"

He held out his hand. In his palm was a cell phone just like hers. Emma dug around in her bag. She was phoneless.

"I found it on the ground," he explained, "just outside the bathroom."

Emma realized the phone must have fallen out of the side pocket of her purse when she was rooting around for a quarter and arguing with Granny.

"Were you talking to your ghost buddies, Emma? Did they follow you into the bathroom?" He shook his head. "Man, don't you just hate when that happens?"

She started to say something but held her tongue.

"Come on, Emma. Let's talk. I'd like to know what you told the detectives. I want to know more about Ian Reynolds."

She stopped and turned to face him. "What? You want me to give you an alibi for last night?"

"First of all, I have—" He stopped short as a couple of older women strolled into the parking lot in search of the public restrooms. He smiled at them and moved closer to Emma before continuing. "I have an alibi for last night. The whole night. When I heard a guy named Reynolds was found dead in the old cemetery, I went to talk to the sheriff—to tell what I knew about him."

"And to point a finger at me."

He studied her. "Do you have an alibi for last night?"

"Do I need one? Am I a suspect?"

"Not that I know of. At least, not yet."

In spite of his abrasiveness, there was something solid, even trustworthy, about Phillip Bowers. But what if he had killed Ian and manufactured an alibi? He could be using her to make sure he wasn't nailed for the murder. Milo didn't think Phil had killed Garrett, but even he admitted he could be wrong.

"And if I do become a suspect, I suppose you'll want to represent me. Is that right, counselor?"

Bowers shook his head. "Sorry, but since I'm a witness, it'd be a conflict of interest. Besides, I specialize in estate planning. Wouldn't do a murder suspect a lick of good."

She looked him up and down, taking in the jeans, knit shirt, boots, and hat. He didn't look like any estate planner she'd ever met.

"So, if you're not my attorney and you're a witness, anything I tell you could go straight to the authorities. There'd be no attorney-client privilege, would there?"

"Afraid not. I just want to know about Ian Reynolds—who he was and where he came from. Seems odd that after all these years, suddenly the two of you come sniffing around that old property. And now one of you is dead."

Phil Bowers took a booted step closer to her. She could feel warmth from his body mingling with the heat of the air. Her nostrils flared, sucking in the earthy and sensual scents of sweat and sweet hay. She shook herself to break its spell.

"I want to make sure my family doesn't go through anything like this again."

"Don't worry, Mr. Bowers." Emma stood her ground, not backing down from his invasion into her personal space. "I have no intention of messing with that property. Frankly, I'd rather see it remain with you than have some cardboard condos destroying the landscape. It's nice out there; it should remain that way. I'm just someone interested in her family's past. Like I've said many times, I didn't know Ian Reynolds even existed until yesterday."

She dug around in her bag. "In fact, I have something for you." She pulled out the Winslow letters and handed him the extra copies. "These are copies of letters I got from the museum. They were written by John Winslow—a confession that he and some others killed both Jacob Reynolds and his wife. They wanted the property because of gold."

Phil Bowers took the letters from her. He fanned through them but didn't read them.

"I have reason to believe," she continued, "that Ian Reynolds saw these same letters, possibly several weeks ago. Maybe he felt the property should be his. Maybe he thought he could bully you and your family into selling it to him. And maybe it wasn't about building condominiums. It could be that he thought there might still be gold out there."

"There's been no gold around here for years."

Emma shrugged and held her hand out for her phone. "Now, if you'll give me back my phone, I'll be moving along. It's hot out here, and I have a long drive ahead of me."

"But you can't go, Emma. We still need to stop him."

At the sound, Emma turned around and faced Granny, who'd disappeared during the initial face-off with Bowers.

"Stop who, Granny?" In her frustration, she forgot about Phil. "Garrett Bell is dead."

From behind her, Emma heard a throat clear. Sweat beaded on her forehead and dampened her underarms. She closed her eyes and wished she could transport herself somewhere, anywhere. She tapped her sneakers together, hoping beyond hope that they could whisk her back to Pasadena.

"Who's Garrett Bell, Fancy Pants?"

Emma slowly turned around, pushing her sunglasses to the top of her head as she moved. With a set jaw, she locked eyes with Phil Bowers. They stared at each other in an emotional standoff for nearly a minute.

"Who's Garrett Bell?" he asked again, his eyes hard as steel. "Or should I go get one of the detectives? They sent three up from San Diego, you know. I'm sure one of them would have time to hear what you have to say. Just don't forget to cop the insanity plea."

"Keep the phone," she snapped. "I'll get another." She started marching out of the parking lot. Bowers was on her heels.

"Who's Garrett Bell, Fancy Pants?"

At the sidewalk, Emma stopped and faced Phil. "Stop calling me that!"

"Then tell me who this Garrett guy is. Is he another partner in this land scheme? Or maybe he's another body—one you have stashed somewhere else."

"Do you really think I killed Ian Reynolds?" The question came out in a half snarl.

"I didn't, but now I'm not so sure."

At the same time, they both noticed that a few people had stopped to stare at them. Bowers took her arm once again and steered Emma back a few steps into the shade behind city hall.

"Do you have an alibi for last night?" He let go of her arm.

"As I told Detective Hallam, I went directly from the Rong Branch to the hotel and straight to bed."

"Anyone see you?"

"Yes, as a matter of fact." Emma stood defiantly in front of him. "Someone did see me. Someone was in my room all night."

When she didn't continue, Phil nudged her along. "And that person was …?"

"Is it any of your business?"

"I'm making it my business."

There, on the spot, Emma decided to slap him with the truth. "Albert Robinson. That's who saw me."

"Albert Robinson." Phil said the name out loud, rolling it over and around his tongue while he searched his memory. Once the name clicked, he narrowed his eyes at her. "Nice act, Mrs. White-castle. Guess being married to that TV freak rubbed off on you."

"Come on, Emma," said Granny, her whispery voice filled with determination. "You can't go now."

Emma held up a hand but looked at Phil while she spoke. "Not now, Granny. One pest at a time is all I can handle." With a huff and a puff, Granny disappeared.

"You're psychotic." Phil gave a little laugh. "Cute but psychotic."

Psychotic. The word jarred her like a slammed door. Emma had used that same word when she'd first found out about her mother and Granny Apples. Thinking about it now, she was ashamed she hadn't been more open minded, especially concerning Elizabeth.

"This isn't an act, Phil."

She spoke in an even tone, forcing herself to remain calm. Let him go to the police with this—with everything. She didn't kill Garrett Bell, and she wasn't the only one in the world who talked to ghosts.

"Last night, I was scared, afraid Ian would find me at the hotel. You heard him; he said he was staying there. When I got to my room, I bolted the door and barricaded it. At some point, the ghost of Albert Robinson appeared."

"And I suppose he watched over you like some guardian angel."

"In a way, yes. I told him I was scared. He told me to go to sleep and not to worry. Then he sat in the chair I used to block the door. He was still there when I went to sleep."

Phil stared at her a long time, weighing her words for both fact and fiction. "So, who's this Garrett guy?"

Emma wasn't sure if she should tell Phil outright about Garrett. She decided to tread soft at first and see where it led. "Another ghost. He came to me this morning after I left the museum. That's how I knew Ian had been killed."

"So this ghost, this dead Garrett guy, he told you? He simply popped in for a visit and gave you a news flash about the murder?"

So much for the soft touch.

"Garrett Bell *is* Ian Reynolds. That's his real name. He's a clairvoyant with sketchy ethics—a real piece of work. You were right to suspect him."

Phil stared at her like she'd dropped from an alien spaceship. "But if you'd never met him before, how do you know all this?"

"A friend—another clairvoyant—told me. I realized last night at the Rong Branch that Ian couldn't be the real Ian Reynolds, so while you two baboons slugged it out, I snapped a photo with my phone and sent it to him. Seems my friend knew Garrett Bell personally."

She started walking away, then turned. "And since I didn't share that with the authorities, feel free to do so yourself. *I'm* going home."

Emma hadn't gone but a step or two when she heard the familiar ring of her cell phone. She turned just in time to see Phil opening it.

"Ghosts'R'Us," he answered, keeping his eyes on Emma.

She stomped back to where Phil was standing. "Give me that."

"No, she's right here. Who's this?" After listening, he said to Emma, "It's some guy named Milo. You in?" He gave her a crooked grin.

Shooting daggers at him, she held out her hand for the phone. Phil handed it to her.

"Milo?" She kept Phil in her sight as she talked. "That was Phil Bowers, the guy who was with me and Ian Reynolds last night before Ian—I mean Garrett—was killed. You know, the bald guy in the photos." She grinned at Phil. He frowned. "Tell me, Milo, is Bowers here the murderer?"

As she listened, Phil made a grab for the phone. She hopped back out of his reach.

"Hmm, too bad. I wouldn't mind seeing him behind bars."

"What the hell?" Phil came closer but made no move for the phone.

"You're *what*?" Emma stuffed an index finger into her free ear to hear better. She couldn't believe what Milo was saying. "No, you don't need to be doing that, neither of you. I'm coming home today. Leaving right this minute, in fact."

"Stay where you are, Emma," Milo told her. "In fact, can you put me on speaker? I want that Bowers guy to hear this."

"Why?"

"He's a good guy, Emma. At least I think he is. You're in danger. Someone needs to help you."

"He doesn't believe me, Milo—about Granny, about anything. And I don't need any help. I'm coming home."

"No! Don't you dare go near your car."

"Why?"

"Do as he says, Emma!" It was Tracy yelling in the background.

Tracy and Milo were on their way to Julian. Since he didn't drive, Milo had called Tracy, getting her number from his client records. It didn't take much convincing on his part to put Tracy on the road to Julian.

Emma looked at Phil. "He wants to talk to us both." After moving close to Phil, Emma pushed the speaker feature on the phone, but with the noise from the street, they couldn't hear very well.

"Hang on," she told Milo, "we need to get someplace quiet."

After looking around, Emma headed for one of the bathrooms with Phil in tow. The one she'd vacated was occupied. She went to the next.

"You have a quarter?" she asked Phil. "Hopefully, we'll still get a signal in here."

He dug one out and fed the lock. Emma entered and motioned for him to follow her. After a slight hesitation, he did. Once inside, Emma shut the door. The tiny room was cramped with the two of them and smelled of disinfectant. The small space grew cold when the ghost of Granny Apples appeared in the corner.

Emma leaned against the sink and held the phone out between them. "Can you hear us, Milo?"

"Yes."

"Phil Bowers is here with me. What's going on?"

"I'm not exactly sure, Emma, but it's enough to worry me. That's why Tracy and I are heading to Julian."

"Who is this guy?" asked Phil.

"A friend of mine. The one who told me about Garrett." Phil shuffled his feet. Taking off his hat, he hung it on the coat hook on the back of the door and leaned in close.

"What about my car, Milo?"

"I don't know, Emma. It's just that I had another vision. I saw a bad car accident. A very bad one."

"A vision?" Phil stepped back. Without realizing it, he'd gone right through Granny, who'd also been listening. "More crackpot crap, Emma?"

He started for the door but Emma reached up, grabbing him by the collar of his shirt. Before he could react, she yanked his head back down toward the phone.

"If Milo says you're to stay," she hissed, her mouth near his face, "you're staying."

"Please, Mr. Bowers," they heard Milo say from the phone. "Just hear me out. Emma's in great danger."

Phil Bowers looked deep into Emma's eyes, weighing common sense against the passion in Milo's voice. He didn't break away from her grasp.

"What about the accident?" he asked Milo.

"It was a white Lexus. Isn't that your car, Emma?"

"Yes, I drive a white Lexus."

"I saw a white Lexus weaving on a narrow mountain road, then going over a cliff." Milo paused. "You were in the car, Emma."

She let go of Phil's shirt as chills shot their way up and down her bare arms. Phil noticed her shaking and put an arm around her, drawing her into his warmth. With his other hand, he cupped the hand holding the phone to steady it.

"I promise you, Milo," Phil said into the phone, but with his eyes on Emma, "that we'll get the car checked out. I won't let Emma drive it until we do."

"Thank God," they heard Tracy call out. "We'll be there in about two hours or so, depending on traffic."

Emma leaned closer toward the phone. "Do you know yet who killed Garrett Bell?"

"I'm afraid not, Emma." It was Milo again. "Has he returned to you?"

"Yes, once more, but he didn't say anything. Granny's convinced that the property is still in danger."

"The real worry is you, Emma. Garrett's killer is still out there. Granny is sensing danger, but she might not have a good handle on what kind. When you get a chance, ask her direct questions about Garrett. See what she knows."

"Will do." She looked around the small room, but Granny had evaporated again. "Call me when you get closer, and I'll give you directions," Emma told them. "I'm not sure where I'll be."

Phil gave them his cell number as a backup.

They were about to end the call when Emma called out, "Wait! What about Archie?"

"He's with us. We're bringing him along," said Milo.

"I didn't have the heart to put him back into the kennel," yelled Tracy over the din of traffic.

"Speak, Archie," Tracy commanded. "Say hi to Emma. Come on boy, speak."

Archie woofed obligingly.

After ending the call, Phil turned his face toward Emma, keeping his arm around her. "Is the dog real or a ghost?"

"Did you hear him bark?"

"Yes."

"Then he's real."

With Phil bent slightly, their faces were just inches apart. Emma could feel his breath on her cheek and the strength of his arm around her. She tilted her head up a bit, just in time to catch his mouth coming down on hers.

twenty-five

TWO LONG KISSES LATER, Emma pushed away from Phil Bowers. She ran a hand through her hair and felt her cheeks grow warm. Phil cleared his throat and looked down at the floor.

Emma was the first to speak. "You don't happen to know a motel around here that allows pets, do you?"

Happy with a neutral topic, Phil thought about her question. "Yes, there's one just outside of town that I believe takes animals. It's not very nice, though. I mean, it's okay, just not what…"

"What I'd be used to?" Her look was challenging, almost a dare.

Taking out his cell phone, Phil made a call. "Hey, Aunt Susan. It's me. Does your friend still rent out that cottage in town? You know, the one with the fenced-in yard." A pause. "I see. Will she rent to people with pets? Just a couple of days. Three adults, one dog." Another pause. "Let me ask."

He turned to Emma. "What kind and how big?"

"Archie's a Scottie, about twenty pounds. Very well trained. The people are average in both kind and size."

"And not well trained, I suppose?"

She responded with a guilty shrug.

Phil repeated Archie's stats into the phone and waited. "It's for Emma Whitecastle." He glanced at Emma. "You remember her, don't you, from yesterday?" Pause. "Yep, she's the one." His face reddened. "You might say we've buried the hatchet."

He closed his phone. "She's going to see if her friend's cottage is available. Cute place, well maintained, two bedrooms—and it's right here in town."

"Good enough for Fancy Pants?"

He shook a finger at her. "That came out of your mouth this time, not mine."

Phil grabbed his hat and opened the door. "I imagine you're the sort who gets snarly when she doesn't eat. Low blood sugar, right?"

"I don't have low blood sugar."

"No? Well, I do. But I'll bet it's been hours since you've eaten."

"Yes, it has, and I'm starving. But what about my car?"

"We'll take care of both." He stopped when they reached the street. Across from them was the Rong Branch. "Let's not go to the Rong Branch, though."

He led her up to the corner and across Main to the Miner's Diner. "You like milk shakes and malts?"

"Sure, who doesn't?"

"They make the best here."

The Miner's Diner was reached by entering the Old Julian Drug Store. Phil waved to a guy behind the register. It was the same man who'd sold her bandages and ointment that morning.

In the next room was the diner, with its old-fashioned marble soda fountain. Lined up at it were customers of various sizes and ages. There were also several sets of tables and chairs scattered about. They spotted an empty table near the window and settled in. Emma ordered a tuna and avocado sandwich with fruit on the side. Phil ordered a bacon cheeseburger and fries. At his urging, she also ordered a strawberry milkshake. He ordered iced tea.

While they waited for their food, Phil made a call about her car.

"A friend of mine is going to take your car to his garage and go over it with a fine-tooth comb. If there's a problem, he'll find it. We'll meet him at the hotel after we eat."

A discomfort settled in on Emma like indigestion. "Phil," she began. "I really appreciate what you're doing for me. You know, with the cottage and the car and all, but I don't want any misunderstandings between us."

He knitted his brows. "You mean about what happened back there?"

"Yes. Let's agree right now that what happened in the bathroom stays in the bathroom."

A corner of Phil's mouth curled upward. "Wasn't it up to your usual standards, Fancy Pants?"

"That's not what I meant and you know it." She huffed in frustration. "What happened was an accident. I was frightened by what Milo said, and you were comforting me. That's it."

"I see. An accident that happened twice, in quick succession."

"First you think I'm here to steal your land." Emma's voice rose in frustration before she toned it down to a whisper. "Then you accuse me of lying and even call me psychotic."

"I believe I called you a liar before I accused you of being a thief."

"Whatever. Now you think one kiss, and I'm going to forget all that and fall into your arms? Please."

Phil held up two fingers. "Two kisses. The first might have been a fluke, but you came back for seconds." He gave her a wide grin. "Did you think it was a two-for-one sale at Saks?"

"You're impossible."

"So I'm told."

She tried a different tack. "Listen, Phil. I'm in the middle of a divorce, and so are you. I came here to find out about my family, not for some quickie romance with a belligerent man who thinks I'm a cheat, a thief, and a nut."

"Now you're the one name-calling."

"What can I say? You bring out the worst in me."

They fell into an awkward silence. Emma looked around, wondering where their food was, while Phil studied her with hooded eyes. She squirmed. She wasn't used to being scrutinized at such close range. Finally, she broke the silence.

"Why'd we come here? Was it because you were ashamed to go back to the Rong Branch after last night's brawl?"

Phil laughed. "Hardly. I've lived here all my life. These folks have seen me do a lot worse, believe me." He looked around before continuing, like he was about to tell her a national top secret. "Truth is, I have a bit of high cholesterol. And my aunt has a lot of influence with the folks at the Rong Branch. Between her and Bev, if I order anything fried, it automatically gets substituted with something healthy. You'd think I was ordering up plutonium with an anthrax chaser. Today I just wanted a cheeseburger and fries with no side of bullshit, just lettuce and tomato. I hope you don't mind."

Emma couldn't help but smile. "But I noticed you didn't order a shake."

"No, but I do intend to have a spoonful or two of yours."

Emma toyed with her silverware. "So, tell me about your alibi last night."

"Why? You jealous?"

"No, of course not. Just that I told you about mine."

The shake and iced tea were served. Emma took a sip of the shake. It was every bit as good as he'd promised.

"You did say you were taking Beverly home. Just wondering if she was your alibi."

Phil dipped his spoon into Emma's shake and took a healthy gob. He stuck it in his mouth and closed his eyes in bliss. "Mmm, didn't I tell you it's the best?"

Their food came next. Emma busied herself with her tuna sandwich while she waited for his answer.

"Yes, she's my alibi." Phil chewed and swallowed his first bite of burger. "Sure you're not jealous?"

Emma laughed. "In a way, maybe. I mean, you spent the night in the arms of a loved one, while I spent it in the company of a ghost. You do the math."

Phil wiped his mouth with a napkin and chuckled. "If it's any consolation, Emma, I spent the night with Beau, Beverly's bulldog. Bev's car is in the shop, and Chad, her husband, is down with a broken leg. She can't drive his truck because she can't drive a stick, so I said I'd make sure she got home. After, Chad and I kicked back a few too many, so I crashed in their spare room. The dog was a bonus."

Phil's cell phone rang. He answered it, grunted a few times, and hung up. "That was Aunt Susan. Your accommodations are all squared away. But she said to bring you home for supper—your friends, too."

They ate in a comfortable silence. In spite of Phil's brusque behavior, Emma found him ruggedly handsome and sexy, and she knew the second kiss had not been an accident, at least on her part. She even liked the friendly teasing. Grant had never teased her in fun. This casual lunch was allowing her to see a different side of Phil Bowers. And it was clear the people in the town respected and cared about him. Perhaps in a different time and different place, they could become friends.

"Tell you one thing that might make you feel better about last night." Phil shot her a pained look. "Bet *your* alibi didn't fart and snore."

After lunch, the two of them walked from the diner down to where Emma's car was parked at the corner of Main and B Streets. Waiting for them next to the Lexus was a short, stumpy man with wild black hair and a full beard. He was dressed in mechanic's overalls.

Phil introduced them. "This is George, but we call him Gopher." After the two said hello, Phil told Emma, "Grab your bags out of the car and give Goph the keys. His garage is just down the road. He'll take the car there and check it over, top to bottom, while we get you settled at the cottage."

The cottage was on Third Street, just a block up and one over from the Julian Hotel. Phil carried her bag up the small hill to a quaint one-story house. It was painted mint green, with a white picket fence surrounding the yard. They were met there by a pleasant-looking woman about Susan's age. She gave them a tour, took Emma's credit card information, and handed her the key.

"Stay as long as you like," the woman told her with a smile. "We don't have it rented until Fourth of July weekend." She handed Emma a card. "That's my number. I live just a few blocks away. Call if you need anything."

The cottage was charming and comfortable. The walls of each room were paneled in pine, and the rooms were filled with painted furniture and antiques. There was a full kitchen and adequate bathroom.

"You were right, Phil," Emma said as soon as the woman left. "It's lovely."

He poked around the kitchen, opening cupboards and the refrigerator. "There's coffee here, but not much else. Why don't I take you shopping so you'll at least have a few things for meals? I'm sure you're tired of eating out."

"Do you really think I need to? I mean, we'll probably go home tomorrow."

He looked at her a long time before speaking. "Why don't you stay the weekend? The cottage is available, and I'm sure your friends would enjoy Julian. I don't have to go back to San Diego until Monday morning, so I can show you and your friends around. Take you riding. Show you Lake Cuyamaca."

It was a very tempting offer, and Emma couldn't think of any reason to rush home if Archie was with her, except that Milo seemed to think she was in danger while in Julian. That was something she couldn't shake and probably shouldn't ignore. After Gopher declared her car safe, she would confer with Milo.

She walked to the window and looked out over the small yard that faced the street. Colorful flowers bordered the fence, adding a storybook look to the house. Phil came up behind her.

"Like you said, Emma, we're both in the middle of divorces. Doesn't mean we can't be friends and enjoy each other's company for a few days." He laughed. "Especially now that I'm pretty sure you're not a thief and a liar, just nuts."

Emma turned around, unsure of whether she should be amused or offended. She didn't like the way Phil Bowers threw her off balance.

"And between your girlfriend, psychic, dog, and my aunt, we'll be well chaperoned. Don't see any more bathroom episodes in the cards, do you?"

Before she succumbed to her urge to kiss him a third time, Emma walked over to a chair next to the sofa and sat down. "And what about the ghosts?"

It had suddenly occurred to her that she could never have a relationship with a man again without mentioning her newfound abilities. It was something that she was sure would cut deeply into the pool of available men.

"They can come along, too, if they like."

"You don't believe I can see and speak with spirits, do you, Phil?"

Frustrated with the way the conversation was going, Phil Bowers sat down on the sofa and crossed one booted leg over the other. "I think that's a lot to ask a guy to believe in such a short time, don't you?"

"Several weeks ago, I didn't believe it either. And now here I am in Julian, looking up long-dead relatives and involved with a present-day murder, not to mention being visited by the ghost of the victim." She sighed. "That was a lot for me to believe in a short time, but I did it."

"Are you saying, Emma, that we can't be friends unless I believe that you're a real-life ghost whisperer, like that show on TV?"

"No, that's not what I'm saying. But I don't know if I can be friends, even for a few days, with someone who thinks I'm crazy."

"Okay, cards on the table." Phil uncrossed his legs and leaned forward. "I'm very attracted to you, Emma. Was from the first time I met you, in spite of how I felt about other things. You're beautiful, smart, and funny. And I generally don't think you're nuts. I know you believe what you're saying. I'm just not onboard with it yet, and may never be."

"Then why did you agree to help when Milo told us about his vision? If you don't believe in these things, then why have your friend check out my car?"

"I wasn't going to take a chance with your safety. It doesn't take long to check the soundness of a vehicle. If that's all it took to give you and your friends peace of mind, then I was going to do it."

All of a sudden, Phil looked around. "Did you feel that? Sure got cold in here suddenly. The a.c. must have kicked on."

"It's not the air conditioning, Phil. The ghost of Granny Apples just came in. The air always turns a bit cold when ghosts are present." Emma shifted her eyes to the table next to the sofa. "She's over there, by the end table. To your right."

After shifting his body a foot or so to his left, Phil turned his head to his right. All he saw was air.

"Didn't you notice how cold it got in the bathroom? She was in there with us for part of the time."

Emma looked over at the ghost. "Granny, we need to talk, so don't you go disappearing on me again."

"You staying to help?" asked the ghost.

"I'm staying because Milo says I'm in danger if I leave. He also told me I'm in danger if I stay. I'm stuck between a rock and a hard place and need *your* help."

Phil Bowers remained on the sofa, watching and listening to the one-sided conversation. But suddenly, before Emma said anything more, she rocketed to her feet. Turning around, she covered her ears with her hands and stared at a place near the window, her face a mask of fright. He heard and saw nothing. If Emma Whitecastle was playacting, she was doing an expert job of it.

The screams pierced Emma's head like an ice pick and sent Granny Apples packing. Standing near the window was the ghost of Garrett Bell, his mouth open as he let out shriek after shriek.

"Stop it, Garrett! Stop it this minute!"

Phil leapt to his feet and pulled one of Emma's hands from her ears. "What's going on, Emma?"

"It's the spirit of Garrett Bell—the person you knew as Ian Reynolds. He's here, and he's screaming over and over. He's scared off Granny."

Garrett stopped. "Isn't that what ghosts are supposed to do, Emma? Or are you only comfortable with Casper-like friendly ghosts?"

"Who killed you, Garrett?"

"The same one who's going to kill you, my dear, as soon as he gets what he wants."

"Who is it, and what does he want?"

"You're so smart, you figure it out."

And then he was gone.

Emma stared at the empty space long after the ghost left. Phil stayed by her side. When she walked over to the sofa to sit down, Phil perched on the arm of the sofa.

Emma told Phil what had transpired between her and Garrett Bell's ghost.

"I see he's just as obnoxious in death as he was in life."

"So you believe me?"

"I believe *you* believe."

It wasn't the answer she'd hoped for, but it would do for now. She gave him a flicker of a smile before sitting up straight. It was time to get down to business.

"Granny, you get back here. I need you." She continued calling for the ghost of Granny Apples until she finally saw a shimmer, followed by the familiar image. Granny sat in a small rocker across from the sofa.

Emma fixed her eyes on Granny's face. "Granny, do you want me to die?"

"No, of course not," answered Granny.

"I helped you. Now it's your turn to help me, even if it means staying around when Garrett Bell comes back."

"Garrett Bell can't hurt you, Emma. He's dead."

Emma gave Phil a running commentary on the conversation.

"Yes, he is, but the person who killed him isn't. Garrett just said that as soon as that person gets what he wants, he's going to kill me, too." When Granny didn't respond, Emma continued. "Granny, do you know who killed Garrett?"

"No, Emma, I don't."

"Wait," said Phil. "Why don't the ghosts know who killed Garrett? He's one of them now, isn't he?"

Emma leaned her head against the back of the sofa. "Billy might have seen it, but I'd have to get into the cemetery to ask him."

"Good luck with that. It's all cordoned off," Phil scoffed. "Of course, we could always hold a séance right here and ask him to join us."

Emma shot him a sour look, then sat straight up. "I just had a thought."

Getting up, she grabbed her phone and her purse and came back to the sofa. After digging out the slip of paper with Ian Reynolds' phone number, she dialed it, putting the call on speaker. After four rings, a message came on. The person identified himself as Ian Reynolds, but the voice was nothing like Garrett's; it was older and thicker. Without leaving a message, Emma closed the phone.

"That didn't sound at all like Garrett Bell, yet that's the number the museum had. That person called them looking for family information a few months ago. It makes me wonder if the real Ian Reynolds was letting Garrett impersonate him to work with the spirits and you to get the land?"

Phil scratched the top of his head. "You thinking maybe the real Ian is the killer?"

"It's just a thought."

She looked over at the ghost. "Did you know, Granny, that when Garrett died, he was posing as Ian Reynolds?"

"Why would he do a fool thing like that? He doesn't look anything like him."

"You know what Ian looks like?"

"Yes. I tried contacting him, remember? He's a much older man than Garrett—or was."

"Was?" Emma got up and went to stand closer to Granny, to make sure she heard her answer.

"Ian Reynolds died, Emma. Not too long ago."

"You're sure about this?"

Granny nodded. Emma noticed that she was starting to fade and hurried with her train of thought.

"Is it possible, Granny, for you to round up Ian's ghost?"

"I'll try." She disappeared.

During the exchange, Phil had gotten up from the sofa and posted himself at the dining table across the room. He watched Emma talking to thin air and listened when she relayed Granny's responses to him. He tried to make himself believe.

The ring of his cell phone interrupted Phil's thoughts. Emma watched as he spoke with someone on the other end, waiting to see if it was news about her car. As the call went on, Phil got more and more agitated.

"That was Gopher." His tone was urgent. "Let's go, we have to get down there."

"There was something wrong with the car?"

"Not really." Phil guided her out the door, and she locked up. "But when his son took it out for a test drive, he got into an accident. Seems there was a sack of rattlers under the driver's seat. Brad was bit while driving."

Phil's truck was parked at a friend's stable near the graveyard. They headed in that direction at a trot, oblivious to the heat and the people staring at them. Phil took the truck slowly down Main but opened it up as soon as he cleared the more populated town area. In less than two minutes and several wild turns later, they came upon the scene of the accident. Phil brought the truck to a stop several yards away and hopped out. Emma followed.

Both paramedic and sheriff vehicles were present, as well as two other trucks. The paramedics had an injured man on a stretcher, getting ready to transport him for medical care. Emma could see his head was bandaged and that the left side of his jeans had been cut away. Bandages swaddled his left ankle. He looked to be in his twenties. The Lexus had gone hood-first into a tree.

As the paramedics hoisted his son into the ambulance, Gopher came over to Phil and Emma.

"I am so sorry, Gopher," said Emma. "Is he going to be all right?"

"Should be," Gopher told them, his face dark with worry. "The scrapes on his head and face are from the air bag. And it's a good thing, or his head would have gone through the windshield."

"What happened, Goph?" asked Phil.

"We couldn't find a single thing amiss with the car, so I told Brad to take it out and see if he could feel anything wrong with the way it handled. The boy's a natural when it comes to anything with wheels."

A paramedic waved to Gopher. "We're leaving now."

"His mother and I will be right behind you." He turned back to Phil and Emma. "Near as we can tell, the snakes probably got loose near the end of Brad's drive. He might even have kicked them with his left foot. Who knows. Fool kid, if he hadn't been playing the radio so loud, he might have heard them first. He received two bites to his ankle, just above his sneaker. Lost control of the car and ended up in the tree." He tried to clear the emotion from his voice but failed. "Good thing the shop's just up this road. We heard the crash and ran down."

"I am so very sorry, Gopher." Emma started weeping.

"Thanks, but unless you keep snakes in your car as a hobby, miss, it wasn't your fault. Animal Control found three rattlers. Someone's out to hurt you, just as Phil here suspected."

"Please don't worry about anything, Gopher," Emma told him, swallowing back bile. "I'll take care of any medical expenses. Just tell Brad to get well."

As Gopher left to follow his son to the hospital, Detective Hallam approached. With her was a man in a suit, whom she introduced as Detective Bill Martinez.

Detective Martinez pointed toward the smashed car. "We're told that's your car, Ms. Whitecastle. That true?"

Emma nodded, unable to speak.

"Those your snakes?"

She shook her head back and forth.

It was then she heard the laughter. No one else paid attention to it, but she heard it clear as clean water. She turned in the direction of the sound and spotted the ghost of Garrett Bell.

Small sparks ignited in front of her eyes. Just as she fell toward the ground, Phil caught her.

twenty-six
· ·

"So this psychic, this—," the detective looked down at his notes, "Milo Ravenscroft—told you he saw you getting into a bad car accident, so you had your car checked out?"

Emma nodded. "Yes, that's right."

"He didn't see the snakes?" Detective Martinez looked across the small metal table at her, his face without expression.

"No. He just saw my car weaving and going over a cliff, with me in it."

"And your car has been parked next to the Julian Hotel the whole time you've been here?"

"Except for when I went to the Bowers ranch and to Ramona. But it hasn't moved since late yesterday afternoon."

"And you noticed nothing the last time you drove it?"

"Not a thing."

"How about today, when you put your luggage in the car?"

"I never opened the car, just the trunk. Same thing when I got my bag out to go to the cottage."

This time the questioning didn't take place in the park but at the sheriff's office. Both Detective Martinez and Detective Hallam were present. A third detective was questioning Phil Bowers separately.

Emma told them everything, holding nothing back. She told them that Ian Reynolds, the dead guy, wasn't really Ian Reynolds, and how she knew. The detectives listened patiently and took notes. One of them left and returned later to confirm that through fingerprints the crime lab had identified the victim as Garrett Bell, a clairvoyant and scam artist.

"You know," said Detective Hallam, "if you did know this Bell character before coming to Julian, we will find out."

"I'm telling you the truth. I didn't know who he was. Before yesterday, I'd never heard the name Ian Reynolds, and this morning was the first time I'd ever heard the name Garrett Bell."

"And the ghost of Bell told you who he was?" asked Hallam.

They'd been over this information time and time again. Emma knew the repeated questions were an attempt to trip her up, but since she was telling the truth, there was nothing to stumble over.

"No," she said, repeating her story. "As I told you, when he first appeared, the ghost of Garrett Bell only said my name. Milo told me who he was after he was already dead."

Detective Martinez looked at Emma. He was a tall, attractive Latino in his late thirties, with thick black hair and chocolate eyes. Eyes that bore into her own without mercy in search of the truth.

"We did confirm that an Ian Reynolds died about a month ago of natural causes. He lived in Woodland Hills—same phone number as the one you gave us. We're following up to see if there was a connection between him and Bell." He looked down again at the notes he'd taken. "Where can we reach this Milo Ravenscroft?"

"I have his cell phone number, but he'll be here shortly," she explained, looking at her watch. "As soon as he had the vision about my accident, he and my friend Tracy got on the road to Julian. They're going to call me when they reach town."

Detective Martinez studied her. "You feeling okay? Just let us know if you feel faint again."

Emma took another drink of the cold soda they'd given her. "Thank you, but I'm fine now."

Detective Hallam paced the small room. She'd removed the jacket to her pantsuit, revealing a gun tucked into a shoulder holster. "We will want to talk to them as soon as they arrive," she said, "especially Mr. Ravenscroft. Where are they staying?"

"We're all staying at a cottage here in town. I rented it today."

"Emma," started Martinez, "why would someone you don't know masquerade as a dead long-lost relative?"

"I honestly think Garrett Bell was impersonating Ian Reynolds long before he knew about me. He told me someone tipped him off that I had met Phil Bowers and was interested in the property. He said he came to Julian to talk to me. He even followed me to the cemetery last night."

"That's where you injured your hand, correct?"

"Yes."

"Did he say what he wanted to talk to you about specifically?"

"No. He never got the chance. He did tell me, though, that he could see the ghosts, same as I could. That's how I knew he wasn't Ian Reynolds." She stopped to take another drink. "He was trying to get the Bowers family to sell him the Reynolds property. I think he was hoping to use his supposed blood tie to the property to get the Bowers family to sell it to him—kind of guilt them into it with the proof that it was stolen from Jacob and Ish through murder. I also think that he was hoping to get me on his side—another blood descendant to help in his cause."

"How would he know it was stolen? Through these letters?" Martinez tapped copies of the letters Emma had given them.

"Yes. The woman at the museum said a man named Ian Reynolds had called her. From the number she had, I think her contact was with the real Ian Reynolds. She told him about the letters, and he said he would get them from the library. It was in La Habra, I believe."

Emma took another drink. Her throat was parched from all the talking, and she felt beaten to an emotional pulp by the repetition and events of the day.

"Is the boy, the young man who was in the car, going to be okay? His father said he would be, but I'm still concerned."

Hallam gave her a faint smile. "Yes, he's going to be fine."

"So if this Reynolds/Bell guy had these," Martinez pressed, "he would know that your ancestors were murdered and the property bought under false pretense. That right?"

Emma shivered in the stale air as a draft hit her. Looking up, she saw Granny. She was alone and came to Emma's side.

"Yes," Emma answered. "And you will note that in his confession, John Winslow says it was for the gold Jacob Reynolds found on the property."

Detective Hallam bent forward, placing both of her hands on the table. "So you believe that these century-old murders have a bearing on the murder of Garrett Bell?"

Emma glanced at Granny, who gave her a smile of encouragement.

"I believe it's highly possible." She stopped to sort her thoughts. "I'm not sure exactly what Garrett Bell had planned, but it has crossed my mind that it isn't about building condos, as he claimed, but about the gold. I mentioned that idea to Phil Bowers, and he said there hasn't been gold found around here for a long time. Maybe Garrett Bell and whoever he was working with didn't know that."

Detective Hallam leaned forward even more. She was almost in push-up position across the table. "You're pretty sure Bell wasn't working alone. Why?"

Emma knew the police had the same idea, but they continued to come at her theories from all angles. But while their thoughts were based on solid police work and calculated guesses, her information had come from ghosts. Apples and onions.

"I've already told you. Someone had to have killed him; my guess is an angry partner. Someone is also trying to hurt me. And the ghost of Ish Reynolds keeps telling me that the property is still in danger. And that was after Garrett was killed.

"Originally," Emma continued, "I thought it might be the real Ian Reynolds who killed Garrett. But when Granny told me he was already dead, I had to dump that idea."

"You'd think," Hallam said, pushing herself up from the table and standing erect, "that one of these ghosts might tell you who did the killing. That would really be helpful." For the first time, she dropped her professional façade and let her tone slip into mockery mode. "Can't you ask the ghost of Garrett Bell who killed him? Or don't you two have that kind of close relationship?"

Emma stiffened at the sarcasm. "I've already asked him. He's not saying. He just said the same person will kill me."

"But he knows who killed him?" asked Martinez.

"Seems so."

"This is ridiculous!" Detective Hallam snapped.

Detective Martinez shot her a look of caution. "Doesn't it make more sense," he asked, returning his attention to Emma, "that if he told you, you'd be able to get help to stop him?"

"You'd think so, wouldn't you? But he was a jerk in real life, and I'm not so sure people change after death. His ghost seems to be taking pleasure in watching me squirm."

She took another long drink from her soda and looked from one detective to the other. "Look, I know this seems hard to swallow. It still is a bit for me. But don't some police departments use psychics from time to time to help them solve crimes? I mean, this can't be all that far-fetched in your line of work."

"*Some* police departments," answered Martinez, "do use unconventional means when a trail gets cold. But the psychic isn't usually involved in the case."

"I'm not a psychic," said Emma, sticking her strong chin out. "For some reason, I can communicate with ghosts. I believe that's called being clairvoyant."

"You tell them, Emma," chimed in Granny, getting steamed up. "You're not a fake."

As much as Emma wanted to say something to Granny, she held back. It was bad enough she sounded like a lunatic, she didn't need to look like one, too.

Martinez glanced at Detective Hallam. "You have any more questions for her?"

Detective Hallam threw up her hands in frustration. "No, not as this time." She arched a brow at Emma. "But as soon as your *psychic* friend arrives in town, we'll want to see him."

Emma pulled out her cell phone. "He might be trying to reach me. May I turn it on now?"

As soon as she got the okay, Emma turned on her phone. There was a voice mail from Milo that had just come in a few minutes earlier. She called him back while the detectives watched.

"Milo, it's me," she said into the phone. "Where are you?"

"We just passed a place called Santa Ysabel. I don't think we're that far away."

"No, you're not." Emma paused before giving him the bad news. "Something's come up, Milo. I'm at the sheriff's office in Julian. There was an attempt on my life—in the car, as you predicted."

He gasped. "You okay?"

"What?" Tracy yelled from the driver's side. "What's going on?"

"Yes, I'm fine. I wasn't in the car, but someone else was. But he's going to be okay."

Emma caught a signal from Martinez telling her to get on with it. "Milo, the detectives handling the Garrett Bell murder want to talk to you. You need to stop by the sheriff's office as soon as you get into Julian."

"Okay," he said, with hesitation.

"They want to ask you questions about your visions and what you might know about Garrett."

"Emma, I really don't like police. They make me nervous."

"I understand, Milo, but this is important."

Emma gave him directions to the sheriff's office, which they'd have to pass as they came into town anyway. She said she would be waiting for them.

. . . .

WHILE DETECTIVES MARTINEZ AND Hallam questioned Milo Ravenscroft, Emma and Tracy walked an energetic Archie. Emma took the opportunity to fill Tracy in on everything.

"You have any idea who killed this guy?" Tracy asked.

"None. But I'm thinking it might be someone connected in some manner to the real Ian Reynolds. Someone who knew about the old family property and its possible value."

Tracy, wearing a long, flowing Indian-print skirt and tank top, knitted her brows in thought. "You really think there might be gold on the property?"

"Not sure, though Phil says no. Says the gold mining here tapped out in the late 1800s, even before Granny was killed. It's one of the reasons Jacob's find might have been so exciting and dangerous."

Tracy thought about it for a minute before answering. "But if these men did finally get their hands on the property way back then, you'd think they would have done the mining at that time. Even if there was gold then, it doesn't mean there's any now."

They had strolled up the street to the small park just past the museum. Archie, drunk with freedom after being cooped up in the car for hours, was pulling on his leash to run. Then Emma saw another reason for Archie's enthusiasm. Granny, who had disappeared right after the questioning, was back, waiting by a picnic table. Smiling, Emma bent down and unhooked the dog's leash.

Archie made straight for the ghost, wagging his tail with gusto. Watching him, Emma was glad they'd brought the animal. He reminded her of home and her parents. His presence assured her that she had a normal life waiting for her elsewhere.

"Well, there has to be something about that land that made Garrett masquerade as a dead man to get it." Emma stretched. It felt good to be free of the intense questioning, at least for now. "You'll see it tonight," she said to Tracy. "Phil's aunt invited us all over for dinner. They live across from it."

Tracy eyed her friend as they walked to the picnic table. "About this Phil guy. What's up with him?"

Phil, after meeting Tracy and Milo, had left for home to help his aunt. Emma and her friends would follow in Tracy's car as soon as Milo was through answering questions.

"Nothing. He's involved with this like I am, on the fringes."

"I don't mean that," Tracy prodded. "I mean what's up between the two of you?"

Emma kept her eyes on the dog. "There's nothing between us."

"Uh-huh."

"You don't believe me?"

"You don't have to be psychic or clairvoyant or whatever to see that there's a spark between you and the ranch hand."

"Lawyer," Emma corrected. "Phil's a lawyer in San Diego. Lives here."

"Lawyer or cowboy, who cares? He's pretty cute and nicely put together. Not a bad caboose for a middle-aged guy."

Emma laughed. "Aren't you forgetting that we're middle-aged, too?"

"And aren't you forgetting that I look at college beefcake almost every day? Makes a woman my age appreciate a fine specimen over forty, believe me."

"Your friend is right, Emma," chimed in Granny.

Emma almost jumped, not realizing the ghost had moved in close to them. She'd been lost in thought about Phil's caboose herself.

"That Phil Bowers is a fine-looking man," Granny continued. "A good man. You could do worse."

Emma turned to the spirit. "In case you've forgotten, Granny, I have done worse."

"Oh my God!" cried Tracy, before catching herself and toning her voice down. "You're talking to that ghost, aren't you?"

Talking to Granny had become so natural, Emma was starting to do it without thinking about who might be near. She would have to watch that in the future, thankful she hadn't popped off in front of the detectives.

"Yes, Tracy, I was talking to Granny Apples. She seems to think Phil's a hunk of middle-aged beefcake, too."

"She kissed him, you know," Granny said to Tracy. "A couple of times." But Tracy couldn't hear.

Emma laughed out loud and plopped herself down on a bench. "Granny's tattling on me," she said to Tracy. "She just reported to you that Phil and I have kissed."

"Damn, I wish I could hear and see her like you do." Tracy sat down next to Emma. Archie settled at the feet of the ghost.

Emma shook her head and giggled. "No, you don't. She can be a real pest." She looked up at the misty image. "Right, Granny?"

"Humph." The ghost moved away but didn't disappear. Archie followed her, his tail wagging.

"See that?" Emma pointed Archie's movements out to Tracy. "The ghost is right there. Archie has a thing for her. Followed her around at Kelly's party, too." Emma thought about Killer. "Come to think of it, so did one of the dogs at Phil's house. Not all of them, though, just one of them. Maybe animals are like people. Some have the gift, some don't. Interesting theory, don't you think?"

"What I'm thinking is that I want you to speak at that class I'm giving next semester. You know, the one I went to the séance for as research?"

"Oh, please, what do I have to say on the subject? You should ask Milo."

"I think the perspective of someone surprised suddenly by this 'gift' would be much more interesting." Tracy patted Emma's knee. "We'll talk more about it later. Meanwhile, I want to know more about this kissing business." Tracy flashed her a devilish grin.

"Okay, you got me. We do find each other attractive. Like me, he's in the middle of a divorce. But he also lives down here, and I live up there. Not exactly conducive to building a relationship."

"Who said anything about a relationship, Emma? Have a fling. It will do you good. Especially after everything you've been through with Grant."

Emma flushed. "I don't know how to have a fling, Tracy. I don't think it's in my makeup. I think I've been genetically programmed to be flingless."

Tracy stared at Emma. "But certainly in college? Before Grant?"

Emma shook her head. "Nope."

"Are you telling me that Grant Whitecastle is the only man who's ever scaled your tower?" Tracy looked at her bug-eyed.

"Pretty much, yes."

"After all the years we've known each other, why am I just finding this out now? Seriously, I figured with all the dating you did in college, you might have … you know."

"Grant was my first and my only. Not that I haven't had the opportunity. A lot of his show-biz buddies hit on me when Grant's philandering became public. Guess they thought I'd be an easy mark." She grinned at Tracy. "One was even a multiple Oscar winner."

"Well, woo-hoo."

In the shade of a large pine tree, the two friends sat in silence enjoying the quiet. Emma watched Granny float about the park. Tracy watched the dog wander about, seemingly following nothing. It looked to Emma like Granny was actually playing with Archie.

After a few minutes, Tracy put her arm around her friend. "Well, Rapunzel, maybe it's time to let down your hair and do some comparison shopping."

twenty-seven
. . . .

"OKAY, LET'S SEE WHAT we have so far." Phil cleared space on the large dining table.

They had just finished a delicious dinner of grilled halibut, rice, and roasted fresh vegetables. Susan Steveson was cleaning up. Her husband, Glen, had retired to another room to watch TV. Archie was outside on the deck, enjoying the evening with the other dogs. After an initial few minutes of growling and posturing, he and Killer had become fast friends.

"Let us help you with that, Susan," Emma offered. She got up and started shuttling things to the kitchen counter.

"No, dear," said Susan. "You all just sit down and talk. Maybe you'll remember something that could help the police. This won't take but a minute anyway, and I can listen while I work. Then we'll have coffee and pie. You know," Susan said, winking at Emma, "strawberry-rhubarb is Phil's favorite."

Emma raised an eyebrow across the table at Milo. He shrugged back with innocent, wide eyes. The three of them had contributed three different kinds of pie from the Julian Pie Company for dessert. Originally, they had ordered just two—apple and boysenberry—but at the last minute Milo felt strong vibrations about strawberry-rhubarb, telling them they just had to get that, too.

Phil Bowers took all of the Winslow letters and fanned them out.

"Do you have some small notepads?" Tracy asked. "We can write clues on them and use them like puzzle pieces."

"Good idea," Susan called from the kitchen. "Emma, there's some large Post-Its in that desk next to the hutch. Those might work even better."

Emma located the sticky notes. They were about the size of an average photograph and perfect for their use. She also brought several pens to the table.

"Okay," she said. "First, let's start by listing the players." She wrote *Ian Reynolds* on a note and gave it to Phil, who stuck it to the top of the table. Next, Emma wrote *Garrett Bell* on a note and handed it off. Soon they had the names of all people involved, both dead and alive, including herself and Milo, in a pattern across the table. Then Phil moved them into two columns, one for the dead and one for the living.

"Hmm." Emma looked at the columns. "I'm not so sure it's that cut-and-dried. Some of the dead were recently alive and have contacts on both sides." She studied the names. "Let's start with Garrett Bell." She took the paper with his name and moved it to the middle. "He's the one we're most concerned with, considering it's his murder that's at issue here."

"Enough's enough, Emma. Go home."

At the sound, both Emma and Milo turned to look at the ghost of Garrett Bell. He was hovering just inside the patio door. Outside on the deck, both Archie and Killer were whining.

"Oh my God," said Tracy with glee. She clapped her hands together like a five-year-old with a new toy. "She's back. This is so exciting! What's she saying, Emma? What's she saying?"

"It's not Granny. It's the ghost of Garrett Bell."

From the kitchen area behind them came a loud crash. Everyone's eyes turned to see a shocked Susan.

"Aunt Susan, you okay?" Phil rushed to her side.

"There's a ghost in my house?" Susan squeaked out.

"Don't worry," Milo assured her, "he won't hurt you."

"It's true, then?" She addressed Emma. "You do talk to ghosts." Before Emma could respond, Susan turned her white face to Phil. "She really talks to the dead, Phillip?"

"Seems so." He cleared his throat. "You'll get used to it."

"But I thought she was just a little crazy. You know, in a harmless, cute sort of way."

"She's that, too, Aunt Susan. Trust me."

Phil bent down to pick up what Susan had dropped. "Well, folks, looks like we're just having boysenberry and strawberry-rhubarb tonight. The apple pie bit the dust."

Tracy went into the kitchen and led Susan out and into one of the chairs at the table. Then she went back to help Phil clean up the mess.

"I'm sorry, Susan," Emma told her. "If this is too much, we'll leave. You've been so kind, I don't want to make you uncomfortable."

"I ... I don't know what to say." Susan was dazed. "I mean, there were always rumors of ghosts in Julian. Take the hotel, for instance. Folks have said for years that Albert Robinson haunts that old hotel. Maybe it's not just an old wives' tale." She paused and placed a hand over her heart.

"Susan, you okay?" Emma crouched down next to the older woman.

Phil dashed in. "Should I call someone?"

"Oh, I'm fine, just a little shocked. All these years—the rumors about that property—it's all real?"

"What rumors?" asked Emma. Everyone moved in to hear the response.

"That property across the way—the old Reynolds property. There were always rumors of it being haunted, too. But we never believed any of it." She looked up at Emma, color returning to her pleasant face. "But it's true?"

"I don't know if that property is haunted or not, Susan."

"It's my home," Granny said, crossing her arms in front of her. "I have every right to be there."

Emma looked over at Granny, who'd recently materialized in spite of Garrett's presence.

Emma patted Susan's shoulder. "But if it is haunted, it's a friendly haunting, I can assure you."

She cast an eye in Garrett's direction, hoping he wouldn't get annoyed while they comforted Susan and disappear before they had a chance to talk to him. But the spirit of Garrett Bell was still there, arms crossed, looking smug and amused by their ministrations to the older woman.

"Oh my." Susan shook herself slightly. "I'm so sorry I caused such a fuss."

"It's okay, Susan," said Milo. "It's a difficult thing for some people to understand."

Throughout the excitement, the two little dogs had picked up their whining, giving off little yips, especially Killer.

"Hush, Killer," Susan told the little animal. "I'm fine."

Emma wasn't sure she should tell Susan at that moment that her dog could see ghosts, too.

"So, who wants pie and coffee?" Susan started to rise from her chair.

"Sit still, Susan," Tracy told her. "I'll get everything, and Phil can help me."

They dished out the pie and poured the coffee while Susan got used to the idea of ghosts in her home.

"Okay," Phil said, as soon as Tracy returned from shuttling pie and coffee to Glen, "back to the drawing board." He bent back over their notes.

"Touching scene, Emma. But you still need to leave." Garrett moved closer to her. Granny moved between them like peanut butter between two slices of bread. Milo watched in silence.

Emma looked at Susan, who sat at the table sipping her coffee slowly, holding it with slightly shaking hands. Then she glanced at Milo, hoping he could read her eyes, if not her thoughts. They needed to talk to Garrett's ghost, but Emma did not want to do it in front of the rattled Susan. Milo was doing his own volley of glances, sending Emma messages with looks over the top rim of his glasses.

After taking several quick bites of his pie, Milo stood up with his coffee. "I'm going to go outside and talk to Garrett. I think it will go better in private."

Susan looked up at him. "Please, don't feel you need to do this because of me. I'll be fine with this as soon as I get used to it." She sounded like she was trying to convince herself more than anyone. "It's actually all very fascinating."

Milo smiled at her. He knew that once people got over the initial shock, they usually did find the idea of ghosts walking amongst them intriguing. It was usually total denial or complete interest. There was seldom a gray area when it came to the living's acceptance of the dead.

"Something tells me, Susan," he said, looking at Phil, who was engrossed in the notes on the table, then at Emma, "that you will have many opportunities to enjoy your new spirit friends." Emma caught the look and threw a frown back at him. He returned a grin as crooked as his glasses.

"Milo's right," Emma said, running her fingers through her hair in annoyance. "Garrett needs to be questioned."

"Maybe I don't want to be questioned."

Milo looked at Garrett Bell's ghost. "It's your choice, of course, Garrett. We can't force you. But for once in your life, why not do something decent?"

Granny was examining Phil. "Milo's right. I think we'll be seeing a lot of these folks in the future."

She nodded with satisfaction, as if judging a job well done, and started for the patio door. "I think," said the ornery spirit, "that I'll go outside and see if I can help Milo."

"What puzzles me," Emma said after Milo and the ghosts left, "is why did someone want to scare me off when I was leaving town already?"

Tracy, Susan, and Phil all stopped and looked at her as if she'd just spoken in Swahili. She took note of their stares. "What?"

Phil spoke first. "Whoever put those snakes in your car, Emma, wasn't trying to scare you off, they were trying to kill you." He said the words calmly but without a sugar coating.

Emma dropped into a nearby chair and covered her face with her hands. Her shoulders began to shake as if with a seizure. Tracy jumped to her side.

"It's going to be okay, Emma." Tracy rubbed Emma's back. "Between us and the police, we'll figure out who did this."

"But why?" Emma stopped shaking and got a grip on her emotions. "Why me? I just wanted to find out about Granny. What reason would anyone have to want me dead?"

"How about that ex of yours?" The question came from Phil.

Tracy and Emma turned their heads toward Phil with the unison of synchronized swimmers.

"Grant?" Emma's voice shook. "You think Grant might have done this?"

Phil shrugged. "Just saying that if it's not the same person who killed Garrett Bell, your ex might be a possibility. I don't know the guy. Is he capable of doing something like this?"

"You are battling over a lot of money, Emma." Tracy plopped down in a chair next to Emma to think the theory over.

"No. It can't be true. Grant's many things, but a murderer?" Emma shook her head. "Besides, he's in Europe with our daughter."

"Sounds like a good alibi to me. Better than sleeping with a ghost."

Seeing Emma's feathers ruffle at Phil's words, Susan broke in. "Emma, dear, it may not be true, but we really should consider all possibilities here. It could be that the murder in the cemetery and the attempt on your life aren't even related."

"The police did ask me a lot of questions about Grant and our divorce proceedings." After a moment, Emma stood up and shimmied her body, ridding herself of the possibility like old skin. "No, I just won't believe it. You guys can put it on the table as a possibility—a long shot, a very long shot—but I'm going to refuse to consider it until it stares me in the face, naked and raw. Grant is vain and arrogant and a total fool, but I've never known him to have a vicious, evil streak." She remembered the way he stroked her hair at Kelly's party. "No, I just can't."

"What about Carolyn?" offered Tracy.

Emma pondered the idea. "Now that's a possibility. But I still believe whoever wanted me—," she paused as another shock of fear zigzagged through her body, "whoever did this—is connected to Garrett Bell and Ian Reynolds."

"I think you're right." They all turned to see Milo Ravenscroft coming back through the patio doors.

"Did Granny or Garrett tell you anything?" Emma's voice was swollen with hope.

"Yes and no," Milo answered. "Granny wasn't able to connect with the spirit of the real Ian Reynolds, but I did get Garrett to confirm that this is all about gold, even the attempt on your life."

Phil stepped forward. "But that doesn't make sense. There's been no gold here for decades, possibly over a hundred years. How many times do I have to tell you people that?"

Milo shrugged. "Garrett wasn't saying much, but he's determined that Emma should go home as soon as possible. Said he's had his fun." On the way to the Bowers ranch, Emma had told Milo and Tracy about Garrett's visit to the cottage and his appearance at the scene of the accident. "Wouldn't say who killed him, though he knows. He's gone now."

Milo walked to the kitchen and topped off his coffee mug from the pot on the counter. "He definitely said it was about gold." He took a drink. "And he mentioned a name—Billy. Said to ask him."

"Billy?" Emma stared in surprise.

"Yes, Billy. Isn't that the name of the young ghost you spoke to? The one everyone thought killed himself?"

"Yes, that's him." Emma sat down again and thought about Billy, his murder, and what he'd said to her. "I was speaking with Billy when Garrett was spying on me in the cemetery. That's when the other ghosts scattered."

Emma stood up and studied the names on the table. Picking up a Post-It, she jotted *gold* on it and stuck it in on the table. Then she picked up other notes and positioned them in two columns under it. Stuck in a row to the right went present-day people, alive and dead, including a note with a big question mark on it to represent Garrett's unknown killer. To the left, she lined up the people from the past. She put the past folks in chronological order. Jacob and Ish Reynolds were first, since Jacob discovered the gold first. Then came Winston, who either didn't know about it or didn't care. Under him went Big John Winslow and Billy, plus a sticky note with Bobcat and Parker written on it to represent Winslow's accomplices. Next came Buck Bowers.

Emma looked at Susan. "Did you ever hear anything in your family's history about gold on that property?"

Susan Steveson shook her head. "Never." She turned to her nephew. "How about you, Phil?"

"Nothing."

Picking up the letters from John Winslow, Emma scanned them once more, trying to find overlooked information or even something written between the lines.

"According to these, we can piece together that John and his gang killed Jacob and hung Ish, and that they did it as part of their plan to get their hands on the gold Jacob had discovered. By hanging Ish vigilante-style, they made sure there were no further questions and investigation. Rumor circulated that she was killed for murdering her husband, and people accepted that, even if some didn't believe it. Granny said that Parker was very mean. A snake, she called him." Emma paused to shudder before continuing. "Maybe some people knew but were afraid of this Parker guy. Either way, it went down in history that she killed Jacob. Winston Reynolds didn't want to stay in Julian, and he trusted Billy's father. He was probably happy to sell the property and move on with his life, leaving behind the double tragedy."

Emma stared at the notes on the table, willing them to talk to her. She tapped a finger on the one with the names *Bobcat* and *Parker*. "Granny said that this Parker fellow owned the property on the other side of them." She looked at Susan and Phil. "What property would she mean? And is there still a Parker family in the area?"

Susan spoke up. "The Parker property was on the other side, just beyond the woods and stream. But the Parker family hasn't owned it in over fifty years. I remember when they sold it and moved. I was just a young girl, and they had two daughters near my age."

Emma looked around but didn't see Granny. "Milo, did Ish leave?"

Before he could answer, Granny spoke up. "I'm here, Emma."

Emma looked in the direction of the deck and saw the ghost's image slowly come into view.

"Granny, did Winston know about the gold Jacob found?"

The ghost paused a moment to think. "I don't believe so. I thought it best he not know right off. And Jacob found it shortly before he was killed."

"Okay," Emma said, moving along on her thought trail. "So Winston was in the dark about the gold and his parents' deaths. He takes the money from the land and leaves town to start a new life."

She paused to look around. Everyone was listening with rapt attention, following her logic as she pieced together the events.

"Billy told me," she continued, "that his mother left because of what his father did. She obviously didn't tell anyone about it, but she left. Then Billy was killed, and it was made to look like a suicide. Billy said he was killed because he knew what his father had done."

"I think Billy's the key," said Milo.

Emma scanned the papers. "I think you're right, Milo. In fact, in this last letter, John Winslow refers to something Billy did. Something 'he ought not have done' but for which his father accepts full blame. That might reference the fact that Billy knew about the killings and was going to tell."

"Or," added Phil, "it could be more literal. Maybe Billy did do something that got him killed. Some action, like already telling someone. Or it could be that Billy interfered in some way with their plans."

Emma thought about the manner in which she was questioned by the detectives. "When I questioned Billy, I didn't have these letters. I also don't think I asked all the right questions in the right way. Plus we were interrupted by Garrett lurking about."

"But what about Ian?" Phil asked. "I mean, that Garrett Bell guy? We know why the old folks were killed, but what about him?"

She walked over to Phil and put a hand on his arm. "Do you happen to know where in the cemetery Garrett's body was found? Did anyone tell you that either in gossip or when you were questioned?"

Phil Bowers patted her hand as he shook his head. "Sorry, can't recall."

"Give me a minute," Milo said. "I might remember."

While they all watched, Milo went into the great room and settled into a large overstuffed chair near the fireplace. He leaned back and closed his eyes.

"What's he doing?" Susan asked.

"He had a vision of Garrett's dead body," Emma explained. "Maybe he's trying to recall where it was."

"Jeeeeeeeeesus," Phil said in disbelief. He threw up his hands and paced a few times. Emma shushed him and concentrated on Milo.

"The grass on the ground around the body is dry and brown," Milo said, lost in concentration.

"That's the whole damn cemetery this time of year," crabbed Phil. "Hell, the whole area."

"Shh!" Emma told him again.

"He's been shot in the chest. Close range." Milo paused. "Very close range, almost like the gun was held next to him when it was fired." He lost himself again in the depths of his mind. "He was struggling with his assailant. The gun went off." Without warning, Milo popped open his eyes and looked at them. "Is there a bench up at the cemetery?"

"There are a few scattered around," Emma answered.

"He was killed by one of the benches—the topmost one. The one that looks down at the town."

Emma ran her hands through her hair as she took her turn pacing and thinking. "That's Billy's bench. I'm sure of it."

twenty-eight
· ·

"YOU ARE NOT GOING to the cemetery!" Phil yelled, following Emma down the hallway. Susan, Milo, and Tracy were hot on their heels. Behind them, the dogs, still on the deck, were barking.

"But I have to. Billy's the answer, don't you understand? I just have to ask him the right questions in the right way."

Emma yanked the front door open and spilled out into the large driveway. Then she froze. Her car wasn't there. The dogs, riled up by the people, had left the deck and run around the house to join everyone in the driveway. Sweetie Pie and Baby reached them first. Archie and Killer brought up the rear, working their short legs into stumps to keep up.

"May I remind you, Fancy Pants, that your car went into a tree today courtesy of a killer?"

Phil took her by the arm. She shook it off. "Let me go. I have to get to Billy Winslow."

"Not tonight, Emma."

"Listen to him, Emma," Tracy added. "It's dark out. Besides, won't the sheriff have it cordoned off like on TV?" Susan and Milo murmured in agreement.

"Exactly," said Phil. "It's not only dangerous, but you can't trespass on a crime scene."

Emma held her uninjured hand out toward Tracy. "Give me your keys. I'll take your car."

"Granny," Phil called out, surprising everyone. "Granny Apples." He stood in the drive and turned this way and that through the barking dogs. "I know you're out there and you can hear me, even if I can't hear you."

Emma stared at him, her mouth resembling a wide-mouth jar. "What are you doing?"

"If I can't talk sense into you, maybe she can." He cupped his mouth with his hands and called out, "Yoo-hoo, Granny, come out, come out, wherever you are."

"Give me your keys, Tracy," Emma demanded again. "Don't worry, I'll be fine."

"I'm coming with you," Tracy told her. "I'm not letting you go alone."

"Neither of you are going anywhere," Phil ordered. "Damn it, Granny, where in the hell are you?"

"He's right, Emma."

Emma whipped her head around to see Granny standing just behind her. Milo saw her, too. The others let their eyes follow Emma and Milo's cue.

The ghost shot a scowl at Phil. "As much as I dislike being bellowed at, the man's right."

While Milo translated for the others, Emma continued talking to Granny. "Then ask Garrett what Billy told him the night he was killed. Or better yet, tell him to come here and tell me himself."

Phil came up to Emma and turned her around to face him. "What are you talking about?"

"I think Billy told Garrett something that got him killed. What's more, I think that's why Garrett was snooping around the cemetery watching me with the ghosts. He was trying to learn what Billy told me, or what he thought Billy had told me." She took a deep breath and pointed in the direction of the Reynolds property. "There's something about that land that Garrett and his friends know about. That's why they wanted it. And I think the reason someone tried to kill me is they think Billy already told me whatever it is that's so important. They want to make sure I don't tell anyone else." She poked her finger into Phil's chest. "Specifically you, the present owner."

Emma ran both her hands through her hair and held her aching skull. "It sounds so preposterous, yet so clear."

Phil put an arm around her. "Take a deep breath, Emma. Take your time, and collect your thoughts. You're exhausted."

She leaned into him for a moment.

"Billy has to be the key. Otherwise, why would a clairvoyant be involved? Based on what Milo told me about Garrett Bell, maybe he learned something in a session with a client. Maybe that client was the real Ian Reynolds."

"But Ian's dead," noted Milo.

"Yes, and isn't it odd that he died about the time he received copies of those letters? Letters that talk about gold and confessions of murder. Letters that specifically say Billy did something he shouldn't have."

Phil wasn't convinced. "The detectives told me Ian Reynolds died of natural causes."

"Me too, but that doesn't mean it couldn't have been rigged to look like natural causes. Especially if Ian was elderly."

Emma left the comfort of Phil's arm and paced. "Phil, when did you start hearing from Ian Reynolds about the property?"

Phil rolled his eyes upward as he calculated the time. "About three to four weeks ago."

"Well, here's another thought. Maybe whoever killed Garrett was his client. Someone who knew the real Ian Reynolds and came to Garrett after Ian's death, letters in hand, to try and contact Billy Winslow or any of the ghosts of the people involved." She paced some more. "I'll bet if we check the hotels around here, we'll find that Garrett, either as himself or Ian, has been here quite often in the past few weeks."

"I know he has," said Phil. "He was out here quite a bit until I finally ran him off." He turned to his aunt. "Remember the well?"

"Yes, he broke into it. We had to get a whole new padlock."

"The well?" asked Emma. "Do you know why?"

"Not a clue. Before I fixed the lock, I checked it out. It's dry. Nothing down there but dirt and debris."

"I think Emma may be on to something," Milo said. "Garrett was quite unethical. He'd use his talents without any thought of right and wrong."

Pieces of information, like shards of stained glass, floated before Emma's eyes, waiting for her to put them together into one tidy picture. She held her head in her hands again to ward off the dull, growing pain.

Emma added, "My guess is they know something about that property that we don't, but they didn't have all the information. That's where Billy comes in. And Garrett. If Billy is the key, then Garrett, or someone like him, is the only one who can turn it."

She looked at Milo. "What about you, Milo? Did anyone ever contact you about trying to reach Billy Winslow or anyone connected with that property?"

"Never. First I heard about it was from you and Granny."

"See," Emma said to everyone, "we have to ask Billy."

Susan stepped forward. "Emma, dear, why don't you get a good night's sleep tonight and go to the police tomorrow?"

"The police aren't going to listen to this." Phil was kneeling, calming the animals. "They'll consider it nonsense."

"And what about you, Phil?" Emma glued her eyes to his face. "Do you still think it's nonsense?"

Even though he couldn't see it in the dark, he looked off in the direction of the Reynolds homestead. "If you'd asked me that this morning, I would have said yes." He looked up at Emma's waiting face. "Now, I'm not so sure." He got up and dusted off his jeans. He looked into Emma's blue eyes. "But since this morning, my whole world's been turned on its ear. So I guess anything's possible."

"Then let me go talk to Billy."

"In the morning. Bright and early, like the crack of dawn. I know you can see them during the day. I've seen you do it."

"Better yet," added Tracy, "why can't Billy come here? Granny and Garrett travel about, why not him?"

Milo didn't look so sure. "Sometimes ghosts don't leave their favorite spot. It's weird. Some go everywhere, like Granny here." He pointed in the ghost's direction. "Others just stay in one earthly place. It depends on Billy's frame of mind."

Granny shook her head. "Billy's like a mule. He won't budge. When he was a boy, he'd sit atop that hill among those graves for hours when he didn't have chores or school. 'Course, weren't no fancy benches then, nor that road. My boy Winston said Billy would just look at the town and daydream." Once again, Milo played the interpreter.

"See, Phil—I have to go to Billy to find out anything."

Phil walked a few steps away. A moment later, he kicked the dirt in anger. "Damn!"

He returned to where Emma and the rest of them stood. "In the morning, Emma. Can't it wait until morning? I can protect you better in the sunlight."

Granny came up to Emma. "Listen to this man, Emma. Billy's not going nowhere."

With great reluctance, Emma gave in. "I suppose you're all right about this." She looked at Milo. "You have anything to add?"

"I vote we go in the morning. And I think I should go with you, just in case Billy won't talk with you. Or in case one of the other ghosts saw something and is willing to talk."

"Good idea."

In the blink of an eye, Emma's headache intensified, and dizziness engulfed her like a tsunami. She was so tired she wanted to drop in her tracks and sleep where she fell. Phil noticed her sway and put an arm around her waist to steady her.

"Why don't you go back to the cottage and get a good night's sleep. I'll bet you're all bushed."

After going back inside to collect their things, Emma, Tracy, Milo, and Archie piled into Tracy's Prius for the ride back to the cottage. Phil bent down to talk to Emma through the open passenger's window. He handed her something in a leather case. Emma opened it and found a pistol.

"I don't want this, Phil."

"Take it, just for tonight. I'd feel better if you had it. It's already loaded. Any danger, just point and squeeze the trigger."

"I'm not sure. It makes me nervous."

Tracy leaned over and checked out the gun in Emma's hand. "That thing will make us all nervous."

Phil took the gun back. "Then I guess I'll have to sleep on the sofa in the cottage. I'll grab a few things and be right behind you."

"No, Phil, don't," Emma told him. "You didn't get a good night's sleep last night. Sleep in your own bed. Besides, we have Archie." At the sound of his name, the dog poked his nose between the front seats and wagged his short tail. "He'll alert us if a stranger comes along. He might like ghosts, but he really is a good watchdog."

"Well, so is Killer, but I still wouldn't expect him to take a bullet for me."

twenty-nine

· ·

ARCHIE SEEMED AS RESTLESS as Emma. He circled the bedroom several times before laying down on a braided rug in the middle of the floor. Soon he was back at it, pacing, trying to find just the right position. Without his own bed, he couldn't sleep. In spite of the comfortable bed she was in, Emma understood his frustration.

Emma, Tracy, and Milo had driven back to the cottage in near silence. And even though it wasn't that late, all of them had turned in almost as soon as they'd gotten back. No ghosts had come with them. Emma figured Granny had used up her power pack and was off recharging. Garrett hadn't been seen since his chat with Milo.

Earlier, before they'd gone over to the Bowers ranch, Emma had taken her friends to the cottage to drop off their bags. The cottage had two bedrooms. One had a queen-size bed, the other contained twin beds. The women and Archie were sharing the room with the two beds. Emma looked over at Tracy. She was on her stomach, dead to the world except for a slight snore.

When Archie started taking another turn just ten minutes after his last, Emma invited him up onto the end of the bed. The dog happily accepted, and the two of them finally fell into a fitful sleep.

· · · · · · · · · · · · ·

EMMA SAT UP WITH a start, her heart racing like a muscle car. The room was completely dark except for the glow from the small clock on the nightstand between the beds. Archie had moved up next to her on the bed and was nudging her. It had been his wet nose against her cheek that had shot adrenaline through her body as if with a hypodermic needle.

Seeing his mission accomplished, Archie hopped off the bed. The black dog in the dark room was not easy to see, but when Archie started lightly scratching at the closed door to the bedroom, Emma knew what he needed. She looked at the clock. It was almost one in the morning. They'd been asleep two short hours.

At home, Archie had a small doggie door for his nocturnal bathroom needs. No such luck here. Emma swung her feet to the floor and felt around for her sneakers. As she slipped her feet into them, she had a thought.

The cemetery wasn't that far from the cottage. And even though it was the middle of the night, what better time to visit a graveyard looking for ghosts? Emma gave a brief thought to the killer but dismissed it. At one in the morning, he'd probably be asleep, too, or else long gone from Julian. She could go, talk to Billy, and be back before anyone knew. Of course, she would catch the dickens from everyone, especially Phil, when they found out, but by then it would be over with and, hopefully, she'd have the information she sought.

Quietly, she slipped on her jeans, tucking her nightgown down into them. Picking up her tennis shoes, she opened the door and tiptoed out into the living room, being careful as she closed the bedroom door behind her. Grateful for the thoughtfully placed nightlights in the bathroom and kitchen, Emma made a quick stop in the bathroom to pee, then she latched Archie's leash to his collar and grabbed her lightweight jacket.

Once again, she thought about the flashlight in her car, but that ship had sailed in more ways than one. Before leaving, Emma went into the kitchen. The doors to the bedrooms were shut tight, so she turned on the overhead light. It didn't take her long to locate an emergency flashlight stored on top of the refrigerator. Blessing the owner for thinking of such small amenities, Emma grabbed the flashlight and made her way out the front door with Archie.

She didn't turn on the flashlight while she walked. She didn't need to. The moon wasn't quite full, but it was bright enough to guide her down the small side street to Main Street. Once there, she felt comfortable walking along the storefronts. Archie trotted in front of her at the end of his leash, stopping here and there to smell and pee.

When they approached the Pioneer Cemetery, Emma had a choice to make. She could go up the steep, winding stairs or go the long way via the road. This time, she chose the road. With a quick glance over her shoulder, she passed under the crime-scene tape that blocked the entrance.

The moon spread a dim carpet of light in front of her as she made her way up the road. To her right were the newer graves, set in a more orderly fashion along the slope. At the top, the road branched to the right and left. It was actually a one-way road that circled the cemetery like a halo. Here, cars could only make a right-hand turn, but pedestrians and ghosts had no such rules to follow.

Emma stopped to get her bearings and to let her eyes adjust. The graveyard, with its awning of trees, was darker than the road leading up to it. Afraid someone up late in nearby houses might see her, she hadn't used the flashlight yet, but now she switched it on and pointed it downward to minimize any chance of being seen. The yellow beam cast a spot of light on the road as she turned right and tried to find Billy's bench in the dark.

Archie let her know the ghosts were there before she could clearly make them out. He pulled her forward, sniffing first at one foggy image, then another. He didn't seem tense or anxious, just curious about them. As Emma let her eyes and mind relax, she began to see what Archie sensed. The graveyard was alive with spirits, even more than the first time she visited. In the inky darkness of deep night, they shimmered with their own kind of life.

Tugging the excited Archie along the curving road, Emma came across her first bench but knew instantly that it wasn't Billy's. It didn't face toward town and wasn't under a large tree. The two nocturnal wanderers kept moving, going slowly in the dark, guided only by the small splash of light. Emma stopped at the next bench.

"Hello, Billy."

The ghost sat on his bench, staring out at the town. He didn't look at her but kept his eyes straight ahead. "Hello, Miss Emma."

"Beautiful night, isn't it?"

"Yes, ma'am. That your dog?"

"His name's Archie." As he was introduced, Archie moved forward and sniffed Billy Winslow's spirit. His tail wagged.

"I always did like dogs. Had one once, a shepherd named Jasper."

As the other ghosts went about their business, Emma sat down next to Billy. She kept still, sensing that he would talk in his own good time, if he talked at all. Archie lay at her feet, waiting, enjoying the evening air. She didn't know how much time passed before Billy spoke again, but it seemed to her several minutes.

"You come here to ask me more questions?"

"You know I did, Billy."

"About the man who died here last night?" He turned to look at her. As usual, his face was passive. "Or about something else?"

"I'm here about a few things. That is, if you are willing to tell me."

"That man," he started, turning back toward the town, "he came here to ask me questions, too."

"Had he been here before?"

"Yes, ma'am. Couple of times."

"Did you talk to him?"

"No. Didn't seem right. He said he was Winston's kin, like you. But I knew he wasn't, even if he did know a lot about what happened."

"He knew why you were killed, didn't he?"

"Yes, ma'am."

"You were killed by your father's partners, isn't that right? Men named Bobcat and Parker."

"You know more than you did last time."

"I came across some letters your father wrote to your mother. In them, your father refers to something you did. He doesn't say what it was, just that you did something you shouldn't have."

"Pa told me to fix it and save my skin. But he's the one who did something wrong. I was just trying to make it right." Billy sighed, his young, broad shoulders rising and falling like a soft wave. "I thought it would bring Ma and my sister back."

"You knew your father killed Winston's parents, didn't you? And that he got Winston to sell him the property so he could have the gold?"

Billy nodded. "It wasn't right, Miss Emma. Pa knew better. Those other men were bad. Made him do bad things."

"What did you do to make them so angry? Did you tell someone about what they did?"

"No, ma'am. I took it."

"Took it? Took the gold?"

"Yes, ma'am. I was going to find Winston and give it to him. It was rightly his. Wouldn't bring his ma and pa back, but it still belonged to him."

"But they killed you to get it back, right?"

"I never gave it back. I hid it."

It was Emma's turn to be silent. In the darkness of the graveyard, she rotated this new information this way and that in her brain, blending it with what she already knew, trying to fit the right-shaped peg into the correct slot. Garrett and his partner must have found out about the missing gold.

"Did you hide the gold on the Reynolds property, Billy?"

The ghost remained silent.

"Where, Billy? Where did you hide it? Do you mind telling me?"

"No, Miss Emma. You're Winston's kin. It belongs to you now."

Emma wasn't so sure about that theory. That might have been true years ago, when Billy took the gold. But if it was hidden on the old Reynolds property, it now legally belonged to the Bowers family. Personally, Emma didn't care. What she cared about was finishing this and getting home.

They fell into silence once more as Emma waited patiently for Billy to tell her where he'd hidden the gold. At her feet, Archie stirred, his pointed ears sharp in silhouette, his body stiff. She looked around. The ghosts were still milling about, but other than them, Emma heard and saw nothing. Even the small creatures in the trees and bushes were still. But Emma trusted Archie's instincts, and the dog was definitely on alert.

"I have to be getting back," she told the ghost. "It might not be safe for me here. Where's the gold, Billy?"

"It's not safe, Emma." It wasn't Billy's voice. Emma turned to her right and saw the ghost of Garrett Bell. "You need to leave. Right now. Or you will never leave alive."

She turned to Billy's spirit. Like a candle burned to the end of its wick, he was beginning to fade into the darkness. "Billy, please tell me." The other ghosts were also vanishing.

"Twenty-five paces north," Billy told her.

"Leave now, Emma," Garrett cautioned. "Go."

"Twenty-five paces north," Emma repeated, ignoring Garrett.

Archie was on his feet, standing at attention, looking off into the darkness. A low growl, like the buzz from an electric shaver, came from his gut. Emma stood up and looked around. Fear as prickly as feasting fire ants blanketed her skin.

"Well." Billy said the single word and was gone.

"Twenty-five paces north of what, Emma?"

Emma jumped at the voice. It wasn't the feathery words of a ghost but the full-bodied sound of the living coming from the depths of night. Keeping a tight hold on Archie's leash, Emma shined the flashlight in the direction of the voice, moving the beam this way and that until it found its mark.

Before her stood a man thick in body, average in height. He held a gun. Next to him was a short, stocky woman also holding a gun. To Emma's great surprise, it was the Quinns, the older couple staying at the Julian Hotel.

"Twenty-five paces north of what?" Mr. Quinn asked again. His wife remained silent.

"I don't know what you're talking about."

"Don't play games. Just tell me what Billy Winslow had to say."

"Who are you, and what do you have to do with this?"

"Let's just say we're interested parties, folks who are so glad you stumbled into this one-horse town when you did. We'd just about given up on Billy."

Archie's growl was deeper now. Emma pulled in a little more of his leash. "Billy?"

"Don't play the wide-eyed ingénue with me. You know I'm talking about the ghost of Billy Winslow. And you know about the gold."

"You killed Garrett, didn't you?"

"That was an unfortunate accident. We argued. He lost. But he'd outlived his usefulness anyway."

"Emma."

She cut her eyes a few inches to the right of Mr. Quinn and saw Garrett's ghost. Quinn noticed her movement.

"You seeing ghosts, Emma?"

"There are many ghosts up here. It's a graveyard."

Quinn gave off a deep chuckle. "So true." His wife also laughed.

"You put the snakes in my car, didn't you?"

"Actually, that was an idea I'm glad didn't pan out. I thought Billy had already given you the information, and we certainly couldn't have you claiming the prize, not after all the time and money we've spent to get to this point. It wasn't until last night, after the snakes were set, that Garrett Bell told us he didn't think Billy told you squat about the gold. But now that Bell's dead, you're our only hope of getting that information. Billy wouldn't talk to Bell—seems Bell had some bad karma or some other shit with the spirit world. We didn't know that when we hired him. They all clammed up every time we tried to get them to talk, especially Billy."

Archie strained on his leash and gave out a short couple of yips.

"If you don't want that dog dead, I'd advise keeping him in line."

Emma tugged the leash and shushed the animal. Archie got quiet but stayed on alert.

"How'd you know I was up here? Did Garrett's ghost tell you?"

"His ghost? Figures he'd come back to ruin everything. But alas, if one of us could see and talk to ghosts, we wouldn't have needed Bell in the first place, or you. But you did save us a lot of trouble by coming up here tonight. We were all set to bust into that cottage and take you by force when we saw you leave for your stroll."

Emma's heart stopped. They were going to invade the cottage at gunpoint? She thought about Milo and Tracy, thankful they weren't in harm's way.

Quinn took a step closer to Emma. The woman stayed where she was. Two guns against a Scottish terrier. Emma was definitely at a disadvantage.

"So? Twenty-five paces north of where, Emma? Tell us so we can all go home."

"He'll kill you, Emma." Garrett stepped closer.

"He's going to kill me anyway." Emma didn't think about the words, they just came out of her instinctively, like a cough or sneeze. But as soon as she said them, she knew it was true. She would die whether or not she told them where the gold was, unless she could convince them otherwise.

In the moonlight, Emma caught Quinn's smirk. "Kill you? Let's just say it's fifty-fifty on that at this point."

"Look, I personally don't care who gets the gold. I didn't know about it before I got here, and I don't care about it now."

Quinn appraised her top to bottom and back to the top. "You know, I actually believe you."

"Then let's make a deal." Emma shifted from foot to foot on the uneven ground. "I'll tell you what Billy said. You get the gold and leave Julian. I won't say anything in return for my life and the safety of my friends, including the Bowers family. Just take the gold and disappear. It's blood money anyway."

"Is the gold on the Reynolds property?"

"Yes."

"I knew it." His voice was smug. "She said it wasn't. Said it would have been too obvious, and Bobcat and Parker would have found it soon after killing Billy."

Mrs. Quinn had the long-suffering look of a wife who'd been told she was wrong most of her marriage.

"Where on the property?"

"We don't have a deal yet."

"It's a deal with the devil, Emma." Garrett drifted between her and Quinn. She ignored him, knowing a deal with the devil was her only chance of survival.

"You're coming with us," Quinn said after giving the situation some thought. "If the gold's there, you can go. If it's not, we'll have to have another talk—this time with a gun to the head of one of those friends of yours."

He started forward to grab Emma, but Archie growled. He aimed the gun at the dog.

"No, please," Emma begged. "He'll behave."

"He's not coming with us. Tie him to a tree."

"But there are other animals out here. It's not safe."

"The tree or a bullet. Your choice."

Emma bent to tie Archie's leash to a nearby small bush, but she didn't fasten it completely. "Stay," she ordered the dog as she walked away. Archie took a step to follow. "Sit. Stay."

This time, Archie sat down and stayed put, his posture vigilant as he watched his mistress being spirited away in the night.

thirty

· · · · · · · · · · · ·

PHIL BOWERS WAS HAVING a bad night. He kept dreaming of pioneer women hanging from trees and snakes driving cars, of ghosts dancing, and bulldogs with flatulence. Or was it dancing bulldogs and ghosts with flatulence? When his cell phone first rang, he thought it was just another crazy extension of his dreams.

He reached for the phone resting on the nightstand. He always kept it on, even when he slept, just in case one of his kids needed him. The last time it rang in the middle of the night, Tom, his youngest, had wrapped his car around a tree on his way home from a party. Like most parents, his heart was in his throat as he answered.

In under a minute, he had jumped into jeans and a tee shirt, shoved his feet into boots, and started running down the stairs.

"Phillip," his aunt called. She was leaning over the banister as he pulled open the door. Her hair was disheveled, and she was in her nightgown. "Is it Tom again?"

"It's Emma. Call 911 and get the sheriff over to the cemetery."

"Oh no! Is she all right?"

"Not sure, just make the call. Tell them to be cautious. The killer might be back."

His truck kicked up a cloud of gravel as it sped down the long drive to the access road. From there, it was nearly another a mile before it turned onto the road that led to the main highway into town. Worried about Emma, to Phil Bowers the drive seemed interminable.

In the middle of the night, the two-lane, twisting highway to town was usually empty. Phil pushed his foot against the accelerator and sent his truck speeding through the deserted countryside as fast as he dared, taking the turns as only a homegrown local could. A couple of miles from town, he saw headlights coming toward him. He slowed down until the dark Honda sedan safely passed, then opened up the throttle full tilt.

. . . .

THE MIDDLE-OF-THE NIGHT PHONE call had been from Milo Ravenscroft. He'd been woken up by Granny Apples. She'd put her face as close to his as possible and yelled his name with her ghostly voice until she got his attention. It was the only way she knew to help Emma. Immediately, Milo had called Phil Bowers.

"Wake up, Tracy." Milo shook her roughly by the shoulder. "Emma's in trouble."

"Huh?"

"It's Emma. She's gone to the cemetery. Granny just told me. The dog's gone, too."

Tracy sat up and glanced over at Emma's empty bed. Seeing the rumpled sheets woke her like a bucket of cold water. "What should we do?"

"I called Phil. He's on his way over there now with the police. He said to stay put until he called us back."

Tracy threw back the covers. "Like hell I'm sitting still." She had been sleeping in a tee shirt. Grabbing a pair of jeans from her overnight bag, she pulled them on and slipped into her sandals. "Come on. Let's get over there."

From the back of the Honda where Emma was bunched like a sack of potatoes across the back seat, she tried her best to conjure up Granny. She'd never called the ghost to her before in silence and wondered if it was possible. There was no time like the present to find out, and she had nothing to lose. If she could get Granny to pay attention, she might be able to send her for help. She had no way of knowing the ghost was way ahead of her. Before stuffing her into the back seat of the car, the woman had bound Emma's hands in front of her.

In the dark of the car, Emma's other senses were as sharp as a stick pin. She felt every turn in the road. Heard every breath of her kidnappers. At one point, she felt the car swerve hard to the right, then straighten.

"Damn fool," she heard the woman say. "That truck had to be going at least seventy. On these back roads, it's a good way to get killed."

Just as Emma was losing the battle with motion sickness, the car came to a stop. She heard both car doors open. The one at her feet was also opened, and the rush of cool mountain air refreshed her. Strong hands grabbed her ankles and dragged her halfway out of the car. As soon as hard-packed earth was under her feet, she was yanked upright by the waist of her jeans.

She turned this way and that, letting her eyes adjust to the night. She looked up. Stars covered the sky like sequins on a soft velvet dress. To her right, in the distance, she could just make out the Bowers ranch house. A whimper caught in her throat at the thought of the lovely meal and good company she'd shared there with friends just a few hours before. She'd wanted to show Kelly this place of peace and history. And her mother—her mother would like it here, at least for a few days. Then she might get restless. But she knew Elizabeth would find it fascinating to explore where her family had settled after migrating from Kansas.

After retrieving a flashlight and shovel from the trunk of the car, the Quinns marched her from the road to the fence. The man held open the wire, and the woman helped Emma through.

"Okay," Quinn said, "we're here. What did Billy tell you?"

"Twenty-five paces north."

"We know that." His voice was heavy with impatience. "Twenty-five paces north of *what*?"

"From the well."

He held the shovel up in front of Emma like a flag. "We thought it might be buried. Never hurts to be prepared, does it?"

The three of them trekked over to the old covered well. "Seems we weren't far off," he said to the woman. He turned toward Emma. "Originally, we thought it might be *in* the well. Bell managed to break the lock and get the lid off a few weeks ago, but there was nothing inside. Would have looked around more, but someone came down the road heading for the Bowers place." He jiggled the shiny new padlock. "Looks like they replaced the lock."

He undid Emma's wrists and handed the shovel to her. "As soon as I say where, start digging."

"Help is coming, Emma." It was Granny, standing almost in front of her. "Don't fret, help's coming." Emma stared straight ahead, not wanting to give any indication to the others that they were not alone.

After gazing up at the sky from several vantage points, the man gave a grunt of satisfaction. He paced off twenty-five steps from the rim of the well and pointed the beam of light at a spot on the ground. "Here."

When she hesitated, the woman nudged Emma in the back with her gun. Emma walked over to where Quinn indicated. She stuck the pointed end of the shovel into the dirt and scooped away a cupful. She repeated the process a few times before he snatched the shovel from her.

"It's going to take all night that way. Haven't you ever used a shovel before?"

"No, I haven't."

"Shit. Just our luck we'd get a hothouse flower."

After pushing her out of the way, the man stuck the end of the spade into the dirt and pushed down on its top edge with his foot, forcing the sharp end deeper into the ground. When he pulled the shovel out, a large chunk of dirt came with it.

"See, gotta use your foot. Put some muscle and backbone into it."

After depositing the dirt to the side, he handed the shovel back to Emma. Granny had disappeared.

Following his instructions, Emma went to work, managing to dig a small, deep hole in no time, but with no results. Quinn instructed her to move slightly to the left, then to the right. She was sweating and tired, and her arms were beginning to ache.

Emma took off her jacket and wiped the sweat from her face. "What I don't understand is who are you people? How did you even find out about this land and the gold?"

"Linda here was old Ian's nurse."

"Peter, don't tell her anything."

"Aw, she's harmless. She knows she'll die if she tells. Isn't that right, Sweet Cheeks?"

Sweet Cheeks—Emma would never complain about being called Fancy Pants again, especially by Phil Bowers.

"That was the deal we made."

"Ian was fascinated by his family history, and when he found documents talking about gold, Linda talked him into going to a séance to see if he could contact the spirits of his ancestors. That's how we met Garrett Bell. He said he could help—for a fee, of course. Unfortunately, Ian died right after receiving the copies of those Winslow letters. Seeing he didn't have any family, we helped ourselves to them and a few other things, and continued working with Bell."

Quinn refocused his attention on the dig. "Can't imagine the boy burying it any deeper than that." He scratched his chin in thought. "Go back to where we started, and dig in a little more toward the well. The boy's paces might've been shorter than mine."

"So the condominiums were just a ruse to cover the hunt for the gold?"

"You can work while you talk, can't you? Or is that something you've never done before, like shoveling?"

Emma went back to digging.

"The condos were actually a real possibility. If we can clear the permits, we know a builder who'd love to build out here. Maybe one of them 55-plus retirement complexes. They're big now with aging baby boomers. But the real goal was the gold."

With every shovelful of dirt, Emma realized she might be digging her own grave.

. . . .

PHIL'S TRUCK HAD BARELY come to a stop when he jumped out. A sheriff's vehicle was parked across Main Street. Next to it was an unmarked car with a flashing light. A few of the townspeople were clustered nearby. Near the unmarked car stood Milo and Tracy talking with Detective Martinez. Archie was in Tracy's arms. Phil headed for the group.

"What's going on?"

"No Emma." Tracy wiped her wet eyes against the dog's long coat and hugged him closer.

"When the deputy got here," Detective Martinez explained, "the dog was wandering down the middle of Main Street dragging its leash. He tried to catch him, but the animal eluded him until these folks arrived and called him by name."

"But no sign of Emma?" Phil looked up the hill at the graveyard.

"None. And no sign of a struggle or anything like it. Of course, it's dark out. We'll know more about what happened up there in the morning. Meanwhile, I've called in some portable floodlights to help."

"Damn her!" Phil paced. "I'm going to wring her scrawny neck when we find her."

"If, Phil." Tracy put the dog down on the ground. "If we find her. She would never have left Archie on his own willingly."

Instead of her usual casual fade-in, Granny used every bit of energy she could muster to pop up in front of Milo without warning. "She's at the homestead!"

The mild-mannered clairvoyant slapped his hand over his heart to quiet his nerves. "Granny!"

All eyes turned to him.

"She's at the homestead digging for the gold." Granny told Milo.

"Emma's digging for the gold?"

"What?" Phil Bowers moved in next to Milo. Tracy and Martinez followed. "She's looking for the gold?"

"Granny says Emma's digging for gold up at the homestead." He held up his hand to silence the living so he could concentrate on what Granny was saying.

"I think," Milo said, trying to piece together Granny's excited message, "Emma's being made to dig. Granny says they're going to kill her."

Before the others could react, Phil Bowers jumped back into his truck and peeled off in the direction he'd come. As he maneuvered the vehicle with one hand, he used his other to call home on his cell.

. . . .

"You lied to us." Peter Quinn brandished the gun in Emma's sweaty face.

"No, I didn't. Billy said twenty-five paces north of the well. Are you sure we're north?"

He closed in on her. "If we had some rope, I swear I'd enjoy swinging you from that big oak. Was good enough for your ancestor."

Emma didn't dare turn to look at the tree. She was afraid she'd faint.

"She's right, Peter, you might be off a bit in the direction. So just keep digging."

"You mind your own business, woman. If I say this is north, then it's north." He looked up again at the stars, recalculating his direction. When he looked back down, he pointed to another spot more to the right of the earlier dig. "Dig there."

Emma had just scooped up her first new batch of dirt when they heard a noise in the distance. The three of them stopped to listen. It was a truck, a large dark pickup, coming down the road from the Bowers ranch like a bullet train. Its headlights were off. Barking accompanied the roar of the engine. Ripping through the barbed-wire fence like it was string, the huge truck bore down on them like Batman gone country.

The lights of the truck came on just as two snarling German shepherds jumped from the back. Linda Quinn froze, her gun down at her side. Her husband screamed at her to shoot the dogs, then raised his own gun. Emma lifted the shovel and brought it down on his gun arm. He screamed. Dropping his weapon, he turned to take a swing at her with his good arm, but the shovel was in motion again. Emma, holding the spade like a baseball bat, aimed for his knees. With her last bit of strength, she felled him like a giant redwood.

thirty-one

"WE NEED TO GO back to the cemetery, Phil."

"We don't need to go anywhere, Emma."

"Well, *I* need to go back. I have to talk to Billy Winslow again."

They were gathered once more around the large pine dining table at the Bowers' home. Heaped on platters were pancakes, scrambled eggs, toast, and one large serving plate with both bacon and plump sausages. The air was heavy with the mingled scents of spicy fried pork and sweet maple syrup. They had all spent the last four hours answering the detectives' questions about the activities of the night, and even though it was only eight o'clock in the morning, for the people gathered around the table, it felt like the day should be ending, not beginning.

As soon as Emma finished the bite of pancake in her mouth and took a drink of orange juice, she cleared her throat. "Thank you, everyone, for everything." She started to tear up. "I don't know what I would have done, especially once that guy realized there might not be gold buried by the well."

Susan Steveson smiled. "Just following Phil's orders."

"My orders were for you to keep watch on the Reynolds place, not for you and Glen to play superheroes," Phil growled as he drank coffee. "And you two," he said, looking at Milo and Tracy, "were supposed to stay in the cottage and wait it out. I had it under control. What if the killers had still been in the graveyard?"

Milo looked sheepish. Tracy gave off a *humph* as she finished a bite of eggs.

"And what in the hell were you doing?" He glared at Emma. "You promised me you wouldn't go to the graveyard until morning."

"It was just an impulse, Phil. I didn't plan on breaking my promise. But if I hadn't, those two would have broken into the cottage. They told me so. Who knows what they would have done to us all?"

Emma speared a sausage with a serving fork and plopped it on Phil's plate, along with two slices of crisp bacon. "Here, go crazy. You deserve it."

Susan walked around, refreshing people's coffee. When she reached Phil, she kissed the top of his bald head. "You can't save the world alone, dear. Sometimes you need help. Even superheroes know that."

Phil finally gave in to Emma visiting the Pioneer Cemetery again. Not that he had a choice. She was determined to go with or without him. The only option he had was whether or not to go with her. He had only one suggestion—a strong one—that she ask the detectives working the case for their permission first. The cemetery was still cordoned off and under their jurisdiction.

It took some convincing on both Emma and Phil's part for Detective Martinez to allow them to bypass the yellow tape, but he finally agreed, with the provision that he go with them. Emma's argument was that she had an idea about where the gold was buried, and that unless they found it, the town might end up crawling with fortune hunters.

Leaving Tracy, Archie, and Milo back at the Bowers ranch, Emma and Phil met Martinez at the bottom of the road to the graveyard. The detective nodded to the deputy guarding the entrance, and he let them pass under the tape. At the top of the hill, Emma asked the men to stay a bit behind her. She wasn't sure how Billy would feel about an audience.

"So there are ghosts all over the place?" Martinez asked, his eyes darting back and forth over the hilly terrain filled with gravestones.

"Right now there aren't any here. So you can relax, Detective." She glanced over her shoulder as she spoke.

She made her way to Billy's bench. "Billy, you here?" She waited, but nothing happened. "Please come out and talk to me."

She walked around the bench and a few paces to the left and right, hoping he would materialize, but he didn't. Stopping, she surveyed the graveyard and noticed there were now a couple of ghosts in attendance. One was the young childless mother. She sat by the tree near the children's memorial rocking empty arms, as Emma had seen her do on her first visit. The other was Garrett Bell.

The ghost of Garrett Bell approached her.

"Do you know where the gold is, Garrett? Did Billy tell you after all?"

He shook his head. "No, he did not. Do you know?"

"I think so."

"Who is it, Emma?" Phil called to her. "Is it Billy?"

"No," she called back, "it's Garrett."

Detective Martinez advanced with caution, his face a marquee of disbelief and curiosity.

"Peter and Linda Quinn are under arrest," she told the ghost. "For your murder and for kidnapping me."

"Have the police look into Ian's death, too."

"They killed him?"

"He was an old man, but I always suspected they expedited things."

"I still don't understand why they killed you."

"I came back here to see if I could get Billy to talk to me, especially after he'd been so chatty with you. The Quinns met me here after putting the snakes in your car. When I told them that Billy still wasn't talking, Pete accused me of lying, saying I wanted the gold for myself. We argued and he shot me."

Emma noticed Garrett's image fading. "You're leaving?"

"Yes, there's no reason to stay."

"Will you come back?"

"No. Never."

Once he was gone, Emma told the men what the ghost had said about the Quinns.

"No Billy?" Phil asked.

"No, but I have a hunch about the gold. Billy told me it was twenty-five paces north. When I asked north of what, he said the word *well*, then faded. Maybe he didn't mean the well at the property. Maybe he meant something else. He might not have finished the word before disappearing."

She started back to Billy's bench. "Granny told me that Billy spent a lot of time up here as a kid. There weren't benches then, but this big tree probably was here, just a lot smaller." She looked up at the sky. It was late morning, and the sun wasn't quite overhead. "North would be that way, right?" She pointed in the direction she thought it should be.

Phil looked up at the sky. "Yes."

She paced off twenty-five steps. "I'm not sure how far twenty-five paces is, but I can't be too far off." When she stopped, she started looking around the ground. "Help me look for a gravestone with the name Well or Wells or any derivative of the word *well*. It should be one of graves set before the first few years of 1900."

The three of them scattered over an arc of space spanning out from the twenty-five-pace mark. Each looked at graves, reading the names and dates.

"Be careful," Emma warned. "Some of the graves are difficult to read. You might have to trace them with your finger."

"I think I found it," called Phil. Martinez and Emma joined him next to a grave several yards to the left of where Emma ended her pacing. The name on the grave was Welles.

"This is it," Emma said with confidence.

"How can you be sure?" asked Detective Martinez.

Without answering, Emma walked over to the bench. Standing next to it was Billy. As she walked away, she heard Martinez yell to the deputy to bring a shovel.

"You buried the gold there, didn't you? By that grave?"

"Yes."

"Why?"

"He was a friend of mine and Winston's. Was killed working in a mine. Just fifteen years old. Knew he'd take good care of it."

"Thank you, Billy."

"No, Miss Emma, thank you. I can go now."

"Go? For good?"

"Yes, ma'am. No sense staying now that you have the gold."

"The gold's not mine, Billy. Seeing that it's on city property, it probably belongs to the town of Julian."

"That's good."

Before Emma could say anything more, he was gone. And like Garrett Bell, he wasn't returning.

thirty-two

"HEY, FANCY PANTS."

Emma dropped her book in her lap as her head snapped up. Standing by the door that led from the patio to the kitchen was Phillip Bowers. Just behind him was her mother, smiling from ear to ear. He wasn't dressed hip and trendy like Grant, given to whims of fashion and vanity, but in conservative tailored slacks, a dress shirt, and sports jacket. Neither did he wear boots or a hat. Today, he looked more like a middle-aged successful attorney than a rancher.

She hadn't seen Phil Bowers since the day she'd left Julian over three months ago. There had been scattered phone calls and e-mails, but both had been careful to keep their relationship bound to friendship. Although it had been her idea originally, now Emma was sorry she hadn't encouraged Phil. But with so many miles between them, and both their marriages coming to an end, she still felt it the best course of action. And Phil had seemed content to leave things the way they were. Lately, though, the calls and e-mails had drifted away.

Emma was still in touch with Susan Steveson. They e-mailed each other regularly. But as Phil and Emma's relationship waned, Susan had been quite careful not to mention Phil, and Emma had been too proud to ask.

Sitting in a chaise on her parents' patio, she felt the contradictory pull of both concern and pleasure at the sight of him. And in spite of herself, even being called Fancy Pants had sent a tingle up her spine.

"Hello, stranger."

Archie, who was rolling around on the grass, stopped his play to greet Phil.

"Hey, boy." Phil sat at the patio table and leaned down to scratch Archie behind the ears. "Got something for you. A gift from Killer." Reaching into his pocket, he pulled out a small plastic bag containing dog biscuits. "From his own private stock homemade by Aunt Susan." He fed the dog a couple. "Let's leave the rest for later, okay?"

As if understanding, Archie took off to resume his play, darting back and forth across the yard with no visible purpose, yet with a definite pattern of motion.

Phil laughed as he put the plastic bag on the table. "I see Granny's still with you."

As if on cue, Elizabeth Miller came out of the house. "Granny, let's leave these young people alone for a bit."

The foggy image of Ish Reynolds started for the patio, Archie on her heels.

"Young people? I'll have you know I'm younger than both of them."

Emma watched the spirit with affection until she disappeared through the wall into the kitchen. Archie used his doggie door. She turned back to Phil Bowers.

"She divides her time between here and Julian."

"And what about you? You ever coming back to Julian?"

"As a matter of fact, my cousin Marlene and I are going down soon for Harvest Days. I've rented the cottage again."

"Going to stop and say hi to your pals at the cemetery?"

She couldn't tell if he was being sincere or mocking her. "Probably."

"And what about your living friends? Were you going to say hello to me while in town?"

"Of course, if you're around when I visit Susan and Glen."

Phil Bowers sighed. "Emma, I'm sorry I've been out of touch lately, but I needed time to think about this, about us." He fiddled with the dog treats as he spoke. "I needed to get you out of my system."

"Gee, Phil, you make me sound like a nasty virus."

He grinned. "In a way, you are." The grin disappeared. "I know you said you only wanted to be friends, and I know the long-distance thing will be a problem, but I'd like you to consider me more than a friend."

Emma took a deep breath and swung her legs off the chaise so that she was sitting facing him. "Phil, it's very difficult to maintain a long-distance relationship, you know that. We're not kids. And I won't be having the free time I used to."

"No?"

She shook her head and smiled. "Milo's offered me a job."

"Working for him as a clairvoyant?" He seemed skeptical.

"No. It's actually a job he was offered but turned down. I'm going to be on TV, hosting a weekly show on paranormal activities."

"Isn't there already a *Ghost Hunters* show on the tube?"

It was the response she'd expected from him. "Not like that show. It will be in a talk-show format and will have scientists and experts in various paranormal fields as guests, along with laypeople who have experienced various phenomena. We are hoping it will be serious and fun at the same time."

"A talk show, huh? Like your husband."

"It will only be on once a week, not every day. They've scheduled it during the same time slot as Grant's show." She winked at him. "*Whitecastle versus Whitecastle* is how some of the early ads are going to play."

"And how is the other Whitecastle versus Whitecastle coming along?"

"We've reached a settlement; the divorce should be final soon. How about your divorce?"

"It was final last week."

Emma studied his face. "Is that a good thing or a bad thing, Phil?"

"I wasn't sure at first, but now I think it's a very good thing." He smiled at her. For a few moments, neither of them said anything.

"I came up here for two reasons, Emma." He pulled a folded document from his inside jacket pocket and handed it to her. "That's the deed to the old Reynolds homestead. It's yours now."

Emma looked down at the recorded deed. "But I didn't want it, Phil. That's not why I went down there."

"I know. But Glen, Susan, and I want you and your family to have it. Though, trust me, my part in this is purely selfish. I figure if you own property down there, you might come down more often. That could solve part of the distance problem."

She blushed, and not just from his generosity.

"You can build a nice cabin on that piece of land. I can help you find the right architect and builder. It could be a vacation home for your family and a solid place for Granny to haunt."

Emma laughed through tears. "I think they would love that, Phil. Granny especially. I just don't know what to say."

"That brings me to the second reason for my visit. How about saying yes to my dinner invitation tonight? We have a lot to celebrate: your new career, my divorce, your settlement, the property. It can be a new start for a new type of relationship."

. . . .

WHEN THEY RETURNED FROM dinner, it was late and the Miller house was dark, save for the kitchen light. They entered through the back door. Archie left his bed to greet them.

"Thank you for the lovely time, Phil."

Putting a hand on each of his shoulders, she reached her face up and kissed him on the lips. It was followed by another, then by a whole series of kisses, until they were wrapped in each other's arms. After the longest kiss ended, Emma pulled away.

In the dim light, Phil chuckled. "Look at us. We're both middle-aged and still living at home."

Emma placed a fingertip on his lips. "Shh, you'll wake my parents."

Taking him by the hand, she led him up the back staircase.

. . . .

"DID YOU AND PHILLIP have a good time?"

Emma jumped at the voice. It was four thirty in the morning, and she'd just said goodbye to Phil Bowers at the back door, sending him on his way with little sleep. Elizabeth Miller was seated at the kitchen counter, reading the paper and drinking coffee. Next to her was the ghost of Granny Apples.

"Mother, why are you up so early?"

"I often get up this early. Granny and I have lovely visits in the morning. You and your father just don't know it because you both sleep like rocks."

Emma looked out the window and watched Phil walk down the driveway toward his truck. When she turned back to her mother, she knew her face was flushed with embarrassment. Elizabeth noticed and smiled.

"You think I never knew about all the times Grant Whitecastle tiptoed up those backstairs? Or the times Nate does it now?"

She turned a page of the newspaper, giving her daughter time to let the information sink in.

"It's different for you girls today. I understand that. Your father may or may not, so I never told him." She looked up. "But the next time Phillip Bowers comes to town, let's put him in the guest room, at least for appearances. That way, we can send him back to Julian with a proper hot breakfast."

Emma wrapped her arms around her mother's neck and kissed her cheek.

"There will be a next time, won't there?"

"Yes, Mother, I'm pretty certain there will be many next times with Phil Bowers."

Emma poured herself a cup of coffee and leaned against the kitchen counter, drinking it and watching Elizabeth. She had weathered losing her son, bearing her grief with dignity and grace. Emma wasn't sure she could do the same if she ever lost Kelly. She glanced at Granny and Granny nodded back, indicating it was time. She disappeared.

"Mother, Granny and I have a surprise for you." Elizabeth looked up, puzzled.

Emma guided her mother to a chair in the dim dining room. She stood behind her and placed her hands gently against the sides of her mother's face.

"Look straight ahead, Mother. Relax your mind and your eyes, release all your thoughts and concerns."

"Is this some sort of meditation exercise?"

"Just do as I say." Emma massaged her mother's temples, willing Elizabeth to see through her eyes. "Do you see anything at the end of the table?"

"No. Wait. Something's shimmering."

Emma looked toward the end of the table. Granny was there, coming into view. "Keep looking, but stay relaxed while you do."

"Oh my, Emma. Is that Granny?" Elizabeth's voice, though barely above a whisper, was filled with awe.

"Yes, Mother, it is."

"I can see her. I can really see her."

"We have another gift for you, Elizabeth," said the ghost.

Another flickering entity started taking shape next to Granny. A smaller image.

"Oh my!" Elizabeth's hand went to her mouth. "It's my Paulie. My dear son."

Emma looked at the ghost of her dead brother as he was when he died at the age of eleven. He was standing next to the spirit of Ish Reynolds, holding her hand.

"Yes, Mother, it's Paulie. He's come to visit, just this once."

The image of the young boy smiled and waved. "Hello, Mother."

Elizabeth slipped a shaking hand over one of Emma's hands as it rested on her face. She squeezed it.

"Thank you, Emma. Once was all I needed."

the end

author's note

· ·

WHILE THE CHARACTERS IN *Ghost à la Mode* are fictional, Julian, California, is a very real place. Located in the mountains an hour north of San Diego and about a three-hour drive from Los Angeles, this sleepy tourist destination is a reminder of the colorful history of California's gold rush days in Southern California.

Readers who visit Julian will be able to follow Emma Whitecastle's steps throughout the town, as I have made every attempt to portray it as it really is today, right down to the pay toilets located behind city hall. See firsthand the Rong Branch Restaurant and Saloon, the Old Julian Drug Store, and the Pioneer Museum. Sit in the park where Emma first encountered the ghost of Garrett Bell, and rest on one of the benches nestled among the graves in the Pioneer Cemetery.

There is, however, one character in the book who is not fictional: Albert Robinson. Albert Robinson was a freed slave who came to Julian after the Civil War. Together, he and his wife, Margaret, started a restaurant and built the Hotel Robinson, which is now the charming Julian Hotel, and it is reported that the ghost of Mr. Robinson does indeed haunt the hotel, especially guest room 10.

Read on for a sneak peek
at the second book in the
Ghost of Granny Apples series
by Sue Ann Jaffarian

excerpt

. . . .

THE WOMAN FROLICKING IN the waves was underdressed for November, even for a ghost. Emma Whitecastle watched as the curvaceous, bikini-clad spirit dashed in and out of the waves, as carefree and untouched by the morning cold as a porpoise. Emma, on the other hand, had pulled her jacket together and zipped it up close under her chin. Then she hovered over the cup of hot coffee she'd picked up from a bakery around the corner. She'd had a restless night, tossing and turning most of it, so just after five thirty she dressed quietly in jeans, a sweater, warm socks, and sneakers, and headed for the beach to watch the sunrise, leaving behind a sleeping Phillip Bowers in their hotel room.

It was Thanksgiving weekend. Emma's college-age daughter, Kelly, hadn't come home for the short holiday, opting instead to spend it at a friend's home in Connecticut. Emma's parents were on a cruise through the Panama Canal. Phil's boys were with their mother, and his aunt Susan and uncle Glen were visiting their daughter. That left Phil and Emma to fend for themselves over the four-day holiday. It had been Phil's idea to go away to Catalina. Emma had been to the vacation spot located just twenty-six miles off the coast of Southern California many times while married to Grant Whitecastle, the bad boy of TV talk-show hosts. During those times, she'd either stayed in the finest island hotels like the former Wrigley Mansion, now known as the Inn on Mt. Ada, or on the yachts of Grant's show-biz friends. When Phil first proposed the trip, he'd booked them at the Hotel Metropole, but Emma didn't want to stay anywhere she'd stayed with Grant. As Phil ticked off the list of the finest island hotels, Emma had said no to each.

Phil had been frustrated. "You can't go through life avoiding everywhere the two of you traveled. If you do, we'll never go anywhere."

He'd been right, of course. But he hadn't been right about why she felt the way she did.

"Are you sure you're over him?" Phil had asked, the vein in his neck tight like a cord, bracing him for news he didn't want to hear.

Emma's divorce from Grant Whitecastle had been finalized at the end of last year. Technically, she'd become a single woman on January first, just eleven months ago. She and Grant had been separated about a year and a half prior to that, and the marriage had been on the rocks almost from the time he'd hit it big with his tacky, tabloid-style talk show. Even before they'd been formally separated, Grant had impregnated Carolyn Bryant, his B-movie, party-girl mistress. Grant had married Carolyn on the first weekend in the new year in a splashy wedding attended by much of Hollywood. Photos of the bride and groom and their toddler son, Oscar, had assaulted Emma from every supermarket checkout. And that's how Emma knew she was over Grant Whitecastle. The photos elicited nothing from her except pity for Grant, for the life he'd thrown away in his quest for fame and his lust for a sleazy wannabe out to grab any man with a big name and a bigger bank account. He'd lost her, damaged the bond between him and Kelly, even lost the respect of his own parents. He'd pretty much flipped them all the bird—in public.

In spite of her protests, Kelly had attended her father's wedding, reporting back that even though it looked like Hollywood had turned out for the circus event, it was more out of deepseated support and respect for Grant's parents, George and Celeste Whitecastle. George Whitecastle was a multi-award-winning director and producer who counted Clint Eastwood and George Lucas among his closest friends. George's parents, both now dead, had been Hollywood legends. Celeste had been a famous starlet known for her beauty and grace. She'd even been dubbed the next Grace Kelly. But like the late Princess of Monaco, Celeste had given up her budding career for love and family. Emma knew that Kelly's summation was probably correct, that most of the A-list guests at the wedding had been there for George and Celeste. Even though Emma was no longer married to Grant, she was still on the fringe of show business, now having her own talk show on television, and gossip managed to filter down to her. Grant Whitecastle was respected for his runaway ratings, not for himself. The minute those ratings dipped, he'd be kicked aside like a pair of old, worn sneakers, just as he had kicked Emma aside.

No, Emma was over Grant Whitecastle. She'd stopped loving him long before the divorce was final. What she tried to explain to Phil was that she wanted to make new and happier memories with him. Many of her past stays on Catalina had not been happy ones. Even on the small island, Grant had managed to cat around, and many of those luxury hotel rooms had been the scenes of arguments and despair.

It was Tracy Bass, a professor at UCLA and Emma's best friend, who had suggested the Pavilion Lodge, citing it as the best value and location on the island. And it was. Though not luxurious, the hotel was lovely and comfortable and just footsteps from the beach. It suited Emma just fine. And it suited Phil Bowers, who, though a very successful attorney and rancher, was as unpretentious as a pair of worn jeans.

Emma took an appreciative sip of her coffee and studied the ghost playing in the surf. She'd first seen the spirit yesterday. It had been Thanksgiving morning, their first morning on the island. After enjoying coffee and a continental breakfast at the hotel, she and Phil had gone for a morning stroll to explore the beachfront shop windows while the village of Avalon was first stirring. The ghost of the young woman had been sitting on one of the tiled benches, her eyes closed, her pretty face turned toward the slow-rising morning sun as if soaking up rays at high noon in July. As they had passed by, the ghost had opened her eyes and looked at Emma with a frank curiosity as solid as the bench on which she sat. She said nothing, but several steps later, when Emma looked over her shoulder, the ghost was still staring after them.

Catalina supposedly has many ghosts in residence, the most famous being that of Natalie Wood. The actress had drowned while yachting off of Two Harbors, the other main town on the island. The accident had occurred over Thanksgiving weekend in 1981, and since then people claim to have seen the ghost of the popular movie star walking the beach. While on the island, Emma hoped to do some research into the local spirits and legends for a segment on Catalina on her weekly television talk show on paranormal theories and activities. Catalina had a rich paranormal history dating back to its original Indian inhabitants, and it included colorful stories about the Chicago Cubs baseball team, who used the island as its spring training camp for nearly thirty years, and the heyday of Hollywood, when movie stars like Clark Gable and Errol Flynn used it as a playground.

Emma Whitecastle was fairly new to the world of spirits and ghosts, only discovering her ability to see and speak with them last year, when the ghost of her great-great-great-grandmother, Ish Reynolds, better known as Granny Apples, had come to her for help to prove her innocence in the death of her husband, Jacob. At first skeptical, Emma reluctantly helped Granny and embraced her ability to see and communicate with the dead. It was during her investigation into Granny's death that she'd met Phil Bowers. On a reference from Milo Ravenscroft, the clairvoyant who had mentored Emma, she was offered a chance to host the talk show, the Whitecastle name no doubt giving as much, if not more, weight to the producer's decision about hiring her as her abilities.

Now Emma saw ghosts all the time. They didn't crowd around her like a swarm of pesky flies, but she was no longer surprised when one presented itself. Usually, they just went about their business. Sometimes they took casual note of her. And sometimes they interacted. Since yesterday morning, Emma had seen the young, bikini-wearing ghost several times, including during Thanksgiving dinner at the country club, where the spirit, dressed in her flirty dotted and ruffled bathing suit, had flitted from table to table unnoticed while guests dined on turkey and pumpkin pie. The spirit hadn't spoken to Emma yet, just studied her with playful interest like a puppy with a tilted head.

It had been thoughts of the ghost that had given Emma a restless night and beckoned her outside at sunrise.

As the darkness turned to gunmetal gray, the ghost continued to play in the surf. Her image was hazy, like a column of smoke molded into the shape of a woman. She'd been blond in life and very curvy, with large breasts, a tiny waist, and a sweetheart bottom. However she had died, it'd been while wearing the bikini; thus she was forever clad. And she had died young, possibly in her mid to late twenties.

When the ghost turned and looked toward the town, Emma raised a hand and gave the spirit a friendly wave. The ghost smiled and waved back, totally untroubled about being seen. Turning again toward the sea, she shot another smile back over her shoulder and disappeared into the waves lapping at the pier pilings.

"Brrrr," a familiar whispery voice said from behind Emma. "Makes me cold as a witch's titty just looking at her."

Emma continued looking at the spot where the young spirit had disappeared. "You're a ghost, Granny, you don't feel cold."

"But I remember it. Felt it plenty in my life. Hunger, too. There were winters in the cabin, felt like we'd freeze to death before spring came."

As a shiver went through Emma, she took a big drink of her coffee. Usually she could tell when Granny or another spirit was near by a sudden chill in the air, but in the cold of the morning, Granny's arrival had gone unnoticed. "Do you know that ghost, Granny? The one just now on the beach?" She turned to look at the spirit of Ish Reynolds.

Just as the young ghost was bound for eternity to wear a bikini, Granny Apples would always be dressed in pioneer clothing consisting of a long-sleeved blouse and long, full skirt. Granny had died over a hundred years ago and had been a tiny but strong woman with braided hair circling her head like a halo, and a pinched face weathered by years of working out-of-doors in every type of condition. Emma caught a whiff of the faint odor of apple pie that often accompanied Granny's presence. In the coolness of the dawn, it was as comforting as a warm fire.

"Can't say that I do."

"She keeps appearing to me. I think she wants something."

"Has she spoken?"

"Not yet. She just watches me in a friendly manner, almost like she's trying to remember me from somewhere."

"Maybe she's an old school mate who passed on."

Emma swallowed some hot coffee. "No, I don't think so. From her appearance, I'd say she might have died sometime in the sixties. That's the *nineteen* sixties," Emma clarified for Granny with an impish grin.

The ghost pursed her lips in annoyance. "I ken what you meant. They didn't wear bathing outfits like that in my day."

"Did you note her hairstyle? The way it's teased on top with the ends curled upward? That was called a flip. And her bathing suit looks a bit old-fashioned with the polka dots and ruffles."

Granny crossed her arms and stood looking out at the water. "Hmph, glad I was dressed when I passed. Hate to think of spending eternity with my backside hanging out like that."

Granny's observation caught Emma's attention. She smiled into her coffee cup, glad she hadn't yet met any ghosts who'd died in the nude.

The town of Avalon was tucked into a crescent-shaped bay on Catalina Island. The main street that ran along the beachfront was appropriately named Crescent. High hills stood on either side of the bay like sentries. Daylight crept over one hill while fog rolled over the opposite one. They met in the middle like tenuous lovers, shrouding the sea in a hazy veil. Palm trees along the beach were ringed with tiny lights, and many of the shopfronts and hotels already had their Christmas lights up and lit. At night, it had been magical walking along the festive beach hand in hand with Phil. This morning, the lights faded into the sunlight, handing the baton of a new day off to the sun.

Both behind and in front of Emma, the town was starting to stir. Ahead of her, people staying on the numerous boats and yachts moored in the bay were wakening. She caught sight of a dinghy making its way from one of them to the pier like a duckling swimming off on its own for the first time. On the long pier that housed several tourist businesses and restaurants, she could make out a few people going about the business of opening for the day. Along Crescent, a few people were out for early morning strolls or heading to work. She heard the soft thunk of metal against pavement, followed by a gentle swoosh behind her. Turning, she saw a man bundled in a jacket and gloves sweeping the street and sidewalk with a broom and caddy, moving deliberately along Crescent, scanning for wayward trash and debris. Catalina was very clean, and its citizens took great pride in keeping it that way. It was one of the things Emma had always enjoyed about the island.

"Mighty beautiful place."

Emma started. She'd almost forgotten about Granny. The ghost was perched on the far edge of her bench, looking out to sea.

"Never saw the ocean until I was dead."

"Never?"

The question surprised both Emma and Granny. Swinging their heads in unison to their left, they saw the young ghost—the woman from the beach. She stood just a few feet away. In addition to her bikini, she wore a small bow clipped to the right side of her hair. Nothing else. It was the first time Emma had seen her so close or heard her voice.

"Came from Kansas," Granny continued, as if she spoke to this new spirit every day. "Settled in the mountains once we got to California. That's were the gold was. So that's where my man, Jacob, stayed put."

"I'd just die if I couldn't go to the beach." Through the ghostly whisper, Emma discerned a young voice that held an almost child-like quality. She changed her estimation of the woman's age at death to be her early twenties.

Granny cocked a thumb in Emma's direction. "This here's my great-granddaughter, Emma."

"Great-great-great-granddaughter, actually." Emma drank the last of her coffee in one final gulp and tossed the cup into a trash bin that stood next to the bench. She knew Granny was sensitive about her age, even in death. And Emma loved teasing her about it.

"Whatever." Granny rolled her eyes. Emma frowned at the response, thinking Granny was picking up far too many modern bad habits. Granny returned her attention to the ghost. "Emma's a friend to those on the other side."

The ghost looked from one woman to the other, from the dead to the living and back again, her face glowing and guileless in the growing morning light.

"My name's Tessa—Tessa North." Before either Granny or Emma could say anything, the young spirit added, "Am I really dead?"

. . . .

If you liked the Ghost of Granny Apples debut, then you'll love investigating the adventures of unforgettable amateur sleuth Odelia Grey, Sue Ann Jaffarian's heroine in her award-winning mystery series that includes:

Too Big to Miss
(Midnight Ink, 2006)

The Curse of the Holy Pail
(Midnight Ink, 2007)

Thugs and Kisses
(Midnight Ink, 2008)

Booby Trap
(Midnight Ink, 2009)

Look for the latest book in the series, *Corpse on the Cob*, in February 2010!

12/09

WW__._____KS.COM

From the _____ _____ ɔs
in the Middle East, it's always midnight somewhere. Join us
online at any hour for fresh new voices in mystery fiction.

At midnightinkbooks.com you'll also find our author blog,
new and upcoming books, events, book club questions,
excerpts, mystery resources, and more.

TM
MIDNIGHT
INK

MIDNIGHT INK ORDERING INFORMATION

Order Online:

• Visit our website www.midnightinkbooks.com, select your books,
and order them on our secure server.

Order by Phone:

• Call toll-free within the U.S. and Canada at
1-888-NITE-INK (1-888-648-3465)
• We accept VISA, MasterCard, and American Express

Order by Mail:

Send the full price of your order (MN residents add 6.875% sales tax)
in U.S. funds, plus postage & handling to:

Midnight Ink
2143 Wooddale Drive, Dept. 978-0-7387-1380-9
Woodbury, MN 55125-2989

Postage & Handling:

Standard (U.S., Mexico & Canada). If your order is:
$24.99 and under, add $4.00
$25.00 and over, FREE STANDARD SHIPPING

AK, HI, PR: $16.00 for one book plus $2.00 for each additional book.

International Orders (airmail only):
$16.00 for one book plus $3.00 for each additional book.

Orders are processed within 2 business days. Please allow for normal shipping time.
Postage and handling rates subject to change.